Alone but for MEDUSA's artificial-intelligence copilot, airborne over the North Sea, Ro Hayes listened with one ear to the radio chatter from the commercial traffic flying miles below, his eyes drifting from his weather radars to the distant, frozen sea, back to the midnight blue of the high sky that MEDUSA had claimed for her own.

He wished he had a clearer picture of what Forrestal had had in mind during that final, unscheduled verbal briefing at Langley.

"Remember, Mr. Hayes, your mission reduces to one single objective: Blow any hostile missile aimed at U.S. property out of the sky," the CIA man had told him. "My girl Amy Brecker, the East German rendezvous, even the lives of our people aboard *Skylab Two*—none of them means squat in the larger context."

"Larger context?" Ro had questioned, not because he didn't understand but because he had to be sure he understood. He felt as if he'd slipped into some alternate universe where all the rules were suddenly reversed—where women, children, and civilians came last; where all games were zero-sum; and where the best thing he could do for his country was take aggressive, preemptive action against the Soviet Union.

MEDUSA

JANET AND CHRIS MORRIS

BAEN
FICTION
BOOKS

MEDUSA

Copyright © 1986 by Paradise Productions

A Baen Books Original

Baen Publishing Enterprises
260 Fifth Avenue
New York, N.Y. 10001

First printing, June 1986

ISBN: 0-671-65573-6

Cover art by Vincent Di Fate

Printed in the United States of America

Distributed by
SIMON & SCHUSTER
TRADE PUBLISHING GROUP
1230 Avenue of the Americas
New York, N.Y. 10020

For Jim Baen, whose spirit imbued
this project with a special life.

*Acknowledgments: To Betsy Mitchell—she knows why.
And to David Drake, for reading the manuscript in
progress.*

BOOK ONE

Chapter One

From her office in the new American Embassy building in West Berlin, Amy Brecker could see the top of the Wall, its electrified barbed wire glinting against the squirrel-gray winter sky, tiny black shapes in a guard tower moving restlessly back and forth before their window as she did before hers.

It was Christmas Eve, and Brecker was working late. The embassy corridors were almost deserted, a skeleton staff of the disgruntled and the depressed holding the fort upstairs while below, in the ground-floor reception room, the last of the senior diplomats buttoned up their coats and dashed for their Mercedes; only the lonely were working tonight.

Brecker had volunteered. Better a desk full of paper work than a cocktail party full of Brits, Berliners, and Frenchmen with eyes only for each other and fake hail-fellow-well-met for everyone else. The international situation was tense; NATO was shaky; everyone in the diplomatic community was walking on eggs because America wasn't: In both hemispheres, American troops were "paving the way for democracy" with blood and bullets, matching the Soviets intervention for intervention, preemptive strike for preemptive strike.

This particular Christmas, there were fifty-three wars in progress around the globe. But that wasn't why Amy Brecker had chosen to work rather than party. Five years in the West Berlin embassy as a second secretary had inured her to crises; as CIA's deputy station chief in West Berlin, she faced potential world devastation every morning with her cornflakes.

So if this particular quick and dirty twilight made the Berlin Wall seem like a memorial to her own fragmented life, it had more to do with personal problems than with professional ones: Amy Brecker had broken up with her live-in lover the night before.

They'd had other fights, and nothing had come of them. But during this one, while Jeremy Pratt, the embassy's cultural attaché, was busy calling her a "horny bitch" and letting her know in no uncertain terms that no wife of a career diplomat of Jeremy's potential could have a second career as "some damn spook," she'd realized he was right.

So Jeremy was at her place, clearing out five years' worth of accumulated "mutuality of interest," and Amy was working the graveyard shift, burying what she could of her emotions.

They'd found out they were in each other's way; it wasn't anybody's fault. It probably would have happened sooner, if sane heterosexual males hadn't been at such a premium in Amy's age group and if she weren't so unwilling to let the relationship fail that she'd made endless compromises and told countless lies.

She pressed her nose to the chill windowpane, fogging the glass, then stood back, her image reflected there like a ghost. Jeremy didn't really want to marry a longhair, anyway. Amy had to be able to connect with the rebels and the peace groups—the Granolas, the Greens, the Soviet-molded marchers and moaners who camped outside Ramstein and smoked dope in dingy cafés, so she came to work in the fatigues and Nagasaki sweat shirts of radical chic.

At thirty-seven, she was getting a little old for it, but she still got results. And she liked herself the way she was. She tried to imagine the small, athletic figure before her in the window transformed: in a chiffon blouse and a Dior suit, teetering on toothpick heels, her shapely legs encased in silk, her wicked grin brightening a pale, freckled face.

"Hell with it," she told her reflection, and settled down behind her gray desk, where she punched viciously at her computer keyboard. She'd cried last night, the first time she'd cried in years. She was still feeling drained, vulnerable, and rebellious. She needed to prove to herself that a man, or lack of one, couldn't really turn her life upside down.

Maybe that was why, when the night desk buzzed and told her there was an "Ivan here who wants to see somebody who can grant him asylum," she said, "Great. Send him up."

The Russian, when he arrived with a marine in full dress who said, "Ms. Secretary, Mr. Azimov," and let Amy know he'd be right outside if she needed him, was a walking cliché.

Azimov—obviously not his real name—was Slavic, overweight, sweating into his dirty, gray-white collar. His overcoat was heavy leather, badly cut, and speckled with melting snow. He held his hat in one hand, a stained manila envelope in the other, and watched her out of round, dark eyes glittering with apprehension.

"Won't you sit down, Mr.—uh—Azimov?" Amy indicated the chair before her desk.

The burly Russian sat, sighing like a punctured tire. Even with the desk between them, Amy could smell an acrid body odor, like copper filings and an old cigar, that let her know the Russian was very nervous about being here.

But then, defections were never routine for the defector.

"What can I do for you, Mr. Azimov?"

The Russian chewed his lip, then said in perfect, unaccented English, "I'd like to go to America, please."

He sounded like a Russian "commentator," the sort who did satellite interviews with the Western press, but she'd never seen him before. She'd expected some low-level mission worker, or at best a poet or a nerve-gas project worker—someone who was fleeing ComBloc for the standard reasons. But Russians who spoke English this well were highly paid and not lacking in creature comforts. She couldn't hook him with offers of his own apartment and freedom of speech.

She stared at him for half a minute, realizing that he'd won the first round, that she was nonplussed, and that she'd better get the ball back into her court. She said, "The next nonstop flight leaves in . . ."—she looked at her watch, her knee pressing the RECORD button on the underside of her desktop—"three hours and fourteen minutes, Mr. Azimov, so we'd better get started. I'll need a good reason to put you on that plane. Tell me who you are, why you want asylum, and what you've got that would interest the U.S. Defectors are a dime a dozen this year, and expensive to support."

The Russian wriggled one scant eyebrow. "Very good, Ms. Brecker." He sat forward, shrugged off his coat, pulled a Cuban cigar from a chalk-striped suit pocket, and lit it when she nodded her permission. Then he sat back, puffed ruminatively like a man at a poker game, all signs of his former trepidation gone, and cleared his throat. "Do you know, Ms. Brecker, what the PKO is?"

"No," she lied. "Tell me." Her pulse was beating hard now; from a simple defection, this was turning into a major acquisition—*if* the Soviet was from the PKO.

Azimov frowned with his whole body: His forehead crinkled; his nose drew down; his mouth, around its cigar, formed a slobbery arc; his shoulders hunched and his arms and legs crossed. "I'd hoped to find someone among you better informed. PKO is a division of the Soviet defense forces, which we call PVO-Strany. PKO stands for Provito-Kozmicheskay Oberona—anticosmic defense. PKO is dedicated to literally 'destroying the enemy's cosmic means of fighting.' "

Amy took a deep breath, visions of promotion and awards ceremonies dancing in her head. "I know," she admitted.

Anger flashed across the Slav's face, then subsided.

In that moment, Amy had realized that this man was unaccustomed to being polite. He was an order giver, not taker. PKO was run by the military; intimately connected with GRU, the Soviet military intelligence agency. For all she knew, she could be sitting across from a master spy. She said, "Go on, Mr. Azimov. Time is of the essence." She tapped her Cross pen on her notepad.

Azimov leaned forward and tossed the manila envelope onto her desk. "Read this, then."

Smart—he didn't want to go on record; couldn't afford to be taped giving specifics, in case no accommodation could be made. She countered: "Tell me what it says—my Cyrillic's nearly nonexistent."

She could almost hear him wishing she were a man. But playing the dizzy broad might be advantageous—if it didn't scare him away altogether.

When he didn't respond, she added: "Someone might have seen you come in here; we've got to expedite this and get you on that plane." She took a form from her drawer—not the right one for a defection request: a CIA blue-bordered priority request for transport.

"If you insist, Ms. Brecker. In that envelope is my dossier—I am a project control officer for the SS-thirty intermediate-range missile system. With it is a copy of an operations plan to 'accidentally' cripple your Strategic Defense Initiative program." He stood up. "As for my person, it is not in danger presently—unless it is in danger from you. No one saw me come in here; no one will notice my leaving. And I know Americans—you will have to consult with some man who is your superior before you make a decision on my case. So . . ."—he smiled nastily, a baring of teeth that showed steel fillings and brown enamel—"I'll leave now, and come back another time."

The big Slav, standing, shrugged into his overcoat and headed for the door.

"Wait a minute—Mr. Azimov?" She'd blown it; the man wouldn't put his fate in her hands. She didn't really blame him—she hadn't taken this thing seriously enough. Now it was too late. . . .

"*Da?*" He turned, a glint of triumph in his eyes.

"How do I know you'll be back? How do I know this report is genuine? Or that *you* are?"

"You don't," he rumbled. "But someone better informed will be able to make those determinations."

"What is it you'd like? How can I persuade you not to leave?"

"Put a geranium in your window when you have permission to spirit me from this country to yours and your superior is ready to talk the turkey with me—money, freedoms, this sort of thing. Until then, my dear . . ."—he reached out, took her hand, lifted it to his lips and kissed it—"have a Merry Christmas."

Dropping her hand, he opened the door and strode out. The marine waiting outside looked in at her quizzically. Amy shook her head. "See him out, if you would, soldier."

She was staring out her window again, the Azimov report still spread out on her desk and her fingernails between her teeth, when ten minutes later someone knocked on her door. It was the marine again, this time with his white hat in one hand and his young face equally white. "Ma'am? Sorry to bust in like this, but . . ."

"Go ahead, soldier." In the distance she could hear the burping wail of an ambulance; out the rear window of the embassy building, the Wall glittered, coldly lit and defiant in its intransigence, a symbol of all that was wrong with the modern world, her job, life in general, and Soviets in particular.

"Well, ma'am . . . that guy, the one who was just here? He got as far as the front gate and then . . ."

"Yes? Then what?"

"We were wondering if he was one of our guys— you know, an agent or something . . . if we screwed up."

"How's that? You didn't detain him?"

"No, ma'am. He cleared the checkpoint, started across the street to his car, and some fool who thought this was the autobahn creamed him. That's who the ambulance is for."

"He's alive?"

"Heck, no, ma'am. This gray Mercedes hit him so hard he went right up in the air and landed behind it—broke his back, we think. Whatever it broke, he was dead when he hit the ground."

"Shit."

The marine flushed up into his crew cut. "Yes ma'am. So . . . did we screw up?"

"No, soldier, you didn't. But you can bet I did."

defense, like we've got now, might effectively intercept a small attack of one or a very few weapons. Such a scenario currently requires a U.S.
retaliation—counterattack price, in the lingo, that the

Chapter Two

"**C**rew rotation complete, sir," Sam Taylor's aide advised over the intercom. "*Skylab Two*'s giving us thumbs-up, and *Discovery*'s on her way back to Vandenberg. Mission Control there says landing will be well within the window of availability."

"That's good to hear, Bob. Keep me informed." Taylor, number three man in the U.S. Space Command and number two man in Air Force Intelligence, turned to the CIA deputy director he was entertaining beneath Cheyenne Mountain in the Aerospace Defense Command Center. "So, Forrey, what's to sweat?" said the balding tank of an air force officer to his leonine, hawkish CIA counterpart. Together, the two men inevitably reminded onlookers of an aging Mutt and Jeff; if they hadn't been two of the most formidable personalities in the American C3I (command, control, communications, and intelligence) community, their presence in the same banquet hall or meeting would have prompted whispered jokes. But they were, and the whispers accompanying their meeting, among those few with need-to-know, were cautious and worried. These days, when Terrible Taylor and Forrey got together, it was never a joking matter.

Taylor paused for a rasping breath, then continued. "Your girl in Berlin made a mistake, admit it. Crew's fine, *Two*'s fine, surveillance—including your own satellites—shows no unusual Soviet activity. Where's your hostile missile?"

"Our reports say it'll come up over the Sea of Japan," the sepulchrally elegant, sixtyish gentleman named Forrestal said nasally, and shrugged. "Interservice rivalry aside, I hope you're right and nothing comes of this." He tapped the black-and-red folder between them on Taylor's graphite desk and let his eyes flicker over the bank of monitors behind the Air Force Intelligence officer's juglike, balding head. "So far," Forrey added softly, "so good. But I wish, just to be on the safe side, that you'd evacuated the old crew and not put any new astronauts up there. I don't like sitting ducks, and I don't like to think about the repercussions if those Soviet PKO boys do try a shoot-down. Hardware we can stand to lose—it's expensive, but replaceable. Four American astronauts, military mission or not, are another story. If something does happen and this thing goes public with human casualties involved, we're staring at Woo Woo Three in the making."

"I know that." Taylor stretched like a cat. "You know that. Don't you think Ivan knows that? I'm betting that the only thing that's going to keep the Soviets from making this plan operational is a manned presence up there: They won't risk murdering American citizens, no matter how much they want to turn *Skylab Two* into space junk. For all we know, that girl was hoodwinked—after all, no high-powered Soviet defector would walk in and casually hand his fate over to a low-level female clerk."

"It's disinformation, that's what you think?" Forrestal scratched in the graying hair behind his ear. "You think the Soviets expect to scare us out of space by merely threatening to harm a satellite? And that they found some guy ready to die on a West Berlin street to give their operation verisimilitude? Bullshit."

"Maybe this Azimov thought it was a real operational plan; maybe they set him up to play patsy. They're capable of it. And maybe, just maybe, it was a real idea they were bouncing around until this Azimov ran with it to the nearest U.S. Embassy—I don't know. But I do know that even the Soviets aren't crazy enough to proceed with an operation after it's been blown wide open. If it ever *was* on the boards, it's not now."

"I hope you're right." Forrestal wasn't convinced. He was deputy director of the CIA's Directorate for Counterintelligence, and Amy Brecker's report had ended up in his lap after a long game of pass-the-buck. His subsection of CIA was barely back on its operational feet; its reputation for dirty tricks and its troubles three decades past still haunted its present. The deputy director of Central Intelligence had handed Forrey this hot potato with a wry smile—nobody else in the Agency wanted to touch it—and Forrestal's best option was Taylor and his spies-in-the-sky. If Air Force Intelligence got a black eye over this one, nobody at Langley would cry about it much.

But you simply couldn't sit on a report like this when a billion-dollar satellite and human lives— not to mention a nuclear exchange—might be at stake.

Forrestal had come to the Agency by way of Air Force Intelligence. Taylor had been his "scope" when Forrestal was a fighter-bomber pilot in Nam in the Sixties. They'd "punched out" together over the DMZ when an incoming round punctured their plane's hydraulics and the stick froze. Then, having ejected and survived, they'd fought their way back through the not-very-demilitarized zone to their own side, saving one another's life numerous times in the process.

To Taylor, Forrestal was still "a hot stick"—a top-notch pilot; and to Forrestal, Taylor was still "my old scope"—the radar man in charge of ordnance and navigation. Twenty-five years later, they still trusted each other implicitly.

And yet now, when it might matter so much, neither man could quite see his way clear to accept the other's analysis. Both of them had seen too many analysts make the wrong decision and too many intelligence professionals become so paranoid that their credibility dissolved.

So they were still sitting there, wrangling about what might or might not be happening, drinking too much coffee and smoking too many cigarettes, when Bob Hendricks, Taylor's aide, came in without knocking and closed the door behind him.

"Yeah, Bob?" The aide's stolid midwestern face, fleshy and square, was impassive. Bob was a career man, attentive to detail and painfully conscious that rank has its privileges; thus if he hadn't knocked first, there was some damned good reason, Taylor knew.

"Sirs, I'd like you to take a look at this." He held out some hard copy with the National Security Agency's scramble at its top.

Taylor scanned it and passed it to Forrestal, who scowled at it as if it had insulted him. "Crap," said Forrestal softly, "I'd hate like hell to be right about this one." He handed it back to the aide and said, as if he were home at Langley, "Shred that. Now. Yourself. And bring me the damn confetti."

Bob looked at Taylor for confirmation. Taylor nodded, and waited until Bob had left before he said to Forrey, "I'd hate for you to be right myself. You've got a full head of hair and I don't; that's all the genetic edge any man deserves."

It wasn't even a good attempt at levity. The NSA report said that there was unusual activity at certain Soviet bases near the Sea of Japan—transport of something very much like a new missile, something with a heat signature that was definitely nuclear. And, NSA reported, as if trying to muddy the water, there were Soviet troops massing on the Sino-Soviet border.

Taylor had two grown kids and six grandchildren. The last thing he wanted to do was see World War III in his lifetime. That was why he'd been a supporter of America's Strategic Defense Initiative from its planning stages. When the program was complete, a Soviet nuclear strike would become impractical: Between three-quarters and four-fifths of incoming missiles aimed at the United States would never reach their targets, but would be shot to bits as soon as they arced up out of the atmosphere on their way from Russia; point defenses on American ground would raise that fraction to nine-tenths. In most cases their warheads would not even be armed before the delivery systems carrying them were destroyed. Of course, each warhead's deadly cargo of plutonium would be pulverized into dust whose grains were among the most poisonous substances known to man, but that was considered a further deterrent: Orbiting dust couldn't be targeted—it couldn't tell a Soviet from an American citizen—and tons of plutonium in the atmosphere made biowarfare nightmares look like pleasant dreams. So kill rate on incoming missiles promised to remain potential: Nobody would chance massive "collateral damage" (civilian casualties) among his own people.

But the program, called "Strategic Defense" within the military and "Star Wars" in the adversary press and in Congress, wasn't fully operational yet. There had been so much opposition from liberal elements in Congress and antitechnology environmentalist types in the streets that the deployment of the full 900 laser battle stations and supplementary conventional weaponry had been delayed by funding squabbles.

Another year, dear God, just give us another year, Taylor prayed silently, not for the first or the last time.

Forrey was staring at him mournfully. Forrey didn't have any kids; Forrey was a dedicated intelligence professional, a man just enough smarter and just enough luckier than Taylor that Taylor had spent his whole life trying to eclipse his old friend just once.

"Well, what say we bring that girl agent of mine over here and have a talk with her, just you and me?" Forrestal said gently. "Maybe if she can convince us that she's right, we'll still have time to send a shuttle up and collect those sitting ducks of yours before the shit hits the fan—if it does."

"Okay, Stick, you win. How fast can you get her here?"

Forrestal was shaking his head: "*You* get her here—you've got the Stealth X-3; all I've got is some support aircraft. At Mach four plus, we could be talking to her this evening over dinner. Also, you've got less channels to go through to clear a nonsched flight than I do, and I don't want more than the minimum number of people to know about this."

Taylor didn't even try arguing that the Stealth X-3 didn't exist. No plane built by Lockheed's Skunk Works could escape the Agency's notice.

But there was one problem: None of the three test pilots who'd made the final cut for Stealth accreditation flights had the right security clearance. And the one Air Force Intelligence pilot with the right clearance and enough experience to be able to fly that high-tech, multibillion-dollar craft with little or no preparation was standing down, on extended leave after a very taxing mission, and probably in no shape to fly an ultralight, let alone an eye-blink-fast, experimental "fly-by-wire" jet with six onboard computers that tended to argue with one another.

Taylor chewed his knuckles, weighing his alternatives: Give emergency clearance to some gung-ho test pilot, or trust the Stealth X-3, called "Thunderhawk" by its supporters, to an intelligence officer who might be facing disciplinary charges for his antics the last time out.

"You're thinking, Taylor, about doing something wicked. What is it?"

"You should pretend you don't know me so well, Forrey. I'm thinking about who'll fly the Thunderhawk. And I'm thinking that the only man for the job is an insubordinate son of a bitch I wanted to forcibly retire three years ago. But there's always some damned thing like this, some reason you need a cowboy when you really wish you didn't."

"Anybody I know?"

"By reputation, maybe, if you counterintelligence boys are all you're cracked up to be. Ro Hayes ring any bells?"

The name must have, for Forrestal whistled softly and said, "What are you expecting, a fire fight on the Ramstein runway?" Before Taylor could answer, he smiled contentedly and stretched his legs. "If you'll co-run a confirm-or-deny op with me, and Munro Hayes is part of it, I'll buy you dinner—I'll buy both of *them* dinner, as soon as we can meet them on the airstrip at Vandenberg."

"You've got yourself a deal, Forrey."

Forrestal of CIA and Taylor of Air Force Intelligence shook hands.

Chapter Three

Munro Hayes was at his cabin in the hills above Vandenberg AFB, out in the California sun, taking revenge on his four-wheel-drive Blazer, when his remote phone began to bleat.

For the third day in a row, the old Blazer had refused to start. It wasn't funny anymore: Ro Hayes liked solitude, when he could get it; the cabin was twenty miles from the nearest store, and the store was his nearest neighbor. He'd run out of milk, then cigarettes, then eggs. If he couldn't get it started today, he was either going to have to call Jenny, his ex-wife, and beg for help, or go hungry. Neither alternative was enticing.

By the time the phone started ringing, the dark, boyish, forty-year-old pilot whose guileless brown eyes and quick smile guaranteed him entry into polite society in Beirut or Boston or Bonn was soaked in sweat, covered with grease, and glaring at the Blazer's carburetor, completely disassembled on an old tarp beside the car, baking in the noonday sun. He knew the problem was in the carburetor; he'd had float-level problems with it since he'd bought it.

He was tempted to let the incoming phone call go unanswered. Short of an emergency, he couldn't be scrambled. He was on extended leave until the brass decided whether the means he'd used on his last mission were too outrageous to be justified by his unqualified success.

Ro hated the way Air Force Intelligence bitched when he won one by playing dirty. The opposition didn't play by congressional rules or worry about what would happen if this or that nasty trick was leaked to a naïve, scandal-loving public.

This time when he'd touched down on a NATO runway, old Terrible Taylor himself had granted him an interview, during which the subject of disciplinary action and/or extended leave had come up. So he was grounded, and he'd had to accept it with polite yes-sirs and no-sirs when he felt like asking Taylor when the last time was that the air force's deputy chief of intelligence had put *his* life on the line.

Instead, he'd come up here to sulk. He didn't like to be disturbed in midsulk; some guys got roaring drunk or skunked on drugs to wind down after action—Ro Hayes sulked. And this time he felt he had good reason: The shoot-down of a couple Libyan rag-heads over the Gulf of Sidra ought to have earned him a commendation, not a four-star dressing down.

By the phone's fifth bleat, he was feeling resentful and guilty, so he reached behind him and felt around for it, wiping sweat from his jaw with his other hand. He keyed the TALK/SHIELD button that supposedly protected the unit from would-be tappers, and said, "I'm not here. Leave a message at the beep. Beep." Then he released the button so he could hear the party on the other end of the line.

A ratchety voice said, "Son? Taylor here. How soon can you get over here?"

"Depends on where 'here' is, sir."

"The base. With your full kit. How long?"

"Walking? Sometime tomorrow. My car's not feeling well."

"I'll send a chopper for you in . . . say . . . forty minutes. Be ready."

Ro grinned and depressed the TALK button once again, but the connection was already broken from the other end. Never mind, he told himself; plenty of time to gloat when I get there. They *did* need him; he enjoyed occasionally reminding them of that.

But he didn't have plenty of time to get ready— not enough to reassemble the Blazer's carburetor. He folded up the tarp with the pieces of machinery inside it, hefted it, and patted the Blazer's grill on the way in to shower and change. "Serves you right, Pig," he told the car.

In the shower, he didn't hurry. Hayes wasn't a big man at slightly under six feet, but he had a wiry athleticism that was never clumsy and a bull's constitution that made him uniquely suited to "special operations," whether behind or above enemy lines. The peculiar combination of mathematical and physical facility that made for good test pilots was obvious only in the fine shape of his head and the glint in his eye as he shaved in the shower with precise, economical movements.

Yet for all his calm, a sensor battery in a space

shuttle or a test aircraft would have detected certain telltales: His pulse rate was in the low sixties, and yet a subtle tremor ran through his muscles. They wanted to put him on line for something and it wasn't going to be a milkrun. "Full kit," Taylor had said. That meant his personal weapons, his high-spy paraphernalia, and a gear bag full of everything he'd need for wherever, since Taylor hadn't deigned to tell him even if the venue was to be arctic, tropical, or temperate. The brass loved to act covert, even when it made things more difficult.

By the time Ro had his coveralls on and his gear bag packed, there was a blue Boeing Vertol 360 hovering over his driveway, its skids less than a foot off the ground and its pilots managing to look impatient despite the flight helmets that obscured everything but their eyes. The Vertol confirmed Ro's suspicion that whatever was about to happen wasn't going to be run-of-the-mill: For a reason known only to Taylor, they were picking Hayes up in the fastest, meanest chopper the air force flew.

Its pilots verified his impression that he was late for some kind of Big Secret Mission, telling him to "Move, man. Let's jack out of here! Terrible's waiting!" But chopper pilots were all cowboys. Ro ignored them and leaned back to enjoy the ride. There was no use getting all pumped up when he didn't know squat about the mission in the offing— not even whether he'd agree to take it.

An hour later, standing in a restricted-area hangar with Taylor, while Taylor offered him a chance to fly the Stealth X-3 Thunderhawk to Ramstein and back and an unhappy-looking Stealth test pilot stood by to brief him, Ro Hayes had forgotten all thoughts of temperament or between-mission sulks.

Even the fact that he was supposed to pick up a woman named Amy Brecker at Ramstein and bring her back for a meeting she, Ro, and Taylor were going to have with some honcho from CIA didn't bother him. He listened with one ear when Taylor told him that this was the beginning of a "confirm-or-deny operation, a joint venture with CIA," and that if Ro had any reservations about it, the time to balk was now, not later: "Once you grab that stick, son, you're in for the duration."

"Yes, sir," he murmured. "That's understood, sir. I'm go, no reservations, sir." If Taylor had wanted him to fly the Thunderhawk to hell, pick up Mephistopheles, and airdrop him into the Kremlin, Ro would have agreed: There wasn't a pilot alive who wouldn't have cheerfully denounced his mother as a subversive to fly the Stealth X-3.

It crouched in the hangar, looking more like a manta ray than the high-altitude, high-speed surveillance and reconnaissance aircraft—and weapons platform—that it was, its composite, low-signature skin matte black, one flowing line from its sharp nose to its wingtips. It seemed to grin at him, as if it knew damn well that only luck had given him the opportunity to take it out on its first real mission—luck and the qualifier that Ro, despite his faults, had an astral security clearance.

When Taylor left him alone with the test pilot and the plane, the pilot said, "Better listen up, old man. I've only got time to show you this stuff once."

And Ro Hayes's preflight briefing had begun.

Chapter Four

Amy Brecker couldn't avoid this particular diplomatic reception: One of the agents she'd picked up as a result of Azimov's walk-in was on the guest list.

The invitations said "creative black tie," and the predominantly West German guests had taken the directive to heart. Amy's tuxedo and chain-mail tie (not to mention her pale, Aryan eyes, shoulder-length hair, and ascetic thinness) blended right in with the slightly outré formal wear of a dozen powerful, aging Greens and their long-haired spouses.

The Greens—the environmentalist/peace/radical socialist party that all but controlled the Bundestag, the lower house of the federal legislature of West Germany—resembled nothing so much as the American hippies of the Sixties, and yet they saw America as their greatest enemy, the fount of all technology's evils. The only American export to win the Greens' approval in twenty years was Amy Brecker. Amy's boss, a vice-consul at the American Embassy, had been adamant that she attend this evening: The Greens' latest firebrand, Reinhardt Dietrich, was the guest of honor, the VC had reminded her, in his best your-country-needs-you tone of voice.

So she was thrown together in public with her new agent, Dietrich, a situation her superiors back home in Langley would have vehemently disapproved of. But Amy wasn't worried; she could carry off the charade.

Ever since Azimov's death, she'd been living a field collector's fantasy: She'd developed a whole new network of highly placed Germans like Dietrich, any one of whom would have been a feather in her cap. Dietrich, in particular, showed great promise: A tall, charismatic Aryan, he was NATO's Carl Sagan, a man with a mission, a popularizer of science rather than a scientist, an idealist with impeccable credentials and all the right friends, who did science specials for the BBC and proselytized for "peace through disarmament" wherever he could.

Tonight Dietrich was in peak form, talking Intermediate-Range Theater Nuclear Force reductions with American NATO generals as if he were West Germany's chancellor, which he might one day become. Every time the chats threatened to become arguments, he would disengage and find Amy, firmly guiding her through the crowd to introduce her to his victims as an example of a "sane American—one of our future comrades in disarmament."

She kept hoping that Vice-Consul Aikins would be able to take all this in stride. Dietrich knew the chance he was taking; his azure eyes sparkled with the excitement of calculated risk.

She was just about to slip away from Dietrich and the red-faced general he had cornered when Aikins, his perpetual bemused Virginia-gentleman's smile replaced by an undiplomatic scowl, threaded his way toward them through the crowd. With the vice-consul was the Federal Republic's assistant secretary for security affairs, an ox of a man named Lutz who had a face as expressive as the Wall outside Amy's office window.

The conversation in which she was enmeshed halted abruptly as the two grave-faced newcomers approached. Before introductions could be made, the vice-consul said in a strained voice, "Amy, dear, I'm afraid I have some bad news for you." Reaching into his pocket, he pulled out a piece of Federal Republic letterhead and held it out to her, adding in a voice loud enough for everyone around to hear, "You've been pinged. You've got twenty-four hours to leave the country by order of the West German government."

Amy stood staring at him, stunned. *Pinged* was diplomatic slang for being declared persona non grata—PNG'd. She couldn't believe it. She didn't understand it—she was doing so well here. And she especially didn't understand why Vice-Consul Aikins would announce the matter publicly.

Her lower lip trembled. She said, "For what reason?" belligerently, while all around her, people drew back. She saw Dietrich's cheeks go pale, his blue eyes dart away, cold and unsympathetic.

Then Lutz said, "For espionage, what else? Will you come with me, fräulein?"

Numbly, she walked between the vice-consul and the German, feeling all eyes follow them as the news rippled through the reception hall.

She'd been so careful; it didn't make sense. None of it made sense. Public humiliation aside, things just weren't done this way. If one was pinged, it was handled quietly: PNGs left behind them very interesting waves, and their governments usually went to great lengths to minimize these incriminating ripples among the spy networks, not—as was the case here—to maximize them.

She was about to demand an explanation from Aikins when he guided her into his study and the German intelligence officer closed the door behind them, punching up a security block on the panel beside the door.

"Sit down, Amy, please," said her CIA station chief, the vice-consul, kindly, running a hand through his thinning red hair.

She didn't remember sinking into the leather club chair. Her career here was ruined, her agents lost or at risk. She could barely think; she just stared at Aikins resentfully.

"We haven't much time," Aikins said as Lutz came around and sat on one corner of his desk, looking at Amy keenly from under beetled brows. "We apologize for any embarrassment we've caused you, but your reaction had to be genuine."

"And it was that, fräulein," the German intelligence officer said, grinning broadly.

"What do you mean, we? Are you two in this together?"

"Let me handle this, Lutz," the American vice-consul told the German agent. Then, to Amy: "There's a plane on its way to Ramstein to pick you up. You're needed in the States. It's possible that you'll be coming back here eventually—not as an embassy staffer, but as a disaffected ex–government employee who's decided to throw in her lot with the Greens. Do you understand?"

She was beginning to, but she was still angry and resentful. They needn't have treated her so shabbily; they could have let her in on their little game. "No, I don't, *sir.*"

"Tomorrow we'll be releasing a picture of you among the demonstrators at last month's 'Kampf dem Atomtod' rally."

"But I wasn't *at* the 'Struggle against Atomic Death' rally!"

"Give us a little credit, fräulein. We know that. And you know that photos can be doctored." Lutz smiled sanctimoniously.

The vice-consul regained control of the conversation. "Whether you were or weren't, we feel it's necessary for your cover that the media think you were."

"But," Amy protested, "my . . . work!" *Her network! Dietrich!*

"You know all you need to know at the moment. We've taken the liberty of having your things packed. A military escort is ready to drive you to Ramstein," Lutz said firmly. Then, as if reading her mind: "Don't worry about Dietrich—we won't have to, after this."

"It's not fair!" she blurted. Aikins, her station chief, had shared her most secret reports with an official of the West German government. Amy was appalled.

The vice-consul rubbed the bridge of his nose, staring at her morosely. "It never is. Comfort yourself with the knowledge that you've done a good job here; and whether you understand it now or not, we're putting you in the position to do an even better job here sometime in the near future." Vice-Consul Aikins stood up. "And now, Ms. Brecker, if you'll excuse me, I have the rest of this charade to play out. Herr Lutz will see that you find your car."

And he left her alone with the German agent, who leaned conspiratorially close and said, "In good time, fräulein, you will see that we've done you a favor—promoted you from a glorified secretarial post to a real operational role."

Amy treated him to a stony silence, trying to control the tears that threatened to spill from her eyes.

Lutz sighed feelingly. "Come along then, if you will."

She went with him numbly, unspeaking. Part of her didn't believe this was really happening; perhaps she'd dozed off in her room and was sleeping through the party, having another nightmare from too much bratwurst.

But at the curb a Mercedes with American Embassy flags was waiting; inside was a marine and her luggage. Lutz opened the door for her gallantly, and it was all she could do not to tell him what she thought of him. Instead she said as scathingly as she knew how, "Thanks for everything."

He smiled with equanimity, said, "Good hunting, fräulein," and shut the door firmly.

As luck would have it, her driver was the same marine who'd been on duty the night Azimov had waddled into her life and out of it so abruptly.

Amy said, "God, what a night!"

"Yes, ma'am," the marine responded, without a

trace of warmth. He'd obviously heard about her troubles. He didn't want to acquire any guilt by association, Amy guessed. Or maybe it was that when you were pinged, you were pinged: In the marine's eyes, she'd failed. She was a flop, a washout.

It was a very long, silent ride to Ramstein.

At the Ramstein gate checkpoint, the marine asked her for her passport. Once the guard had looked it over and handed it back to him, Amy expected the marine to return it. He didn't.

She said, "Soldier, my passport."

He said, "Sorry, ma'am. Orders."

She didn't know whether to cry or hit him with her purse. "But I'll need it, to get on the plane. . . ."

The marine shrugged, saying again, "Orders." But as Amy slumped in the back seat and, sniffling, hunted for a tissue in her bag, a trace of humanity came through and he added, "You won't need it. Don't worry, ma'am. It's going to be okay."

"Sure. Easy for *you* to say."

The marine said, "Yes, ma'am," with infuriating calm.

Amy subsided into stony silence, watching dully as Ramstein's long, low buildings gave way to hangars and radars and control towers spiking brightly lit runways. As they pulled out onto one runway, a plane was landing. It taxied to a stop and the marine drove the car right up to it.

Amy was nonplussed: She hadn't cleared Customs—even at a military installation, you probably had to do that. She hadn't had a chance to go to the bathroom or wash her face.

Still, she'd had quite enough of playing the idiot tonight. She didn't say anything at all, just flexed her aching hand on the sweaty handle of her purse and gritted her teeth.

"This is it, ma'am," yelled the marine above the roar of the plane's engines. "Let's go."

Outside, a wind was blowing, and as the marine got the balance of her luggage from the Mercedes' trunk, the jet's engines fell silent suddenly. Amy looked up in time to see the canopy roll back and a figure in flight suit and helmet scramble out onto a still-deploying ladder and jump to the ground.

She certainly hadn't expected to go home in a fighter plane, or whatever this was. She vaguely remembered that fighters didn't have transoceanic range. Then she noticed that there wasn't any American flag or even an air force star on the plane, and that it was black as night.

The pilot ambled toward them, a ball of international-distress-orange cloth wadded up under his arm, unlatching his oxygen mask as he came. "Brecker, right?" he said as he reached the Mercedes. He threw her the wad of orange cloth. "Put this on."

"*Here?*"

In the Mercedes' headlights, she could see the pilot's eyes narrow despite the shadow of his raised visor. "Over your clothes. If you don't mind." He was looking at her luggage doubtfully. He said to the marine, "Want to help me with this stuff, buddy?" And to Amy, "You really need all of that? It'd make life easier if you could do without . . ."

Amy had one leg in the flight suit; her foot was stuck, her high heel snagged in its narrow opening. She looked up at the pilot and said, "Fine. I'll leave it all. Have them send it, soldier. It's the least they can do."

"Send it where, ma'am?" the marine asked as the pilot watched her struggle with the flight suit, a spreading grin on his face.

"Ask *him*," Amy puffed, finally realizing there was a zipper on the leg of the suit, and bending inelegantly to open it wide enough to get her foot through.

"Vandenberg," said the pilot.

Amy straightened up. "*California?*"

In back of the pilot, a fuel truck pulled up to the black plane and began to pump. Over the noise the pilot said, "If it pleases Your Ladyship . . ."

"Look, mister," Amy snarled, "don't get cute. I've had a rough night and you're not the end of it. As far as I'm concerned, you're just a taxi driver."

"Affirmative." The pilot nodded gravely, his jaw squaring. "Understood." But she saw the commiserating look he exchanged with the marine.

Sometimes she hated men, the entire sanctimonious, cocksure race of them.

Ten minutes later, when it turned out she couldn't scramble up onto the jet's ladder without his help and he made his hands into a step and boosted her up as if she were mounting a horse, she kicked him—accidentally, of course.

Then she was in his world, full of toggle switches and green and black display monitors and things she shouldn't touch. The oxygen mask was uncomfortable and the headset in her helmet came down too far below her ears to hear his voice well as he told her, "Fasten your harness, Ms. Brecker. You're about to have the ride of your life."

Just before the engines screamed and something like a giant, invisible hand pushed her back into the padded seat and tried to crush the breath from her, she said fliply, " 'Amy' will do fine. And you—you've got a name?"

She thought he said "Ro" as the g force hit her. But maybe he said "No."

As her vision became grainy and she struggled for breath and the plane leaped, impossibly, almost straight up into the air while in her ears pilot's jargon and control-tower banter buzzed unintelligibly, she decided that it was fine with her if this nasty bastard didn't want to tell her his name.

First she thought she was going to faint, then vomit into her helmet. Then she knew she was going to cry. Breaking up with Jeremy Pratt had been traumatic. Azimov's walk-in and subsequent death—probably her fault for not being able to persuade him to stay in the embassy—had made things worse; she'd thought she'd managed to salvage something by acquiring the network of PKO agents Azimov's documents had revealed, but the result of all her efforts had been the destruction of her new network and the end of her own career. She felt terrible about Dietrich; she felt worse about herself. She felt used, abused, and useless. Whatever lay ahead for her wasn't going to make up for what had happened tonight at the reception.

Whatever the reason for it, whatever the explanation, if she wasn't fired, she was going to tender her resignation. Then maybe she'd crawl back to Jeremy—he was right; she wasn't cut out to be a spy. She'd give him his 2.2 kids and learn to hire the right caterers. It couldn't be that hard. . . .

The pilot picked exactly the wrong moment to

reach out and touch her knee. "If you're feeling a little giddy, Amy, don't breathe so deeply," advised his crackling voice in her helmet.

She didn't answer, just stared straight ahead at the plane's windshield, where ghosts of the green instrument readings below it hovered mysteriously. She blinked through her tears, but the ghost readings didn't go away.

The pilot said, "Are you okay, Ms. Brecker?" without turning his head. In profile he looked like something from a science-fiction movie.

"*Okay?*" she replied scathingly. "I've just been pinged. Does that sound 'okay' to you?"

"That depends on how much it pays and what the perks are, doesn't it?" came his response in her ears.

"PNG'd, you moron. No perks, no job, and no damned sympathy from the likes of you, fuck you very much." The last thing she wanted was pop-psych from some throttle jockey.

"Sorry," the pilot said. "But don't take it so hard. Look outside, down to your right."

Amy craned her neck. There below was the corona of the earth, gilded in moonlight. "My God," she breathed. "What kind of plane did you say this was?"

She heard a metallic snort. "I didn't. But believe me, if you were any kind of security risk, you wouldn't have a ringside seat for a flight like this."

"A lot *you* know." Beyond the windshield were the stars, so much fiercer in their endless night than she remembered that she gulped a lungful of oxygen-rich air. Giddy, she reached out toward a lit panel whose indicators were red, not green. "What's this?"

"*Don't touch that!*" he snapped urgently, and flicked a switch. The little fluorescent-red letters that said LASER ARM/READY winked out.

Chapter Five

"What the hell is that?" wondered Canfield, *Skylab 2*'s mission commander, aloud to Robinson, the black who was his second-in-command.

The mission specialists were both asleep; Canfield and Robinson had been floating dreamily in the middle of *Skylab 2*'s electronics-laden Forward Control, just holding the fort, talking about their kids and what they were going to do with their hazard pay once their six-week tour in orbit was done.

"What's *what*, whitey?" Robinson's voice was velvety, the racial slur delivered with casual good humor. The graying-blond commander and his eggplant-black pilot/mate were old friends; they'd flown NASA shuttles together and they'd flown other, more classified air force missions.

Canfield was actually relieved to hear Robinson call him "whitey." The "woman and the Jew," as Robinson referred to the two mission specialists, made Robinson uncomfortable: In the presence of that pair of double-doctorates, Robinson was all academy charm—his southern accent disappeared, and so did his easygoing nature. It was going to be one hell of a six weeks. Canfield had been hoping he could find out, during this sleep rotation, what the two brains had said to mortally offend Robinson.

But looking at the scopes of infrared, low-light, side-looking, and counterjamming radar as something arced very high and very fast up over West Germany, headed in a beeline for the United States, Canfield's personnel problems were forgotten. Pushing off against a rack of electronics, he drifted toward the control panel of C3I equipment that could give him a readout on the bogey: Heat signatures would tell him if the UFO carried nuclear warheads, what its skin temperature was, whether there were any biological weapons or human beings inside.

Robinson beat him to the panel of knobs and toggles. Punching and twisting the controls, he said cheerfully, "Is it a bird? Is it a plane? No, it's . . ." His voice dropped an octave. "It's . . . *gone*, whitey. Just like that. Off the scopes."

"That can't be right." Canfield maneuvered his way in beside Robinson and did some quick calculations. Then he said, "It's still there. Watch the projections on its trajectory." And there, along a path calculated from the bogey's speed and arc, were temperature readings fractionally different from the upper atmosphere around its path.

"What are *you* reading there, Robinson?" Canfield asked for a second opinion.

"Exhaust; afterburner temperatures from something that isn't there. God bless those guys at the Skunk Works." The temperature-variation monitor that gave them the telltale had come out of Lockheed's countermeasures-development program, a spin-off of their Stealth research. Robinson turned to Canfield, button eyes widening. "Betcha that's what this is—the Stealth X-3. Or the Soviet equivalent."

"Jesus, let's hope it's not Ivan's." Both superpowers were currently at a state of readiness called Launch on Warning. Canfield most definitely didn't want to be the guy who gave the warning. With the world at stake, you just weren't eager to cry wolf.

"I think we ought to report it, commander," Robinson said slowly. "It's our job."

"Right. But let's remember it came up from West—not East—Germany when we do." All Canfield could think about was his family; his wife and children's smiling faces appeared like ghosts before him, interposing themselves between him and the monitors.

So it was Robinson who whistled, pointing: "*Look* at it! Leveling off at what? . . . Eighty—no, ninety thousand feet! If it ain't ours, they're going to tell us to shoot it down." As he spoke, he started the laser-targeting process.

"What are you doing? Easy, big fella!" Canfield protested. "I've got to call this in first."

"Call it in," Robinson agreed magnanimously. "If they tell us to shoot, we'll be ready." His eyewhites gleamed. "I've been wondering for a long time if this laser crap will really work."

Canfield was already trying to raise Mission Control at Vandenberg. When he did, the answer came back: "Abort. Repeat: Abort alert. Your bogey is classified, U.S. flight X3-1, nonsched."

Robinson heard it and sat back. Canfield, for the first time in minutes, looked up at his first officer. There were sparkling beads of sweat on Robinson's brow. That was comforting, Canfield thought as they shut down their war-making electronics and went back to standard C3I observation mode. He'd hate to think that he was up here with a trigger-happy fool.

Ten minutes later, sipping tepid coffee through a straw, he thought about the track from Ground Control: U.S. flight X3-1. That was the Stealth, all right. For some reason or other, Thunderhawk was on the wing.

Chapter Six

It was 1950 hours in California when Ro Hayes put the Stealth X-3's nosewheel down on the Vandenberg runway.

By the time they taxied to a stop before a ramp with a black limousine drawn up to it, CIA's Forrestal was making his summation to the president of the United States in a similar-looking car parked under the new Vandenberg Executive Complex overlooking the California coastline.

"So it's my feeling, sir, that the operation I've proposed offers the greatest probability of success with minimum risk." He looked at America's charismatic commander in chief, ex–New York governor Hamilton Stewart, expectantly.

Stewart's brooding, owlish eyes met his, reminding Forrestal that CIA was traditionally "the president's intelligence service" and that if Counterintelligence's verbal recommendations were disregarded or overruled, there was no appeal.

In this situation, at this moment, Stewart's word was law. Like a Roman caesar or a Russian czar, Hamilton Stewart held the fate of nations in his hands. And he knew it. Stewart's goatee-fringed chin jutted forward. His shoulders were hunched. His deceptively soft body was absolutely still and his peaches-and-cream complexion was yellow in the courtesy lights of the presidential limo.

"Minimum risk?" Stewart's voice was sensually soft, intimate with an awareness of the stakes in this global poker game. "Two intelligence people and the four up there in *Skylab*, you mean? That's not how I count it, Forrey—I count it in the millions. If the USSR thinks it can terrorize us out of SDI, that we're so weak-willed that we'll cut and run, give 'em everything at Geneva, say we're sorry, we didn't mean to build a protective system for America . . ."

Forrestal shook his head nearly imperceptibly as Stewart continued warming up like a pitcher about to throw a sinker.

Stewart noticed, scowled, and pulled himself up short. "This is a crazy thing you're asking me to sign off on, Forrey. As crazy as the Cuban missile crisis response was. More so, maybe, because it's just you and me, no National Security Council to blame if things go wrong. So I'll be candid." The president sat back, fingers playing in his salt-and-pepper beard. "If you screw this up, I didn't know a damned thing about it. That's the good news. The bad news is, if they go bang, so will we. You reading me, Stick? If they shoot, we'll shoot back—just as accidentally, of course. Saying that it was an uncontrollable response, if we have to. But we'll shoot back. You read me loud and clear?"

Forrestal took a deep breath and the chilled air of the limo bit his lungs like fire. The president wasn't stupid—not this one. He was, however, prideful and quick-tempered, a man of confrontationist ideology. He'd just this morning sent U.S. ground forces officially into El Salvador at the "request" of the Salvadoran government, turning an already volatile situation into the world's fifty-fourth ongoing shooting war. The press was having a field day.

"Clear, sir," said Forrestal. "But the purpose of this mission is to avoid that circumstance." He took a second deep breath and began a lecture the president shouldn't need, probably didn't need, to hear—began it for his own conscience, because you never knew how much these administration types really understood from their briefings.

"Mr. President, Geneva aside, there are good reasons to assume that if we counter this feint by the Soviets forcefully *but covertly*, so that no public response is necessary, neither side will have to 'shoot,' as you say. The Soviets know we'll be operational with a high-kill-rate, space-based defense within the year; that their arsenal will soon be, let's say, decimated, if not neutered. Their own military must be pressuring the leadership to 'use it or lose it.'"

"I know that, Forrey. Where do you think I've been for three years, asleep at the wheel?"

"Yes, sir, I'm sure you do. SDI—any ballistic-missile defense more sophisticated than the Galoshes they've got around Moscow—will reduce the probability of nuclear war by protecting the U.S. from a 'small' nuclear attack. Even a thin defense, like we've got now, might effectively intercept a small attack of one or a very few weapons. Such a scenario currently requires a U.S. retaliation—an attack price, in the lingo, that the

Soviets ought not to be willing to pay, *if* they're sure we'll make them pay it. That, sir, is what this operation's all about."

"Like I said, Forrey: They shoot, we shoot back."

"Yes, sir. We're trying to avoid that necessity, sir." *Patience*. "CIA won't be giving such an order, in any case. We want only an order, now, to source and confirm, and to place an armed Air Force Trans-Atmospheric Vehicle—TAV—in a position to monitor and intercept any 'runaway' Soviet missiles. Any launch order will have to come from you—that's why we need to have this talk, sir. If such a request is made by me or by Hayes, it can't go through normal channels."

"That's fine, I told you. As a matter of fact" —Stewart leaned forward in his seat and the glitter in his eyes made Forrestal even more nervous than he'd been previously—"it's about time. I'm proud of you, Forrey. You're a man of action like myself. If this works . . ." The president trailed off, his eyes focused on some personal horizon, then continued: "If it works, it'll be a different world."

Forrestal looked at the man who'd just put thousands of American boys into Central America's jungles and remembered Nam and a surge of fury rose in him. For a moment he actually considered killing Stewart, here in this car. But the vice president was a wimp. And Stewart, for all his bellicose rhetoric, understood the responsibilities of his office.

So Forrey added, for the record and the sake of his own conscience, to be certain that the president did understand, "It already is, sir. So-called small attacks, launches of one to ten warheads, are part of both sides' strategic arsenal now. The Soviets may well feel they can field one and get away with it as a bargaining strategy: They don't want us to finish our SDI umbrella—it's too much better then theirs. We have to consider that they might be serious about demonstrating their resolve and confident that we won't respond, lest the war escalate to unacceptable levels. A space war is the last thing either side really wants."

Stewart snorted and bared his teeth. "We'd hold a lot more cards than in a ground war in Asia, wouldn't we, deputy director?" Unlike the CIA man, the president had seen service just before the Nam mess and had always been a bit pugnacious on the subject.

Forrestal's stomach tied itself into a knot. "If we've been in a more delicate situation with regard to nuclear conflict, sir, I don't know about it. Consider that including our point defense—antimissile batteries on the ground—and SDI's space capability, we can raise the Soviet attack price to twenty Russian warheads per U.S. target. We've got one hundred critical fixed C3—Command, Control, Communications—targets alone. That's two thousand Russian warheads right there, instead of the one to two hundred the USSR would require without SDI. That would leave the Soviets about four thousand warheads for the entire U.S. in an all-out conflict."

"But nobody wants an all-out conflict," said the president. "Even with SDI, in an all-out spasm exchange we all die. SDI's job is to prevent the spasm."

"That's right, sir," said Forrestal. "And nobody wants to concede space. So, thinking in intelligence terms, it's probably better to let the Soviets test our system—that's what they're doing, sir, in a deniable fashion. As long as we can counter the feint, we'll be golden. If we can't dissuade them and they make a 'mistake' and launch a missile, then we'll shoot it down for them, publicly, and reap the publicity bonanza and probably real rewards at the arms-control negotiations. It'll be stabilizing, not destabilizing."

Stewart frowned so deeply that his eyes seemed drawn toward the bridge of his nose. "Are you trying to give me a lesson in military strategy, deputy director? Telling me that I can't afford to shoot back? That's it, isn't it?"

Thin ice, this, Forrestal knew. A revamping of the president's *High Noon* approach to space defenses had to seem like Stewart's own idea. "Sir, I'm not doing any such thing. I'm just pointing out that we'd be the world's heroes if we demonstrated that we could shoot down a runaway missile without losing our heads and launching anything in retaliation. It would be the propaganda coup of the century—worth the cost."

"The cost?"

"Surfacing the TAV, sir. Not even the man who's going to fly it knows about it yet. You remember what we discussed doing with it?"

This point was the stickiest: A super–secret weapons platform like the Trans Atmospheric Vehicle was at risk in Forrey's plans, a plane so secret that its forerunner, the Stealth X-3 Thunderhawk, was still ultra–classified. He needed a clear go-ahead from Stewart before he started up his operation. Once it was started, there would be no turning back. And many of the specifics he needed to discuss with Taylor, Hayes, and Brecker he hadn't broached to the president: Counterintelligence rules were simple—you said as little as possible to as few as possible.

Stewart understood that. He even appreciated the fact that this way he could claim ignorance of specifics that might be illegal, immoral, or embarrassing politically. What Stewart didn't understand was that Forrestal had a personal score to settle with Marcus Wolfe, his East German counterpart, and that Forrey was intent on doing that during the run of "Classic Thunder," as he'd dubbed the operation taking shape.

Stewart said cautiously, "You've got your okay, Forrey. For all of it. The only thing that bothers me is, what happens if your plan doesn't work?"

"Damned if I know, sir," said Forrestal honestly, thinking of thousands of warheads, or the alternative, ceding the game to the Soviets. "Damned if I know."

The restaurant where Munro Hayes and Amy Brecker met Forrestal and Taylor was on the top floor of the new high-rise that housed Vandenberg's Officers' Club as well as its executive suites.

The lounge, still sporting its Christmas tinsel, was full of artfully crafted black leather sofas, $3,000 coffeepots, and aerospace execs from Lockheed and Rockwell with their blonde and expensive ladies tipping Baccarat highball glasses.

Ro ushered Brecker through, feeling out of place and underdressed beside the woman in her black and silver tux, although Taylor's aide was waiting for them at the door with a smooth "Good to see you, major, Ms. Brecker. Right this way," and a space manager sitting with a Lockheed engineer gave him a friendly wave.

He'd just keep his flight jacket on and nobody would offer to bring him a tie, he decided as they approached Terrible Taylor's table and both men sitting at it rose.

"Full kit" hadn't meant dress blues, not until today. He hadn't thought seriously about "dinner"; he hadn't thought about much but Thunderhawk, all g's and sleek speed. He hadn't even thought much about Brecker, once he'd been airborne on the flight home. He was still full of adrenaline from the ride, in love with Thunderhawk, his soul back on the runway.

So he went through the formalities of handshakes and pulling back Brecker's chair absently, looking at the ten-page parchment menu without really seeing it, until the unspoken imperatives of his situation began to sink in as he listened to the small talk that wasn't really small and realized that this table, in its dark nook, was about to be isolated from the rest of the room by sliding panels behind his back.

He'd seen this sort of thing before: honchos from nobody-asked-where in one of these high-security conference alcoves—seen backs briefly while waiters brought food in and dishes out. He'd never wanted to be in one of these meetings.

While the other three were chattering about "the gravlax here," he sneaked a look at Brecker. There was nothing of the sniffling, overwrought girl about her now. She tossed her head flirtatiously and laughed at her CO's joke about the weather in Berlin as if she were at some embassy function. He realized for the first time that she was attractive, professional, and assuredly competent, or she wouldn't have been here.

He also realized that he'd signed onto something interagency and complex when he'd assured Taylor that he was "go."

At the time, he hadn't thought any further than flying the Thunderhawk—anywhere, any way he could.

He studied Forrestal, CIA's legendary deputy director of counterintelligence, over the top of his menu. There were stories about Terrible and Forrestal; there were more stories that left no doubt that Forrestal had "teeth." He ran offshore counterintelligence and ran it well enough that the private war he'd been fighting with the East German spymaster Wolfe rocked NATO periodically.

Again Ro looked at Amy Brecker, who somehow managed to seem completely at home here, where she'd never been, in her chain-mail tie and her high heels, and remembered the way she'd told him he was just her "taxi driver." For people who would probably be working together, they hadn't gotten off to a flaming good start.

When his eyes returned to Forrestal's craggy, aristocratic face, they met the spymaster's with a jolt.

"And what do you think, Munro?"

"Sir?" Ro hadn't been following any of the conversation.

"About the menu," Amy Brecker said, her voice barely audible on his right and her lips unmoving.

"I'm a meat-and-potatoes man, sir. Steak and fries after a . . . flight . . . like that's sort of a tradition with me."

Play country boy, Forrestal's glance said with

paternal amusement. *Agents and pilots aren't that different.* "Steak and fries—*pommes frites,* hereabouts—it is, then. We'll order and then get down to business, unless anyone objects?"

Taylor said, "Nobody does, Forrey. Ro, we can talk about the plane's performance later."

"That's fine, sir. I'll write it up, anyway. . . ." Taylor wasn't himself, either, Ro realized, wondering what Taylor was trying to tell him.

"No, son. Not this time. You'll give me a verbal when I give you your technical briefing—no writtens. It wasn't a test flight."

"Yes, sir. I think I understand that, sir." Out of the corner of his eye, Ro caught Amy Brecker looking at him and wondered why he had to be here for this.

"The test flight's later," Taylor said with a cold and wicked grin on his wide flat face as he summoned the waiter with a beeper to order drinks and dinner.

It was a long dinner, full of NATO talk and half-datums, which made Ro realize that although Taylor and Forrestal were old friends and co-running this operation, neither wanted to be candid with his own player in front of the opposition. Like CIA's budget, hidden in the air force's, what was crucial here was buried in what was not, and intimacy didn't guarantee trust.

For Ro, the endless meal full of innuendo and half-confidences was comforting: Some things never changed. Forrestal and Taylor had set the meeting here because they felt the place was secure, but didn't trust it, or each other, enough to turn their cards faceup.

Ro was doing something that involved another

classified aircraft, and Brecker—something that probably would involve NATO airspace. He watched Forrestal draw her out and surmised that she, too, would be asked to make no written report.

When names came up—names like Wolfe, Vice-Consul Aikens, somebody called Lutz, and another vaguely familiar name, Dietrich—he paid close attention. When Forrestal asked Brecker, point-blank, "Did you understand what Lutz was trying to tell you, my dear? Are you ready to go back into Berlin as a traitor, playing Dietrich and the net you picked up from Azimov?" Brecker put down her fork.

"Sir," she said, looking first at Hayes, then at Taylor, "I assume we're free to discuss this here in detail? Then," she continued after Forrestal smiled expansively, "I'll do what I'm told, of course, but I don't see where you're taking this—how penetrating one of Wolfe's East German operations is going to help stop the PKO gambit. . . ." She trailed off, as if some mechanical governor had cut in, keeping her from speaking of things she'd been trained to hold back.

"We'll be giving you great bona fides, for a defector: Hayes here, and perhaps his plane."

"*What?*" Ro burst out, then sat back with all eyes on him. He put up one hand, palm toward Forrestal. "No objection. You just surprised me, that's all." His mind was racing, wanting to object. This wasn't what he did—he wasn't any penetration agent; in fact, he wasn't great with people, period, let alone women. He didn't like it on America's ground, let alone foreign soil. He'd signed on to fly whatever they'd give him, though, and he'd given Taylor his word. Objections couldn't come from him.

He looked squarely at Taylor, distress squelched so that his face was as impassive as his CO's. And Taylor gave him an infinitesimal shrug, which Ro hoped meant "We'll talk later."

Brecker was more forthcoming. "Director Forrestal, I'm not sure I see the point of this. PKO's not going to take out *Skylab* now that we know about the plan and they know we know. . . . Oh, I think I see."

"We'll talk at length later, Amy—if I may call you Amy. This operation, you both may have gathered," Forrestal said as he picked up his brandy, "isn't the sort where you'll have briefing books. There'll be no time to read in or send up dissenting opinions. There's no reporting chain beyond the four of us here. You'll have secure equipment, of course, but—"

"Jesus," Ro said softly, reacting as much to the mention of PKO in the same sentence with *Skylab* as to the high-security procedures. Then he looked at Brecker. Go into some game of NATO hardball dependent upon this woman?

It better be one hell of a plane, and one hell of a plan.

Two hours later he was convinced that it was both.

Coming out of the restaurant with Taylor's aide and the pilot, Amy was giddy from wine and success. What a day! A long one, given the time gain, of course. But still, only hours ago she'd been sure that her career was in ruins. Now she knew it was just beginning.

Forrestal himself! She'd never even *met* the counterintelligence chief; now she was reporting directly to him.

Taylor's aide and her pilot stopped, their heads together, under the modernistic concrete of the entryway, talking about cars.

"Her" pilot: She was already thinking of him that way.

". . . take my four-wheeler for tonight," the aide was saying. "It's got civilian plates; the Old Man suggested you do."

Munro Hayes said, "Fine with me, if Ms. Brecker doesn't mind fending for herself. . . ."

The aide whispered something Amy didn't catch, and Hayes, listening to the other man, scratched the back of his neck ruminatively, then nodded: "Right, I'll take her."

Amy was watching the California sky, soft and mild and full of stars. The warmth of Vandenberg, compared to Berlin's clawlike cold, was making everything seem surreal. She hugged herself, thinking she'd never sleep, not with a personal verbal briefing by Forrestal scheduled for tomorrow morning.

When Hayes came toward her, touched her arm, and said, "Right this way, Ms. Brecker," it seemed the most natural thing in the world to go with him. He was part of her future, her good fortune. It was all she could do not to gloat where Taylor's aide could see.

As soon as she was in the passenger seat of the turbocharged air-force-blue four-wheeler and Ro started the engine, she let out a triumphant laugh. "We were great back there," she declared.

"You were," he amended as the seat-belt buzzer

sounded angrily. "Buckle up." Still the pilot, his head bent to the unfamiliar car's cockpit, he adjusted the steering wheel and found the headlights. The road blossomed before them.

Then, unpremeditatedly, she leaned across the seat and kissed him.

He froze, then responded tentatively, politely. As soon as she disengaged, he went back to setting the car's climate control with one hand as he wheeled it out into the slow, departing restaurant traffic. Amy sat back uncertainly, feeling a flush rise in her cheeks.

"For the audience?" he asked wryly, flicking a glance in the rearview mirror at the high-rise they were leaving behind, where Taylor's aide and valets and brass could be seen under the portico.

"For the record," she said defensively. "Because I felt like it. Forrestal, no less . . ." But her expansive mood was evaporating. She sat sideways, her back against the car door, and there was a thunk as he locked it from his side. "We're going to be working very closely together, Munro," she began.

"Ro," he corrected. "Nobody calls me Munro but my wife and your boss."

Wife? Of course he'd have a wife. Probably kids. She didn't know why she felt so disappointed. Then she did: He was hers for this mission, hers the way an agent was hers. But it shouldn't matter that he had a wife. She chided herself and tried to summon some of her lost ebullience.

"Ro, then. You can drop me at some motel close to where you live. I'll rent a car there. We'll need to spend a few hours together tonight, detail stuff, and we're supposed to look like—"

"Lovers, yeah. Terrible's aide made that clear."

"Terrible?"

"Taylor," he said. " 'Terrible' Taylor, the general. We'll have time to compare notes."

"As soon as I get a room and shower," she proposed as he headed the car toward the gate with its guards and she realized she had no passport, no ID. But this was America. . . .

"What's wrong?"

"My passport, I left it behind."

"No problem, I bet. They said they put everything you'll need at my place."

The dark was deep here, the car ambiently lit by its console's lights, his face intermittently bright in the headlights of approaching cars.

"Your place?" He wasn't wearing a wedding ring, she noticed. "A motel will be good enough for—"

"It would be, if there were one within twenty miles of my place, or if Taylor's aide hadn't given me my orders. Look, Amy, this is more your business than mine. You can stay at my wife's, but that will entail lots of explaining and it's not within walking distance. Or we can play it by your rule book and you'll bunk in with me. Everything you need is there, remember? If it doesn't bother me that your people broke into my house to make you comfy, it shouldn't bother you. I'm a nice guy. I won't jump you. Spooks scare me to death."

His gaze flickered quickly to her, returned to the road, where he was in line to be passed through the first of three gatepost checkpoints.

"Fine," she said, though it wasn't. She didn't like being forced on him. And she didn't like his reaction. They'd have to do better together than this, and much better than they'd done on the flight over from Germany. "I'm sorry about the way I behaved on the Ramstein runway," she said. One of them had to take control, and if Hayes was trying to tell her anything with his remarks, he was saying that this was her area of expertise, not his. "I'd just been pinged, and I didn't realize it was for cover."

"I know, remember? I told you to wait and see what the perks and the pay were." Now he grinned boyishly, toggled his window down, received a salute from the guard, who obviously knew him (and craned his neck to look at her), then accelerated toward the next gate. "No hard feelings here. We'll start from scratch. Maybe you can help me with this playacting stuff. I just fly planes."

I bet, she thought, and said, "And space shuttles? Do you think you're going to be the one who brings those astronauts down? Is that what Taylor wants to brief you on?"

His head swiveled and he stared at her for a long moment before looking back at the road. "No space shuttles. Too long a turnaround time. I don't know half what you do, Amy, but if those guys up there are in danger, somebody'll bring 'em home. Aren't we supposed to find out the whens and ifs?"

"We'll know more tomorrow night. Tonight I'll tell you about the PKO and what I know, and you'll tell me about the planes and what you know. And we'll figure out how we're going to float this legend of being so much in love that you'll follow me anywhere, even to the Soviet Union, and bring your plane with you."

Ro grimaced but said nothing.

"What?" she demanded. "What were you thinking?"

"I was wondering which was worse—having my ex-wife find out I've got a woman up at the cabin, or my friends find out I'm a Commie-lover."

It sounded to her like it was his suddenly "ex-" wife he was most concerned about.

They drove through the two remaining gates in silence, and Amy reached for the radio. "Look," Ro said as she turned it on and jazz tinkled from the speakers, "until you get my files . . . I just splash bogeys, mostly—you know, shoot down enemy planes. I haven't done much cloak-and-dagger. So I'll need some coaching. The TAV— trans-atmospheric vehicle"—he enunciated the long form slowly and clearly—"is a class of fighter plane, or weapons platform, if you like. Every inch of it and every piece of paper relevant to it is a black project—you know, top top secret, and certain other clearances required. We flew over here in the only one anybody's been talking about, even people with clearances. But whatever they've got is probably a faster, meaner incarnation of the same thing—transatmospheric. Understand?"

He had good instincts, waiting until the radio was on, though it was tough for anyone pursuing them to take microwave readings off the glass of moving cars. Tough, but not impossible. One thing Berlin had taught Amy was the seamy side of tradecraft: Wolfe's East Germans played by the old, dirty rules.

"I understand," she said carefully. She had to treat him like an agent; he was being pushed like one by her boss and his own, General Taylor. "You need to check my clearances. I bet everything we need to know about each other will be waiting for us. We're going to find out the differ-

ence between military and civilian intelligence,
that's for sure."

"That's how you think of yourselves?" Hayes
said disbelievingly. "As civilians?"

"Yes, of course." There was that defensiveness
again, instilled in her by Jeremy Pratt, as if what
she did were somehow obscene or immoral. It
wasn't, not by her standards. She didn't take designer drugs or smuggle heroin for the narco-
terrorists of the Middle East. She just tried to
keep West Berlin free. Or had, until today. "Do
you think this gambit has anything to do with
Nicaragua, some sort of lateral escalation?"

"Jesus, you're asking me? Remember, I'm just a
pilot. Your PKO contact was prior to President
Stewart's move into Nicaragua, I assume, since we
just got official about it today. Can you tell me
what you found out?"

"Not yet, Ro. After we get to your place."

"Okay."

And so they fenced in the car, neither telling
the other anything as the blacktop sped by and the
four-wheeler climbed into the hills.

Amy sat, listening to the radio, wondering if she
could handle all the responsibility Forrestal had
heaped upon her. The pilot beside her, intent on
his driving, obviously didn't understand just how
much or what kind of pressure was going to be put
on him, or how grave a risk he'd be taking. She
had no doubt of his physical courage, but the kind
of operation Classic Thunder was shaping up to be
demanded moral courage, the ability to be the
person that the situation demanded. He was going
to need help, but he'd said he knew that.

Dreaming in her seat, silent, listening to the

jazz and watching the gorgeous country, moonlit and wild, as they sped through it, she found that her palms were sweating. Did he understand that to pull this off, he was going to have to live his cover? *Be* what he advertised himself as, as closely as he could? She didn't think he did. She wondered how far she'd go to teach him what he needed to know.

If the operation could be run without someone like Munro Hayes, she knew, he wouldn't be here. He was pivotal to everything. She was merely a guiding hand. Hayes—what he knew and the spaceplane he'd command—would be the bait. It didn't matter if she liked it or not, trusted him or not, or thought he was the right man for the job. But she did.

Or she did until he wheeled the Chevy into a driveway and pulled up before a fieldstone-and-log house too big to be a cabin, a ramshackle place where someone grew trellised roses, and stopped the car. She reached for her door lock, but he said, "We're not there yet. I've got to get some things, see my wife and kids for a minute."

Something must have showed in her face, for he added, "Don't worry. I won't tell them anything. And Jenny's bound to see you, which will back up our story." He chuckled sourly.

He strolled up the flagstone path to his ex-wife's house, hands jammed in his pockets, head hunched between his shoulders. The door opened; he was silhouetted in its light. There was a woman's shape there to greet him. He pecked her on the cheek, went in, the door closed.

Twenty minutes later, just as Amy was considering shutting off the car's engine to conserve fuel, the door opened again and Hayes emerged, carrying a gear bag in one hand and a paper bag in the other. He went around to the rear of the Chevy and opened the tailgate. "Clean sheets," he said with strained insouciance. "Sleeping bag. White wine. Cigarettes, milk, and cereal in case the store's closed."

Even to him, the excuses must have sounded lame. But Amy didn't say anything. The man had a right to see his wife, ex or not, and kids. Especially when he might not see them again for a long, long time.

When he'd slammed the tailgate and come around to slide under the wheel, a dog came bounding and barking, at a dead run, and tried to climb onto his lap, a big Labrador with slobbery lips. He fondled it briefly, then said in a tight voice, "Go on, Buddy, go take care of mama."

The dog whined but got down on all fours, then trotted obediently up the walk, where it scratched at the front door as Ro closed his and started the motor.

"Home?" he said. "Or do you need something I didn't think of—aspirin I've got, but . . ."

"Home," she said uncomfortably, thinking that she'd take the sleeping bag tonight and when she saw Forrestal in the morning she'd make sure she didn't have to impose on Ro further until it was absolutely necessary.

His wife was standing in the window, the curtain pulled back, as they drove away.

Chapter Seven

New Year's Eve in *Skylab 2* was a study in make-do psychology, Canfield thought as he prepared to take his turn at the visual com-link Houston had thoughtfully arranged for the four astronauts.

It was a tough time to be away from home. Holly Gold, the woman crew member, had cried openly when her kids had come on screen. The other scientist, Alpert, who had crippling arthritis, was taciturn and glum because the best Houston had been able to dredge up for him as well-wishers were his sister and brother-in-law.

Robinson had the perfect family, of course: a son at Yale and a daughter at Duke; a loving, plump wife who showed him the mince pie she was freezing until he got home to eat it; and a grandmother who remembered all too well when blacks couldn't have been given the red-carpet treatment at Houston because one of their own was an astronaut.

The whole event was making Canfield distinctly uncomfortable. He wasn't much for open emotional display. He didn't like the mix of civilian

and military missions that had put Holly Gold and
Alpert aboard and in his charge. Canfield was a
military man through and through, and although
the two specialists were military consultants, on
the payroll, and represented the crucial university
linkage SDI needed, anything that smacked of
public relations made Canfield nervous.

Canfield's wife, herself a government scientist,
was showing signs of strain when at last he saw her
face, pale and distorted by the long-distance transmission. And the time lag made the conversation
awkward. They talked about their kids and they
talked about the weather on Earth: "Looks beautiful up here, honey. Wish you could see it."

Her delayed response, this time, was due to
more than just time lag. She had been as qualified
as Holly Gold for this flight—more so, because
there was some pressure to test "fertility in zero
g." But nepotism couldn't be tolerated; fertility
testing would have to wait for an all-civilian or
all-military mission—for the bigger, NASA station.

"Wish I could too, Can," said his wife bravely,
blinking fast, her lips twitching. "Come home safe
and sound, okay?"

The long pause was on his part this time. His
gaze locked with his wife's. They couldn't talk in
this fishbowl atmosphere; both of them knew it.
He wanted to ask her about the U.S. troops in
Nicaragua and how things really were down there,
but he couldn't bring himself to do it. In fact, his
throat seemed to be closing up. He had three
weeks more of this tour and suddenly it seemed
like a lifetime.

"Happy New Year, baby," he said, despite the
ears listening. "Happy New Year."

"And many more, Can," came her voice so quickly she must have blurted it.

He blinked, and when he opened his eyes again, she was already getting up from her seat before the monitor.

Behind him, Robinson was waiting with a drink carton full of champagne.

Chapter Eight

At 0500 on New Year's Day, Taylor's staff car picked up Munro Hayes to drive him to a classified test site north of Santa Barbara, where General Sam Taylor waited with the TAV in its hangar.

Alone with the spaceplane, but for its guards and mechanics, Terrible Taylor had too long to wonder if what he and Forrestal were planning was worth the risk of the TAV's security envelope. Worse, Taylor had time to wonder whether Forrestal was leveling with him—whether what Forrey had in mind for Hayes and this billion-dollar aircraft was similar in more than surface features to what he himself had in mind.

You don't work closely with a man for a quarter of a century and learn nothing about him. Forrey was a snake. But Forrey was Taylor's snake, and in this business you had to have one, or you'd be bitten by the other guy's.

The differences in mission of their two services seemed to have disappeared in this one instance; interservice rivalries seemed to have been put aside. The Strategic Defense Initiative had brought elements of the air force and CIA into the closest harmony anyone could remember. It was the nature of SDI's mission itself—protecting American interests in cislunar space (everything between the atmosphere and the moon)—that had done it, not executive orders or outside pressure. Both services had the responsibility for certain components of space-based and airborne surveillance; both were deeply involved in the design and implementation of the Keyhole 12 generation of spy satellites; both felt the massive and hostile National Security Agency nipping at their heels.

The Strategic Defense Initiative Office, in its attempts to woo contractors, implement project security, and coordinate the armed services' efforts, as well as lobby Congress, impeded rather than facilitated progress. Moments like this, when decisions could be made without the involvement of numerous consenting agencies—when decisions could be made, in fact, by just Forrey, Taylor, and President Stewart—were few and far between.

It reminded Taylor of the old days, of the good memories that time had burnished. But 40,000 American boys in El Salvador and Nicaragua also reminded Taylor of the old days, of the bad memories that night exhumed like ghosts.

SDI had involved an enormous effort: wrangling about its viability; billions of dollars in cost overruns alone spent to design and emplace it; multilayered defenses, from ground-based kinetic-kill Gatling guns for point defense to chemical, excimer, and even *Excalibur*'s nuclear-driven lasers in orbit to strike enemy missiles in their boost phase and in space—not to mention *NAVSTAR*'s global positioning network, which could pinpoint a moving target to within a meter anywhere on earth or above. With all this, SDI was going to find its make-or-break dependent on the steadiness of an American president in a prototypical Soviet face-down, the cleverness of CIA, the tactical and technical competence of the air force's most closely guarded secret, and the nerve of a single pilot.

If it was a matter of who blinked first, Taylor was determined that it be the other guy: the Soviet Union, not he or his.

That was why Munro Hayes had been the only choice, once Taylor had factored in what Forrey wasn't telling him, along with what the CIA chief *had* said. As soon as it became clear that Taylor wouldn't be allowed to bring the astronauts aboard *Skylab 2* home early, Taylor had understood what was implicit, as well as explicit, in this international game of chicken into which he'd been drafted.

So would Hayes, once he saw the TAV. No matter what Forrey's honey-haired agent said or did, Hayes was, now and forever, a pilot—a prime example of what the air force could offer that would beat any technical means or convoluted arms-control strategy hands down. It was a shame to ask Hayes to go through all this cloak-and-dagger; if Forrey hadn't been a confirmed bachelor, a heartless son of a bitch with no kids of his own, he'd never have suggested linking the pilot to an espionage mission. It should have been enough to put Hayes and the TAV together, on alert, and stand back when the buzzer sounded. Munro Hayes was the Air Force's top gun, not only in war games but in action. The TAV was the natural child of the F-15 ASAT (antisatellite) launching platforms—the only satellite killer that had proved reliable in the field.

One of the laser battle stations dotting the sky (barely noticeable alongside 4,000 other satellites that made the belt from Low Earth Orbit to Geo-synchronous Orbit seem like a diagram of New York's rush hour when you saw the data come up under Cheyenne Mountain at the tracking center) *might* be able to take out one missile coming up from the Sea of Japan, all by itself. But they were complex, computer-driven systems and they could not, under any circumstances, be allowed to fail. If the target had been an unmanned satellite, the response might have been different. In that case, the Russian ploy would have stayed subsurface—just a test of equipment, not of national will. But the subtle difference in target choice, the threat of public outcry at the loss of American life, made the stakes too high to risk leaving the outcome to an incomplete computerized system.

Next year, they probably could have done it—left the TAV unexposed, the outcome to semicon-ductors. But it wasn't next year, it was this year, an election year. And the Soviets wanted Stewart out of the White House.

So man and computer would work together, with as little as possible left to chance. The F-15 ASATs had been flown, in essence, remotely, the missile in control of the fighter plane, in its turn controlled by men deep under Cheyenne Moun-tain, the pilot (for much of the flight) along for the ride.

The TAV in the hangar beside Taylor was of a more advanced generation; Ro would have many options. Unlike the F-15s, and equally unlike the interim X-29A canard-winged fly-by-wire aircraft that were inherently unstable and needed six onboard computers to stay in the air, the TAV had seven computers aboard that Ro could override. Those seven computers had earned the plane the designation and the acronym *MEDUSA*. Three of its onboard brains were digital; three were analogue; and one, the tie breaker, was of a new breed, an "artificial intelligence" computer—a silicon copilot.

If the lesser computers argued, the AI copilot was the decision maker. It kept the pilot out of the unenviable position of being able only to make suggestions to computers flying his aircraft when his butt was strapped to the iron. It could recognize 200 verbal commands, perform autopilot functions and all human copilot functions. But it couldn't correlate data like a human being. It would still be Ro's job, at closing speeds of 15,000 miles per hour, to hit the LASER ARM/FIRE button. Through a specialized helmet, the pilot's eye—the most accurate targeting mechanism nature had ever designed—assisted by the AI and its computer slaves, would determine the hit or miss.

The spaceplane could deliver as much as 2.5 million pounds of thrust. It could carry a 20,000-pound payload into Low Earth Orbit or half that to a Geosynchronous Orbit. But on its own, it couldn't be trusted any further than the 1400 components of the space-based SDI: It couldn't be trusted not to miss.

Ro Hayes had never lost a dogfight. He'd seen more action in the air than any currently qualified American fighter pilot, and he'd handled the Stealth X-3 Thunderhawk as if it were a riding-school nag.

But still Taylor faced lingering doubts. Nobody had ever flight-tested the weapons-platform aspects of the TAV. *MEDUSA* had never had to make a decision in a crisis. The life-support capabilities of the spaceplane hadn't been tested either.

If something went wrong with the life support, the computers could probably bring the plane home, with assistance from Cheyenne Mountain—unless what went wrong had to do with electromagnetic pulse or holes in its fuselage. . . .

Taylor lifted his head at the sound of his staff car approaching, then glanced into the hangar at the TAV. His spirits rose, looking at it, three times the size of an F-15, fluid as a woman, black and white and awesome with its detachable canard and its narrow nose.

Then he strode out to meet Hayes.

The pilot, even as he slid out of the car's back seat, was judging the length of the runway, 7,000 feet of manicured flatness, stretching away toward the end of the bowl in which the test facility was situated. Where mountains crouched around the two-mile flat, a control tower was nestled; closer to hand, three long, low buildings sat, squat and utilitarian; dirt tracks of deeper brown crisscrossed the plain, leading to the six hangars before which the staff car had drawn to a stop.

Ro's salute was precise, but his eyes were narrowed, scanning the distance, as Taylor said, "No need for formalities, Ro. Let's go see her."

"Her?" The pilot faced him, kit slung over his shoulder. "The TAV, right, sir?"

"*MEDUSA*," Taylor affirmed, conscious that he now had the tall young man's complete attention. There had been no preflight studying for Hayes, no books or even a spec sheet. As with Thunder-hawk, Ro was coming in cold. Taylor searched for doubt in the pilot's face, found none. "How was your New Year's Eve, son?"

"Uh . . ." Ro looked puzzled; then, pulling sun-glasses out of his windbreaker's pocket, said, "That's right, sir. Happy New Year."

Taylor was wondering why Hayes wasn't already hurrying into the hangar to get a look at the plane. When they'd offered him Thunderhawk, he'd been mesmerized.

"To you, too, major. Is there some problem?" Taylor crossed his arms, suddenly conscious of the chill in the early-morning air.

"Not exactly a problem, but . . ." Hayes rubbed the back of his neck, then turned from the hips to face Taylor, a habit some pilots displayed in stress, learned in high g, when the pressure was so in-tense that a man couldn't simply turn his head but had to swivel his torso.

"Let's hear it, Ro." Taylor waved impatiently at the staff car and his aide got out, closed the back door, got back in, and drove away toward the rear of the hangars, leaving the two men, general and pilot, as alone on the barren flat as they'd have been at the end of the earth.

For nearly a full minute, the only sound came from inside the hangar, where a mechanic was manhandling something large and metallic.

Then Hayes said, "I lost track of time, what with all the spook stuff. . . . New Year's was that woman telling me what she thinks I'm supposed to do. I'd like to hear your version, sir." Ro's head came up, his chin jutting. For the first time he seemed to be peering into the shadows, where *MEDUSA* waited.

"What did she tell you, Ro?"

"About flying over to Germany with whatever you've got here and letting the cat out of the bag. About playing defector with her, giving out data on what the TAV can do, about maybe taking it into Berlin or—"

"*No!*" Taylor snapped, fury rising to make the veins stand out blue on his reddening forehead. "Ramstein, yes. Cat-and-mouse games, if you can handle them, yes. But this plane doesn't go farther east than Ramstein, if you have to crash to avoid it. Clear?"

The pilot puffed out his cheeks, expelled the breath as he took off his sunglasses, and stared fondly at Taylor. "I was hoping you'd say that, sir. This whole business with Brecker isn't really my style. You'd better talk to her CO, sir. She thinks she's running this whole show."

"That's exactly what I'll do, Ro. Exactly. We've got lots of briefing time, but let me ease your mind: I expect we'll have you up there"—Taylor pointed skyward—"for a good bit of this mission. There's still a chance that we might be able to evacuate *Skylab*. *MEDUSA*'s being converted to hold them, if we decide that's what we'll do. Remember, we've got two chains of command, here— yours to me; Brecker's to Forrestal. You don't take orders from her."

"That's good to hear, sir. Let's take a look at what we've got, then."

Just like that. No further questions. Not an eyebrow raised at the possibility of evacuating *Skylab*'s personnel, though Taylor was willing to bet that

Hayes knew enough about the difficulties of such a maneuver to have plenty of questions.

Sure that he'd picked the right man for the job, Taylor trailed the pilot into the hangar, where Hayes stopped, hands on hips, his sunglasses dangling from still fingers. Hayes whistled softly.

As the pilot slowly circled the spaceplane, Taylor was tempted to follow and give a running commentary on the technological advances incorporated into *MEDUSA:* the Teflon-and-composite skin, the low-signature shape, the scramjet boosters, the electronic countermeasures, the underwing arsenal.

But Hayes knew what he was looking at.

Taylor felt just a twinge of jealousy for the man who was going to fly this billion-dollar craft into space for the first time. Fly her from a standard runway, no piggyback required, into a combat situation among the stars.

The general's eyes got misty. It was a wonderful time to be alive if you loved technology the way he did. Wonderful, if technology could be used properly. If everybody stayed alive. And free.

Taylor had started flying crop dusters on his daddy's farm. When he'd been Forrey's scope in Nam, the high-tech bug had bitten him, had bitten all of them who realized that they were just learning the ropes, that they were at the tricycle stage of the space age. You could get killed on a tricycle, true. But if you mastered the art of bike riding, there was a ten-speed in your future.

And the TAV before him, with its revolutionary avionics, was tomorrow's ten-speed.

Give the Soviets hands-on, indeed! Not while Taylor was alive. Let 'em use their spy-eyes. They had *Salyut 10* in a polar orbit, low-orbital photo-return satellites, and Lenin-knew-what kind of ground penetration at Ramstein. That was plenty, all they were going to get.

Taylor fully expected to scramble Ro and *MEDUSA* out of Ramstein into orbit, to put his manned space fighter into a contest against a Soviet missile. And perhaps to lose it, if luck was against him and *MEDUSA* was buffeted by electromagnetic pulse. But he wasn't going to *give* the TAV away. And he wasn't going to give Hayes away. Taylor had a son nearly Ro's age, and was life-conserving by nature. He was going to grab Forrey by the nose and not let go until the division of command for this mission was clear. Absolutely and perfectly clear.

Hayes came around from the plane's offside with a wistful, half-dazed smile on his face like a bridegroom's. Taylor chuckled and said, "Go on, check her out."

Without another word, Hayes hit the button on *MEDUSA*'s nosewheel and with a whir from above their heads the boarding ladder started to descend, while from behind the plane a man in coveralls came trotting toward them with a three-ring binder under his arm.

An hour later, alone in the TAV on the runway, engines fired up and waiting only for Ground Control's final okay to take *MEDUSA* up, Ro Hayes checked every gauge and readout one more time. Then he just breathed deeply through his helmet's oxygen mask and waited for the word.

MEDUSA was an acronym for military earth-orbit-defense undetectable strategic aircraft. She was stealthed, armed and dangerous, and more powerful than Ro had dreamed she could be. She was single-pilot-capable, although there was room for a copilot/scope/passenger. "Single-pilot," in this case, begged the question: *MEDUSA* was the next generation of fly-by-wire aircraft, with an electronic copilot aboard.

His head was full of last-minute instructions, but the part of him that flew aircraft wasn't consternated. He was going to override the computers wherever possible; he was going to keep his voice instructions to a minimum. In short, he was going to fly the plane under him with as few bells and whistles engaged as possible. Once he was in the high sky and they sent up the drone for his shoot-down, he could start making deals with computers. Before that, he had to know what he could do with this bird if her high-tech accouterments were disabled or malfunctioned. And Taylor had to know whether, under imperfect field conditions as opposed to contractor testing, *MEDUSA*'s laser battery could splash a target.

Behind the copilot's seat was a sealed-off cargo area, filled now with fuel for the onboard lasers. If something went wrong, he wouldn't even feel the heat before he was vaporized along with the plane.

He'd been relieved of the worst of his qualms when Taylor had confirmed that no one was going to ask him to fly *MEDUSA* into Berlin: It just wouldn't wash. If he got it there, the opposition would be justifiably skeptical of his veracity: Anybody taking a plane like this east should be shot out of the sky by American chase planes before he made any unauthorized airspace; otherwise they might as well hang a sign on him that said "phony." He didn't want to give his life for Amy Brecker on foreign soil. Miles above the earth in an experimental aircraft, though—that was a different matter; he accepted that sort of risk as a part of his life.

There was a punch-out button that would jettison the canopy, then the pilot in his seat, if Ro wanted to try a long, slow roast-and-fall. He felt for it, and the movement made him very aware of the pressure suit he was wearing. It was almost a space suit. It had to be. *MEDUSA* could make him pull thirty g's or better; her top speed was thought to be Mach forty-two; she could surveille the earth from orbital distances. It would be one hell of a long fall.

He resolved, in those final moments, not to try it if the plane glitched up on him.

Then he got his okay from the tower and everything kaleidoscoped. His enemy was gravity, his own pulse rate, the dark at the edges of his vision as a giant sat on his chest and *MEDUSA* leaped under him, straight at the stars.

Chapter Nine

As soon as she'd deplaned at Langley Field, Amy Brecker had begun to sneeze. There was snow on the East Coast, and by the time her driver had deposited her at the imposing front door of someone's very private and very country stone-and-oak estate, her nose was running and she had chills.

Forrestal himself came out to meet her, looking like something from a Victorian novel in his red velvet smoking jacket with a butler hovering behind him on wide granite steps. He called her "my dear" and fussed over her with sepulchral charm as she realized that there were too many cars parked along the long, circular drive for hers to be a private interview.

Inside, under twelve-foot ceilings and glowering, cracked portraits of long-dead men, a woman in a starched white apron brought her chamomile tea in a cavernous sitting room in which she was totally alone. Not for the first time during this operation, panic began rising in her throat. She waited for Forrestal or someone, anyone, to come in and explain to her what was going on, what she was doing here, what "things" of hers were "already upstairs in your room, dear," since she had brought no "things" and had no "room" that she knew of. She'd fight off the sniffles by a mighty effort of will, she decided. It was something she could do, or try to do, to affect her own fate. Not much, but something, when everything seemed out of her control.

Ro Hayes certainly was. They'd fenced and worked at being achingly polite in his cabin. She'd taken time to read his file, saying that they'd "have to get to know one another, you understand," and suggesting that he read hers.

He was more of an operator than he'd let on; a cowboy, in the vernacular—combat-trained, qualified with all manner of weapons, some sort of air force specialist in the kind of intelligence Amy didn't want anything to do with: covert action, counterterrorism, things that went bang in the night. She'd felt as if he'd betrayed her, tricked her by omission. She'd resolved to teach him respect, and more—that there was more to her kind of intelligence than he thought.

She'd pushed too hard, and he'd reacted with careful silence and raised eyebrows as she tried to teach him some rudimentary German facts of life and set up deep context for their operation. When, well before dawn, someone had come to collect him, he drove off for a "check-out" ride, leaving her in the strange cabin, alone.

Neither of them had realized that it was New Year's Day until the air force man who'd come for him had wished them a Happy New Year. Her own orders had come shortly thereafter, delayed only by the length of time she let his phone ring, wondering if she dared pick it up. It might have been his wife, his girlfriend, or one of the good ol' boys he hung out with.

It wasn't. It was her summons to the opposite coast and her promised personal briefing at the hands of Forrestal. She'd never expected, when she'd gone into this sort of work, to be in such a position. She thought of Jeremy Pratt, and what he'd say if he could see the gentleman's country estate with its snowy grounds and her being treated like a dignitary, sipping tea from a porcelain cup worth what her Berlin weekly paycheck totaled.

She began to take stock of her surroundings, noticing the secure phone with its thick cord and video/hardcopy/computer capability; a blank wall with buttons set into its molding; an absolutely clean desk with locking drawers.

Was this Forrestal's house? Or an Agency house? She couldn't ask; she'd never been privy to the machinations of power at this level. She'd never been more than a glorified secretary, a paper-pusher, a cog in the wheel, efficiently doing what she'd been trained to do and waiting for the right man to come along. This was a different CIA than the one she'd joined, at entry level, years ago. Then, she'd been disappointed that her job wasn't glamorous, or as exciting as spies' lives in the movies. Secretly, she'd been relieved. Now, after the lack of equanimity she'd displayed at the start of this operation in Berlin, when she'd been pinged, she was wondering if she had what it took.

But it was too late for that. She had to rise to the occasion. And so she would, though she felt rather like she'd made a dentist appointment and kept it: surprised that she was doing this to herself.

She was sipping her tea, finally fatalistically accepting of whatever lay ahead, when Forrestal came in and, with a Vincent Price smile, said, "My dear, we don't have much time, so let's get to it." He sat at his desk and began to tell her, very gently, that she'd screwed up with Hayes.

"Taylor called me, hot as a pistol. Seems that Hayes wanted assurances that the TAV isn't going into Berlin—in fact, is going nowhere but Ramstein. I had to give it to him."

"I didn't—"

"I'm sure you didn't, dear. But you've got to realize that this is a co-run, that the air force doesn't like being bossed around, that you're dealing with a hotshot pilot who doesn't take easily to being ordered about by a . . ."

"Woman?" Amy supplied bitterly.

"An agency functionary," Forrestal corrected. "I brought you here for your final briefing, and you'll have it, though I'm afraid I must ask you to pretend to be socializing with my guests—it's a holiday, after all. But you're up to that, having served us so well in Berlin."

"I'm not dressed for—"

"Upstairs, dear. We have the simple matters well in hand. However, there is a kicker of sorts. Taylor has his back up. He wants you range- and punch-out-qualified. I had to agree." Forrestal spread his hands.

"Range?" That was shooting, no doubt. She could manage that; her father had insisted she be the son he'd never had. "Punch-out?" She had no idea what the term meant.

"I'm sure you'll do very well. We'll have someone with you who's coached raw diplomatic personnel, so you won't be alone. You're about to learn that where this sort of operation is concerned, you'll never be entirely alone. But do be careful."

Coming from Forrestal, accompanied by a concerned and paternal stare from accomplished eyes that chilled her, the simple words were terrifying: *Do be careful*.

What did he expect her to be, cavalier? Devil-may-care? She didn't like the sound of the warning, where one shouldn't be necessary. But somehow she couldn't bring herself to ask him what he meant.

She listened to the arrangements made for her return by commercial carrier to Berlin, her well-thought-out cover story, her arranged meeting with Hayes and the one she'd have to arrange for herself with Dietrich. And she listened to cautions about the strains on interagency personnel (Munro Hayes) and a clear division of command—hers on the ground, "wherever action or countermeasures aren't involved"; his in the air. She memorized the timetable and bit her lower lip to still the desire to take notes when Forrestal punched the button that slid back the wall-sized wooden panel and began explaining, with visual aids, about the manned space station and the personnel on board.

"If Hayes is scrambled," Forrestal concluded, "it doesn't necessarily mean that you've failed in your mission. But from that point, you're on your own—you'll have to handle your own extraction if you're in enemy territory."

It was numbing to hear East Berlin referred to

as "enemy territory." Of course, it was. The borders of the two Berlins had never been officially fixed; the four occupying Western powers technically had jurisdiction over both Berlins, according to the NATO Status of Forces Agreement (SOFA) and its supplement, over "U.S. servicemembers" accused of offenses "arising out of an act or omission done in the performance of official duties."

That subsection of SOFA might be all Amy had to protect her if Hayes had to fly off into the wild black yonder.

It sucked, she knew. And she knew Forrestal knew, too. But it wasn't worrying her as much, somehow, as shooting qualifying rounds and executing a "punch-out."

"Questions, Amy?" Forrestal prompted.

At least he'd dropped the "dear." "May I—is there any objection to my seeing old friends? I had a fiancé in West—"

"Jeremy Pratt? I don't see why you can't visit whomever you choose, as long as it's behavior compatible with your cover. Might not help the young man's career, but that's not our business, is it?"

"I—no, I guess not." She was beginning to feel like a spy, like one of those by turns arrogant and furtive types who dropped in occasionally for money or passports or a safe place to sleep.

"If that's it, then," Forrestal, obviously a busy man making time for her, said conclusively, "I'll go back to my guests while you go upstairs to make yourself presentable. When you've changed, come down and I'll put you in the hands of the person who'll be with you during your qualifiers."

"Fine, sir," Amy agreed.

And everything was, after that, fine until she met the hard, thin woman in the blue chiffon dress who'd be "with you every step of the way, honey, tomorrow morning," and found out that a "punch-out" was something you did to save yourself when the plane you were in was crashing.

To the woman, she whispered over her wineglass, "But I'm not going to *be* in that plane, am I? I'm flying over commercial—"

"Ours not to reason, honey." The older woman winked. "And listen, with the full-auto rifle, if you disengage the back end of the sling and stand on it while you're shooting, you'll have as much control as a three-hundred-pound man with wrists the size of your knees."

Amy wanted to ask the older woman, Mary Smith, if this punching out was the air force's revenge—or Ro's—on CIA in the person of Amy Brecker, for taking the reins of this operation.

But something inside her knew the answer: Of course it was.

BOOK TWO

Chapter Ten

Amy Brecker said, "Hi, Jeremy," with more insouciance than she felt when the cultural attaché opened his apartment door.

At least there wasn't another girl in there. Jeremy Pratt's apartment in Berlin's new American Embassy compound was tiresomely Bauhaus, sterile and expensively furnished in bachelor modern—black leather, Italian lighting, a desk made from a BMW's bonnet. Amy had always hated the place, but tonight it was reassuring—more so than the carefully arranged face of the man, who for once seemed at a loss for words.

"Well, darling," Amy said brightly, shifting her heavy pocketbook into the crook of her arm, "aren't you going to invite me in?"

Indecision, frustration, then embarrassment paraded across Jeremy's neat WASP features. He even flushed before he stepped uncertainly backward, motioning as he did so in a parody of welcome meant to avoid the necessity of even a polite embrace: "Surely, come in, come in."

The jilted woman in Amy considered allowing

Jeremy no time to recover, pressing her advantage and involving her ex-lover inextricably in what he most feared: a real intelligence operation. A sense of power filled her as she stepped over the marble threshold and saw that with every step forward she took, Jeremy retreated before her.

Then she got hold of herself. She needed a friend; it wasn't entirely spite that had brought her here. She needed somebody she trusted to know that she *was* here. *You're going to have to handle your own extraction,* Deputy Director Forrestal had said to her. If something went wrong while she was east, there had to be somebody outside the normal chain of command to help her. And Jeremy was perfect: real diplomatic personnel capable of unfeigned upper-class umbrage, well connected, and well meaning in the extreme. Jeremy had access to powerful friends in the Bundestag; he'd survive any scandal unblemished—his sort always did.

And besides, he owed her one. At least one.

They murmured small talk: She thanked him for his kindness; he responded that she was quite welcome. They sat on opposite ends of his feather-stuffed leather sofa, a sea of hide and her pocketbook between them.

She hadn't really expected to come here when she'd asked Forrestal about it; her instinct had been more accurate than she knew. Coming into Tegel on a blue civilian passport, she'd found herself in a world subtly and frighteningly changed. She'd been terrified while she waited in line to clear Customs, certain that one of the blue-uniformed officers of the BGS (Bundesgrenzschutz—Federal Border Force) Individual Services branch was going to haul her off for interrogation or deportation. After all, she'd been pinged less than a week ago; her passport wasn't exactly kosher, nor exactly fake. Forrestal wouldn't give her fake ID.

It was the first thing Jeremy asked her about: "But how did you *get* here, Amy? What's going on? Are you all right?"

"Get here?" she said in a hard, bitter voice: She'd thought this part out, and Jeremy was reacting as if he'd been coached. "I flew. On a blue book—a civilian passport. The Amy Brecker who was pinged had a black book—a dip's number. They didn't even blink."

"Oh, good Lord," Jeremy breathed, his lips going white, his eyes sliding furtively from side to side. "I was hoping you'd gotten things straightened out. I—"

"No you weren't. You knew damned well when you asked how I got here that nothing like that could have happened. For all *I* know, you knew when you broke up with me that this was going to happen. . . ." This wasn't part of her game plan. She didn't want to fight with him.

Jeremy stood up. "Let's have a drink. A little brandy won't hurt you. We've got to think."

She'd been doing plenty of thinking. What he wanted to think about was the security of his Princeton-educated butt. He'd soon be asking her if she thought anyone had seen her come here.

"Does anyone else know you're in Berlin?" he asked on cue. "How did you get here? Where are you staying? What's your legal . . ."

Crossing to his wet bar in a play for time, Jeremy's motions were jerky. The crystal decanter clinked loudly against the snifters as he poured.

Amy gave him his moment. She wanted him to be willing to help her. She didn't want to coerce him, didn't know if she could. She picked up the remote on the lamp table and tapped a sequence of buttons with casual familiarity. Miles Davis's "Sketches of Spain" welled up out of Jeremy's four wall-mounted speakers. The digital recording was cold and the piece itself loaded with anxiety—perfect for her mood.

He came back with the drinks, sat down on his side of the sofa, and held out her glass with a trembling hand. She took it, calmer now in the face of his hard-held panic. She was the spy; he was just a fly in her web. It seemed fitting that all the fears that had driven him away were turning out to be well founded. He didn't have guts, that was what was wrong with Jeremy. He'd say he had different priorities, of course; that his value structure was at odds with hers. He'd say he wanted different things from life; that courage had nothing to do with the matter at hand.

Oh, she knew him well. What Jeremy Pratt didn't have was guts.

But he had pride, she thought; some self-respect and certainly a well-developed sense of responsibility. Those were the qualities in him she was counting on. For both their sakes, she hoped he had them in as large measures as was necessary.

Over the last few days, she'd found out she had more reserves to draw on than she might have imagined—during her "punch-out" when she'd seen God and touched the sky and then met the earth with a jarring realization that gravity was not just a concept. She'd used her memories of the punch-out test flight to get her through her panicky wait at Customs: They weren't going to shoot her out of hand, not the Federal Border Force, anyway.

Once she'd cleared Customs, she'd had to find the locker that matched the key Forrestal had given her, then get a cab, still half-expecting to be apprehended, her mind, supercharged with adrenaline, conjuring up the heavy footsteps of the BND (Bundesnachrichtendienst—the Federal Intelligence Service) close behind.

Of course, she'd thought then, *that's why the BND didn't grab me—I'm not committing a crime until I'm loose in Berlin, doing what I'm supposed to do. Then, it's an intelligence matter.*

But the BND didn't grab her. If they were aware of her, through Forrestal or the opposition, they were merely watching. Waiting. Biding their time. Help or hindrance would come later. She wished Forrestal had been more specific about her not being alone.

Time was something Amy had less of than anyone. She had to set up her fallbacks before Munro Hayes flew into Ramstein. In fact, she had to do what she could now, tonight, before she went to Dietrich's lecture. Once she did that, she'd be swimming in the deep end of the pool, way over her head. And it was a very murky pool, indeed.

"Do you want to tell me why?" Jeremy asked quietly, his tender voice meant to summon up memories that he hoped would protect him from this dangerous ex-lover.

"Why what?" she said innocently, sipping her brandy. She looked very good tonight, she knew, vibrating with excitement, her cheeks flushed and her skin pale.

Outside Jeremy's window a Federal Police patrol car, its distinctive siren wailing, raced by. He shivered and said, "Come now, Amy. I deserve at least an explanation. Are those state police going to be breaking down the door any minute? What's going on? What do you want?"

"Slow down, Jeremy. That's a lot of questions. I'll take the important ones first. . . ."

He nodded and leaned back, imitating calm. Jeremy was a good diplomat. Whether he was a good human being remained to be determined. "I'm all ears," he prompted.

"What I want from you," she said carefully, "is a set of false ID, including driver's license and resident cards, the whole nine yards. I told you, I'm here on a civilian passport in my name. And I can't go east on that without your help. Getting back, I may have to be somebody else—"

"Go *where?*" Jeremy blurted, his calm shattered, raw horror beneath. "Listen, Amy, whatever happened, you can't take revenge on the entire U.S. Tell me you're not. You know you get irrationally angry when you're . . . well . . ."

The look on her face must have penetrated. He shook his head miserably, sitting ramrod-straight now. "I won't help you do anything that endangers national security, you must realize that."

"Fine. I'm not asking that. I'm asking you to help me ensure national security, not endanger it. Think for a minute, Jeremy. Would I be here, after what's happened, on my own? Without help? Or for personal reasons?"

"I—oh, Amy, you're not saying you're still working for—"

"I'm saying I need your help. I can't tell you any more than that right now. I want to go east incognito. That's simple enough. I want fallback documentation, and I want it from you."

"I can't get you that sort of—"

She stood up, put the snifter carefully on his lamp table, and said quietly over the bleating of a coronet, "Of course you can. And you should, after . . ." *After all I've done for you*, she wanted to say, but didn't. Instead she said, "After all we've been to each other." She paused. "Are you telling me you think I'm lying? A traitor?"

"I . . ." Jeremy rose, too, misery on his face. "Amy, don't ask me this. Not now. Give me some time. . . ."

"Fine. I won't ask you this. Now." She was trying to keep her lip from curling. She'd been worried that he just didn't have the intestinal fortitude to put his precious, ordered world in jeopardy for her—or for anything or anyone else. She didn't want to threaten him. It wouldn't help, anyway. "Meet me at Dietrich's lecture tomorrow night and we'll talk again. And use your head, Jeremy. Don't have me paged."

"Where are you—"

"I'm not going to tell you that, not until I find out whose side you're on." She was heading for the door, pocketbook under her arm.

He followed. "Whose side? What side? What's going on? You can't expect me to say yes to something I know nothing about."

"*To me?* You can't say yes to *me?* You don't know anything about me? You don't trust me? Jeremy, I said think about it. Be there if you dare."

She'd reached the door before him; she let herself out and closed it, putting a firm barrier between them, unwilling to give eye contact or even another word in her own cause.

Downstairs, on a wet, cold street where she'd have to walk to a corner for a taxi, she wondered if she hadn't laid it on a little strong: *if you dare*. But that was what it came down to, wasn't it? That was what the handgun she'd found in the airport locker, courtesy of Forrestal, seemed to signify, a deadly heaviness nestled in the bottom of her pocketbook.

Lutz was in his BND staff meeting in Munich late the next afternoon when Dietrich called.

Dietrich knew better than to call him there. Lutz stared at the note on his desk: "S. called. Expects to see you tonight."

It was nearly quitting time and the sky was turning dark, brown and hazy from the pollutants underlit by the night lights just coming on. Munich was an ugly city, downtown.

Lutz hadn't been planning on attending Dietrich's lecture after all, not since he'd been called into headquarters on what seemed to be routine business. But Dietrich wouldn't have called him here, even with so cryptic a message, if it hadn't been urgent. Damn, it was going to be a busy night. Lutz ran fingers through graying hair, still staring out at the skyline.

Somewhere above the pollution and the deep cloud layer that so frustrated the Greens, who wanted all Germany to go solar despite an inarguable lack of sunlight, the European Space Agency's *Spacelab* joint venture was in its last construction phases. Lutz wanted Germany to have its own access to space, but of course everything was done jointly. It was the only way to keep pace with the

Americans, whom he detested. He also detested the French and the Italians and the Scandinavians, and even the Russians. At least the Russians didn't have a stake in *Spacelab*, though the Americans did.

And, of course, BND did. BND was an intelligence collection, analysis, and counterintelligence service—it did whatever was necessary to counter threats to the republic's borders. Lately that had come to mean threats from above, as well as from beyond. And Lutz, whose position dictated that he was the single administrator in BND to be dealing with BND's sister service in America, CIA, on "Line X" matters of Soviet high-tech espionage fielded out of its Illegals Directorate, was well versed in all going on "above."

Thus he knew that an experimental American aircraft due to land at Ramstein under ultratight security couldn't be as routine as the U.S. Air Force was pretending. The question was what, if anything, he wanted to do about it. It would be nice to discuss the matter with Dietrich, he decided.

Perhaps the trip to Berlin would be worthwhile, after all. Dietrich was one of Lutz's most important agents, if not the single most important one. But Lutz didn't like being at Dietrich's beck and call. Lutz would make it clear that the spaceplane's arrival was a matter of the highest priority. He, not Dietrich, would set the agenda.

Girding himself for a quick snack, a long ride, and an interminably boring lecture on the virtues of disarmament and the peaceful utilization of space, Lutz said *"Guten abend,"* to his headquarters staff and left them to lock up and turn out the lights.

Chapter Eleven

By the time Amy Brecker got there, the Hansa Library in West Berlin was packed so full that it was hard to see the trees in the atrium or the stone-block floor.

Under a slatted wood ceiling, Reinhardt Dietrich held forth on the wonders of peaceful science and the horrors of space militarization to a packed house guaranteed by the cosponsorship of the Protestant church and the Greens. Behind Dietrich was an appliquéd banner on which a united Germany floated beneath a dove with spread wings. Dietrich, tall and Aryan, with a square face and liquid blue, oversize eyes, spoke intimately, as if a half-dozen microphones weren't placed along the podium's edge, as if this were a coffee klatch in a private home, as if the hundreds gathered to hear him were all close friends.

His audience was primarily young, primarily Greens, spattered with gray-haired church types who went along with the fantasy every young German here had embraced—that there had been no Hitler, no atrocities, no concentration camps. Their textbooks had told them the real truth—that the Holocaust was an Allied invention, an excuse to tear Germany asunder and steal her greatest scientists and engineers; a horrid exercise of power by the criminal, inferior Russian and American mongrels.

This canon of the New Germany subsumed everything Dietrich said, everything he did. He didn't have to proclaim it to these listeners; they knew he knew and believed what they knew and believed. He was their hope, their salvation, their rising star whose access to the world's media assured them representation among their oppressors. When Dietrich talked, Germany listened. And Dietrich, called by the American press the "German Carl Sagan," always said what was in young Germany's heart. He talked of peaceful cooperation in the same breath with German reunification; he spoke of tearing down the Wall and linked it to a new German nationalism making itself great in space.

Space industrialization was the key, and Germany was the only nation clever enough to turn it: Space would make them free, extract them from the superpowers' grip, now squeezing the life out of their partitioned nation.

"The Stewart doctrine," Dietrich said, judging his audience sufficiently mesmerized by the promise of sci/tech to be reminded now of the obstacles on their path to the promised land among the stars, "a doctrine of adventurism the American president does not even repudiate—a doctrine that proclaims the United States the world's peacekeeper, which baldly states that dictatorships lead to communism and neither will be tolerated in the entire western hemisphere—is plunging the world into war.

"Even now, U.S. soldiers machine-gun the Central American *campesinos* in the jungle while their Keyhole Twelve satellites tell officers on the ground not only how many are hiding in a particular shack but how much coffee is in their pot, how many pesos in their pockets, how much ammunition they carry."

Dietrich paused for the hiss of hostility his words had evoked, then tossed his head so that the lock of flaxen hair fallen over one eye would not obscure the vision of Germany's savior.

Amy, making her way through those standing in the aisles, had to admit that Dietrich was good. The best, perhaps, among the young idealists of Europe. He'd be chancellor one day, everyone agreed. And he'd been her agent, her finest moment. What she could expect from him now, she wasn't certain. But she had to try.

As she sidled toward the front, where Dietrich would be sure to notice her, she looked in vain for Jeremy among the crowd. The knot in her stomach had as much to do with whether Jeremy would show up as with Dietrich and her plan to enlist his aid. She didn't want Jeremy to fail her; it would make the years she'd spent with him so much garbage, devalue her worth as a human and a woman, make a lie of their friendship. She wanted to think they still had that—a friendship.

Dietrich was evenhandedly berating the Soviet Union now, the other irresponsible superpower racing the U.S. for control of the earth and space.

"The moon, my friends—think of the moon. You look up now, at night, and the moon is a light for lovers, a guide to farmers, a beacon over the Rhine. Think what it will be like if the moon is partitioned, like our beloved country, by the superpowers, turned into a staging area for space war. Think how it will be for our children, to regard the moon with fear instead of awe."

The crowd fairly growled.

Dietrich shook his Teutonic head commiseratingly. "And we, what are we doing? Are we demonstrating against the enemy? No, my friends, we are helping." He raised his hands as the crowd's voice began to deepen. "Would I lie to you? Every space scientist we have works in concert with the European Space Agency. The best minds of Germany slave over engineering problems common not only to Europe's space industrialization but to her strategic defense—yes, that's right: laser battle stations, killer satellites, and particle-beam-weapons platforms are on the agenda.

"And who benefits?" Dietrich shouted over the crowd's hoarse "No!" "Not Germany, who has nothing of its own, who is still being punished for the alleged crimes of World War Two! No, Germany will have not a single national advantage from all the help she gives NATO's child, the European Space Agency. We cannot be trusted with rockets. We cannot be trusted with our own fate! So the Allies think."

Amy saw, as she pushed into the front row, a short, graying man of peasant stock, fingering his beard: Lutz! Her heart stopped. Lutz, who had been there when she'd been pinged, who'd known more of her fate than she had that awful night. Coincidence? Amy's head spun. She couldn't believe it was innocent. Lutz . . . And Forrestal had said she wouldn't be alone. But Forrestal couldn't have known she was going to be here; nobody knew but Jeremy. Jeremy wasn't part of the intelligence community. Jeremy wouldn't have betrayed her—she was almost sure.

Lutz *was* part of the intelligence community, though, as well as an unabashed German nationalist. Amy stepped back a pace, willing herself to disappear into the crowd from which she'd just emerged.

She looked up, and saw Dietrich wink at her as he launched into his climactic paragraphs on Germany's patriotic duty to disengage from the European Space Agency as soon as possible, in order to save Germany's secrets for Germany and as a prologue to uniting the two Germanies into a force with which the world would once more have to reckon.

Uncertain, Amy paused where she was as the crowd began to cheer. She'd come here to see Dietrich. Lutz's presence was something she'd have to deal with. What could Lutz do to her?

Report her presence to the Berlin authorities and have her deported was what. Unless she could persuade him otherwise, which she must. She stole a glance at him and froze in her tracks: Lutz's cold eyes were resting on her face.

She'd refer him to Forrestal, she decided. Forrestal would smooth things over.

The crowd around her was shifting as Dietrich came down off the podium, some in the back heading for the reception room in which sausage and beer would be served, some surging forward to touch Dietrich's hand or try to engage him in dialogue. Amy suppressed the urge to disappear into the crowd, leaving Lutz wondering whom he'd seen. But Dietrich knew it was really Amy, not someone who simply looked like her. And as he made a beeline for her, smiling and nodding determinedly to those who tried to intercept him, she realized she couldn't simply tell Lutz to talk to Forrestal: Forrestal didn't want any connection surfaced between her and the Agency.

She must *be* the disgruntled employee looking for revenge in the East. So, unless Lutz had been briefed by someone higher up and was here to help her, she had no choice: She'd have to pretend to be the illegal she was supposed to be.

She had the gun to prove it: No one in the republic was allowed a handgun for simple personal protection. The weapon Forrestal had left for her in the Tegel airport locker was proof of her renegade status. The penalties for possessing it were stiff.

But not as stiff as making a wrongheaded judgment call in the espionage game. *Good hunting, fräulein* had been Lutz's parting words to her that night the marine had driven her to Ramstein. Lutz had probably been in on this all along, she told herself as Dietrich disengaged from a stubborn female admirer and took the last few steps toward her, arms outstretched to welcome her into his embrace. She let him enfold her, thinking that her former agent had guts: The last time he'd seen her, she'd been pinged in public.

"Acht, fräulein, your troubles are over?" Dietrich murmured as he pressed first one cheek, then the other, against hers and leaned back to gaze fondly at her. "What a pleasant surprise." Dietrich's English was impeccable, his manner innocent, but there was a shadow of concern hiding behind his eyes.

Amy shrugged off the serious question behind the amenities. In Berlin one assumed that every public event of this sort was bugged by both superpowers, by any number of technical means or by human ears. And yet, she had to say something.

"Reinhardt, you're the first person I wanted to see—and the most important. Can we talk later? I don't want to impose, but—"

"You mean, my dear, you haven't an escort tonight?" Dietrich's blue eyes sparkled with mischief. "Then I proclaim you the property of the Fourth Reich, held by me in trust henceforth." And he took her arm and squired her through the crowd toward the reception hall.

Amy had to go with him, though with him she was too obvious: Men with cameras blinded them, flashing pictures; women looked at her with unhidden envy. Lutz paced them, off to the side, his face inscrutable.

So much for secrecy, she thought, beginning to understand why Forrestal had refused to give her false ID: She was too well known to too many players in this weird game of face-down that America's CIA chief had concocted. The method in Forrestal's madness was to "show our weapons so we won't have to use them, Amy. In this case, you're part of our arsenal—you, Hayes, and the TAV."

It hadn't made sense to her then; it was only now beginning to dawn on her that she was a key figure in a game of show-and-tell on which the world's very survival might hinge. And Dietrich was crucial to her success. With her hand on his arm, she was winning, she told herself as they headed down the long, book-lined hallway to the reception room and the linen-covered refreshment table at one end of it.

Occasionally, she caught sight of Lutz's expressionless face, but for nearly an hour he didn't approach her. She was too visible, part of the centerpiece, basking in Dietrich's reflected glow and telling herself it would protect her.

Between conversations with gymnasium instructors and earnest young women with steamy eyes and purple hair, Dietrich managed to promise, "Soon we'll go for dinner. Be patient. I understand we've got to talk."

So she looked for Jeremy, wishing she weren't wishing so hard he'd show up, and clutched her pocketbook, feeling very illegal, armed, and dangerous here, and watched Lutz watch her.

As the crowd began to thin, just when she was thinking that she might get through this whole evening and never have to talk to the BND man who was one of the republic's most feared intelligence professionals—or better yet, that Lutz had somehow failed to recognize her—Lutz made his way toward her, with all the subtlety of a tank on the Ku-Damm.

"Ah, fräulein," he breathed, his beard hiding what movement of his lips his raised glass could not, "we meet again. I must say I am not surprised."

Amy said, "Oh?"

Lutz tsk'd. "You must admit, I predicted your . . . resurrection, shall we say?"

"You can say whatever you want, sir," Amy responded carefully, the words coming hard and slowly through her suddenly constricted throat. *What did he know? What should she say?* "I'm

here as a private citizen, seeing an old friend."
She wanted to ask him what he meant, beg him
not to interfere, tell him to talk to Forrestal if he
got officious, enlist his aid if he was here to help
her. But she couldn't do any of those. She had to
play by the book. She said, loudly enough that
Dietrich, back half-turned but still beside her,
would hear: "I've got feelings of my own, you see,
and I'm tired of suppressing them. I don't owe
anybody anything, least of all *you*."

She didn't know if Lutz was a good guy or a bad
guy in the game she was playing. She did know he
ought to have understood disinformation when he
heard it. And he ought to know better than to
make innuendos about her status here, where spy
dust was probably all over everything and every
apple was likely to have a bug in its core.

Lutz nodded and smiled as if Amy had just
voiced a pleasantry. "Absolutely, fräulein. I couldn't
agree more."

Non sequitur. Amy's skin horripilated. She wasn't
cut out for this sort of major-league ballplaying.
She delved into Lutz's face for a clue to his meaning, found none.

Then Lutz said, "You'll call on me for help,
certainly, whenever you feel the need. Whenever," and went his way with professional ease.

Amy felt a rivulet of perspiration, formed under
her hair, run down her backbone, although in
January no dwelling in Germany was ever warm
by American standards.

And then Dietrich drifted away, toward the group
of three into which Lutz had just insinuated himself, leaving Amy alone by the buffet. She was still
standing there, picking at hand-cut radishes on a

decimated tray, when a voice behind her said, "So? I'm here."

She whirled, startled.

Jeremy's face was white and pinched. He said, "You left your sweater at my place," and thrust an Icelandic cardigan with roomy, stuffed pockets into her hands, then wheeled on his heel and stomped away.

Amy squeezed her eyes shut, forcing back tears. Suddenly she felt despicable. The look on Jeremy's face had been so accusatory, so frigid, so full of dull and hopeless anger. She hadn't blackmailed him. He could have refused. He could have stayed home. She wasn't going to get him into any trouble. She was sorry. She was . . . doing her job.

She opened her eyes, the sweater clutched against her breast, thinking to go after him. But he'd disappeared into the thinning crowd.

Gone. Remorse buffeted her, then fury. She couldn't let him get to her. He didn't have to make such a big deal of this. He was still a gutless wonder as far as she was concerned. For all she knew, the bulging pockets of the Icelandic sweater she'd never seen before could have been filled with nasty notes, warnings to stay away from him, or American cigarettes. She felt inside one pocket, and her fingers found the shapes of permits and a passport's embossed cover.

She breathed a sigh of relief: American passports had computer chips in them; they were nearly impossible to fake. Jeremy was the only acceptable source for false documents—the only source that wouldn't unmask her as a current employee of the Central Intelligence Agency rather than a former one.

By the book, she'd managed to acquire documentation. It was no small triumph. It was, in fact, the first step toward becoming a defector who might be believed, rather than branded as a provocation agent.

She stood there, just holding the sweater, breathing deeply, taking stock. Lutz had seen the exchange, she was certain; he was alone with Dietrich now and twice he looked her way. God, she wished she knew whom Forrestal had set up for her contact. She wished she knew whether Lutz's presence, his private chat with Dietrich, meant that Lutz had a stake in Dietrich. Was Dietrich now Lutz's agent? She tried to remember how much Lutz had known about her relationship with Dietrich. One of the easiest ways to acquire an agent was to find out he was somebody else's. It was called doubling.

Dietrich would have been vulnerable, once she'd been pinged. If he hadn't been vulnerable beforehand.

Amy put her hand to her forehead, an unconscious gesture. She was too confused, too tired to think it out. Damn Jeremy for getting her emotions in an uproar. Damn herself for letting it happen. And damn Forrestal for asking so much. Playing defector wasn't going to be easy. She didn't like trying to add up so many unknowns. And yet, before Munro Hayes touched down at Ramstein, she had to be securely in place.

Somehow.

Again, she hugged the sweater. She really wasn't doing badly, her first time out. She'd gotten what she needed from Jeremy, no matter how much his abruptness had hurt. And she had no doubt about her ability to handle the next phase: She wouldn't have any trouble with Dietrich, once she got him alone.

Chapter Twelve

Post–New Year's depression had spread through the four-person space station like the cold that Holly Gold had been incubating.

As *Skylab 2*'s commander, Canfield had already had his hands full, keeping the NASA civilian mission specialists' noses out of his military business, before the two scientists had begun feeling under the weather. Every time Gold or Alpert found some excuse to glide into the command module of the four-module station, Robinson's black back would go up and morale would go all to hell.

Now finally, with Gold in the science module, remotely piloting the orbital maneuvering vehicle (OMV) toward the ailing target, *Arabsat*, with Alpert inside the supposedly automated space truck to make sure that the OMV managed to retrieve the satellite for servicing, Canfield had time to talk to Robinson about the tension on board.

"What's with you and Holly Gold?" Canfield asked casually as, on his scopes, he zeroed the OMV's twelve-sided shape, widened his field of view to include the target satellite, asked for vector confirmation, and watched plot lines appear on his monitor.

"Gold?" Robinson asked with tight-lipped innocence. "Me? I don't know what you mean, whitey. She's a well-bred, well-meaning young lady."

Gold was right on course, Canfield's instruments were telling him. If she hadn't been, the OMV had eight pairs of rockets for attitude correction, especially comforting on this mission, when *Arabsat* was in an almost direct line with *Salyut 10*. The Soviet station's orbit brought it to within fifty miles of *Arabsat*—too close to risk the chance that someone in *Salyut* might misconstrue a vectoring error as aggression. The Russians were very nervous lately.

"Come on, Robinson, this is me. What's the trouble between you two? We're stuck with both those civilians for the rest of the tour. She can't hear you, not now—tell papa what's wrong."

"She screws this up, those *Salyut* boys'll probably fry us where we sit, that's one thing," Robinson said quietly, with the age-old resentment of a professional whose job was being done by an amateur for political reasons.

"Oh, that's it. Christ, I thought it was something serious." Canfield was candid in his relief. He'd been worried that one of the two scientists had made some racial remark, or that Robinson had the hots for Holly Gold, or that his first officer was intimidated by the two certified geniuses who'd never had to learn the most basic skills of human interaction. Or worse, that Robinson was just coming unglued.

Ever since they'd sighted the Thunderhawk on a nonscheduled flight and Robinson had been so quick to arm the laser battery, Canfield had been worrying about Robinson's psychological profile. This was no place to have serious personnel problems, let alone try to deal with a trigger-happy psycho—especially not with civilian observers on board. Canfield had enough trouble just trying to keep the two NASA specialists out of his SECRET/NOFORN command module, where their educated eyes would learn more than the air force wanted known about just how militarized *Skylab #2* was. All he needed was those two "concerned scientists" going home screaming that *Skylab's* mission definition was being perverted by the odious military.

Quieting such rumors was one of the main objectives of this shared mission; Canfield didn't want to be the guy on whose watch a carefully structured PR plus turned into a disastrous minus. Soon enough, *Spacelab* would be up and running. He could just make out the sun's reflected glow on the half-assembled station, floating like so many pieces of a child's puzzle, waiting for the children to arrive.

Low Earth Orbit was becoming a very crowded place to be.

"*Achoo!*" Robinson sneezed, managing to get his hand to his mouth.

"God bless," Canfield said absently, still watching Holly Gold's pilotry and the progress of the OMV toward *Arabsat*. With luck, the remote arm would function properly and Alpert wouldn't have to space-walk. It was bad enough that the scientist was stuffed into the OMV's cargo bay like so much equipment, hanging from a cable in his space suit and just hoping for an EVA (extravehicular activity) opportunity. Canfield couldn't imagine what

NASA had been thinking of, saddling his mission with a cripple who had too much to prove and a woman who was determined not to have to prove anything.

"Thanks, sir," Robinson replied, fumbling for a cold capsule in the console's medicine chest. "For asking, I mean. Let's see if we can keep these two from making just enough mistakes to buy themselves a little adventure."

Canfield shot a look at his first officer, startled. But then, Robinson had always had a knack for reading his mind.

"Yeah, I was thinking that myself. Nothing Alpert would like more than to perform some superhuman feat in zero *g*."

"That's right. Make a man out of him, sir, at least in Holly's eyes."

There it was again. Holly Gold *was* getting to Robinson. All right. Canfield would talk to the woman, who had a tendency to shake her butt in everyone's face, sure she could get away with it. If it weren't such a cute butt, it might not have been a problem.

"Maybe I'll sit in with her, make sure we don't have any nonsched space walks," Canfield began. "It's not that I don't trust her. . . ."

"Hey, sir?" Robinson floated free, his lips pursed, staring at the high-magnification monitor. "The Sovs have any scheduled EVAs today?"

"No, not that I—oh, boy."

Canfield was looking at the scope, which showed *Arabsat* and, beyond, *Salyut 10*. From the Soviet station, something small was separating, red dits on the scope indicating intermittent rocket bursts of the sort used for minute course correction.

Spy satellite! Canfield didn't need to say a word to Robinson; both men knew what they were looking at. And there was nothing they could do about the surveillance blip headed toward the OMV for a better look. Space being what it was, you couldn't keep the Soviets from looking. And any craft under way revealed much more about its capabilities than its secrecy-sworn designers might like. Once you powered up a system and let it do what it was built to do, surveillance electronics could read data from it as easily as reading the manual.

It was just one of the perils of working in space, and one reason that military hardware wasn't powered up for orbital testing anymore: When you went operational with your equipment, you were telling the other side half your secrets, whether it was ground radars tracking bogeys, or satellite-borne lasers blasting space junk.

So you didn't do it, except in an emergency.

There wasn't an emergency status on the *Arabsat* retrieval, except that NASA was using a military component, the OMV, to bring the prodigal in for service. Therefore, there wasn't a damned thing Canfield and Robinson could do about the Soviet flyby in progress, presuming that was *all* it was, except call it in on a back channel so that the U.S. could register an unofficial protest. There was no space law to protect your secrets, nothing you could do but smile and wave.

Canfield was about to tell Holly Gold to do just that, figuratively, when out of the corner of his eye he saw Robinson push off toward the armaments console.

"Robinson!" Canfield snapped.

Robinson turned his head slowly, a gleam in his

eye, his long, dark hands caressing the controls. "Readiness, Can, that's all. Readiness. That's the name of the game, ain't it?" said the weapons specialist, his velvet voice grating against Canfield's nerves like chalk on a blackboard.

"Affirmative, Robinson," Canfield soothed, all notions of leaving the command module for the science module evaporating. "Readiness. But that's all. You know that, buddy."

"Yeah, I know that, Can," Robinson said. "You're not worried about *me*, are you?"

Canfield tried to keep his tone casual. "You? Never gave it a thought."

But he couldn't keep his eyes off those long, black fingers on the weapons-control console.

Chapter Thirteen

Munich was celebrating Fasching with 2,000 masked balls. Costumed crowds were abroad even now, in early morning, ending their all-night revel with weisswurst and beer.

Lutz glowered at the celebrants through the smoked glass of his limousine's rear door. They had no right to be partying when he could not be. From January 6 through Mardi Gras, Munich was on holiday. He, however, was not.

Lutz had seen the American woman, Brecker, at Dietrich's rally and known then that he'd have to work straight through. He was on a particularly treacherous tightrope: At one end were the Americans and at the other the Soviets. But he was not alone there, blowing in the wind with only his luck and balance to save him from crashing to his death if he fell. Dietrich was out in the wind with him, and, to a lesser extent, so was Marcus Wolfe, East Germany's spymaster.

Brecker had shown up before any orders about her were forthcoming from Lutz's superiors in Western Intelligence, or EastBloc Intelligence. This in itself was disconcerting. Lutz had known of CIA's plan to reinsert Brecker as a penetration agent— he'd been part of the setup; he'd been the man who was to inherit her agents, especially her new PKO contacts. Of course, he had also been the man who made sure that Azimov didn't tell too much to Brecker, his American contact.

Lutz was a central figure in both Western and EastBloc machinations—a trusted minion of BND's liaison group; a double agent for Marcus Wolfe and, through him, the Soviet politburo. Lutz was a man of both worlds, and of neither. He plays his own game, Germany's game. "The East plays to win; the West plays not to lose," went the saying. But Lutz played for higher stakes: a reunified Germany.

It bothered him substantially that no orders from Brecker's American spymaster had preceded her. Could she be what she pretended, after all? Had she balked at the game? Could it be she was striking out on her own? There was always the human element in such operations, the wild cards of personalities.

Amy Brecker had gone to Dietrich for help. It was confusing. She should have come to Lutz, if the Americans' game plan was intact. If she was playing her country's game and had not, as he was beginning to fear, struck out on her own.

He'd made inquiries and found only one anomaly, and that, too, might have been motivated by personal, rather than professional considerations: Brecker had had a public spat with her erstwhile lover, Jeremy Pratt. Lutz had seen this with his own eyes, and it had troubled him so much that his suspicions about her had nearly obliterated his previous intention, that of alerting Dietrich to the American spaceplane—the military aerospace vehicle about which Lutz had been told so little— the arrival of which was imminent. He'd wanted Dietrich to begin a campaign of demonstrations against the presence of an advanced tactical fighter in Germany. Her designers might call her, euphemistically, a transatmospheric vehicle, but everyone knew that the American military's most highly classified weapons platform was not so innocuous as its acronym.

It bothered Lutz, a seasoned intelligence professional, that Amy Brecker had left Germany in a classified aircraft and that now, almost simultaneous with her return, another such plane was due to land at Ramstein. What troubled him more was that he didn't understand why the coincidence bothered him so terribly: He couldn't find a rational connection to make between the two.

Yet there must be one, if Brecker was still an agent of her government. Although, if she were that, he should have been running her—he would have been the middleman, the contact, the person to whom she'd necessarily have to turn for help. He was the single German national to whom the U.S. would have disclosed her mission. This was dictated by the wiring diagrams of the machine called the international intelligence community. Not to inform him of or enlist him in such a mission as that planned for Amy Brecker would have serious interagency repercussions.

Therefore, Brecker was not acting according to plan.

Lutz shifted in his seat as the limo stopped at a cross street and a tall figure in a bear costume, escorting a masked woman in an eighteenth-century ball gown, knocked with drunken ebullience on his window. He ignored them and picked up his shielded car telephone. Pressing the SECURE button, which scrambled the transmission that went not into Germany's normal cellular network but into its military communications net, he dialed Dietrich's home number.

The phone rang three times before Dietrich's voice said sleepily, "*Ja?*"

"It's me," said Lutz in English, another precaution. "How is Brecker?" No preamble, no pleasantries. Dietrich was his agent—his and Wolfe's. Dietrich must now give his report.

"She—wait, please. The door, I must close it."

While Lutz waited, the revelers beyond his window were left behind as the car accelerated.

It seemed too long before Dietrich came back to the phone, an interval in which Lutz listened to the hiss of the satellite-bounced silence, imagining all the distance the signal was traveling. Then Dietrich's voice returned, saying uncomfortably, "She's here, you see. Staying here. She wants to work with my people—for peace, she says. She wants to meet those of us in the East who also wish peace."

Dietrich was being very careful, but still the words made Lutz's head spin. *Was* Brecker still a player?

"Yes?" Lutz made his voice brusk and impatient, as if Dietrich's words held little significance. "And what else?"

"She has a lover for whom she waits, another American. When he arrives, she wants to take him

into East Germany with her, to meet someone of
. . . importance. To help the peace effort."

"And you believe her?"

Dietrich's sigh was deep. "I am not certain, my
friend. She is a lovely woman. She needs comfort,
you understand. I want to believe her. Her tears
in my arms, when she told me of her lover, seemed
very real. She is distraught, bitter at her treatment by her . . . former employers. I have said I
know nothing of such people, only of those who
seek peace. I have promised nothing." The ner-
vousness in Dietrich's voice was infectious.

"She'll know you'd know people—the right sort
of people. Tell her you'll help her as best you
can."

"I will. But what if—"

"What if, what if—who knows what if? We'll
protect your status if you do your part. Say only
that you'll take her to a rally in East Berlin. See
what she does then. Get back to me."

Before Dietrich could answer, Lutz broke the
connection. Even on a secure line, he'd not dared
ask Dietrich whether Amy's lover was still Jeremy
Pratt. If it was Pratt, Lutz would consider it proof
that the Americans were running a game without
his knowledge, and make a formal protest. If it
was someone else, Brecker's story could be true.
Americans were all spoiled children; they had no
national allegiance, no backbone. And women were
vindictive by nature.

Giving Amy Brecker to Marcus Wolfe would be
a feather in Lutz's cap. Even if later she proved to
be a penetration agent, or a provocation agent
meant to gum up the workings of East German
intelligence, it would serve Lutz's ends: Let the

East and West be at each other's throat; while they struggled, Wolfe might fall. If Wolfe fell, East German intelligence would be temporarily paralyzed. If that happened, reunification's timetable could be pushed up by years. Perhaps even to this year.

Lutz stretched out in his limo, fingers laced behind his head, trying to fit Amy Brecker into the puzzle. He understood the Soviet strategy that had brought Azimov to Brecker's night desk—he had been part of it. PKO wanted to force America to put its space-based defense system on line, to either fail in an attempted shoot-down, or succeed. Either way, the intelligence and propaganda value to the Soviet Union would be great.

The USSR did not want war; they wanted an intelligence coup. Knowledge, in this case, was preemptive: A forewarned America would not push its nuclear button. But the U.S. must still respond in some way, or be seen internationally as either lacking in will or lacking in technological competence: The United States would have no choice but to power up its entire space-based defense grid to operational levels.

No one in Moscow actually cared what course the U.S. took, as long as it was not the nuclear course or the course of total inaction. And the presence of Americans aboard the target, *Skylab 2*, assured that the U.S. must try to stop the "runaway" missile. The intelligence coup forthcoming was all but a *fait accompli*.

Thus, letting Azimov run to the American Embassy had been a no-lose situation for the Soviets— as long as Azimov didn't understand what use his masters were making of him. And as long as he wasn't allowed to actually defect.

Making sure that Azimov never made it to the West had been relatively simple for Lutz. Making sure that Amy Brecker made it to the East was fraught with difficulties, unknowns the magnitude of which Lutz was hesitant to contemplate alone.

There was only one safe course, Lutz decided, beginning to perspire in his air-conditioned limo, beginning to feel that he was, finally, in danger of getting his coattails caught in the revolving door between East and West that he'd been so accustomed to using with impunity. He would have to talk with Marcus Wolfe himself. He would lay before Wolfe his suspicions, his doubts, his sense of danger. Then, if Brecker still wanted to see "someone" in the East, she would see *the* someone, the man who made East Germany run.

She *and* her lover, Lutz amended, wondering who it might be as he pulled his notepad out of his jacket pocket and began jotting cryptic notes.

Chapter Fourteen

Once airborne, it took Ro Hayes twelve minutes to fly *MEDUSA* from Vandenberg to Langley Field, where he encountered an intransigent traffic controller and found himself stacked up over the air base for twice as long as it had taken him to travel coast to coast.

He smothered his irritation at the delay, cursed the bureaucracy under his breath, and rode out the groundside glitch, telling himself that you couldn't have too much shake-out cruising in an experimental craft, and wondering how long it would take Taylor or CIA to burn the butt of the poor fool who'd put the TAV's priority clearance behind that of the visiting Aggressor squadron, some kid on his first solo, and a couple of C-130s.

Meanwhile, there was *MEDUSA* and there were the stars, barely dimmed by the Northeast Corridor's city lights. He had fuel enough, and an aircraft under him the like of which he'd never flown before.

The air-breathing weapons platform known as *MEDUSA* didn't seem to mind being asked to circle meekly over Langley in the traffic pattern; all of Ro's instrumentation read nominal and the AI computer didn't even beep.

That was good—sometimes these hot rockets couldn't idle at traffic lights. He sat back, breathing shallowly through his oxygen mask, and watched the stars visible beyond his heads-up display. America's ASAT grid was out there, among the brighter lights of suns and the reflected lights of planets, invisible to his naked eye. He could have punched up a computer-assisted view of them in any quadrant the TAV could "see" with her complex of radars, everything from OTH/B (over-the-horizon backscatter) to IFLTR (infrared lock on target), or he could have initiated spacecraftlike telemetry options.

But he didn't. He'd checked out every CMC3I (countermeasures, command, control, communications, and intelligence) component of the trans-atmospheric spyplane to his satisfaction—*MEDUSA* was everything she was touted as being.

The SDI components orbiting the earth with their American designators were somewhat less than as advertised—unfinished, untested as a system, and with a mission capability different from that which her early proponents had envisioned. In the early days, SDI had been hailed as an antinuclear umbrella that technology could place above not only the entire U.S. but also her NATO allies. Reality and kill ratios being what they were, pragmatism and funding battles had altered America's SDI strategy. The space-based components of America's ballistic-missile defense were now concentrated on "area denial": Laser and particle-beam defenses were programmed to shoot down

enemy missiles before those missiles could enter
American airspace, hopefully before or during boost
phase; but there would be enough leakage that
only some strategic assets could be expected to
ride out a strike.

Because the total "nuclear umbrella" had proved
an impossibility, defense postures had pivoted: The
best defense was a strong offense. Opponents argued that SDI's projected ability to hit enemy
rockets as they reached ignition in their silos would,
once operational levels had been reached, force
the Soviets to new, more dangerous, less controllable countering strategies.

As things stood now, the Launch on Early Warning doctrine was considered barely time enough
by many war planners on both sides.

Operational levels for America's SDI were scant
months away. What new escalations would follow
were all in the realm of command and control—
computer war, the disarmament-minded Western
liberals cried, was imminent. And there were more
and more of those, more people suspicious of technology because men were always afraid of what
they did not understand.

Even Ro, who did understand the trade-off between risk and security, was uncomfortable with
SDI this evening, staring out at the stars from
MEDUSA's ultrahigh-tech cockpit. Uncomfortable
not because SDI threatened him or his family in
some abstract or conceptual way, but because
Munro Hayes had become a component of America's strategic defense arsenal, a crucial and all too
human bit of RAM in the computerized U.S. defense network.

He'd tested too many aircraft, flown too many

hazardous missions, to be worried about his personal performance—his ability to fly the mission, fry the target, and get back home in one piece, with or without his plane. But *MEDUSA* was as much a part of the SDI network as she was an aircraft, and the ejection seat he was strapped to was just a psychological perk. If his luck ran out and he failed, what was at stake this time was somewhat more than Ro Hayes's reputation as a top-gun fighter jock.

If Langley—supposedly friendly territory—could leave him stacked up in traffic in *MEDUSA* as if he were hauling air cargo and not flying the most secret plane America had on a highly classified mission, what worse was in store for *MEDUSA* once she left American airspace?

He told himself not to sweat it. He told himself that the lack of priority landing status was just a function of security: Nobody had told Langley control that there was anything special about *MEDUSA*.

On the ground, when he finally got there, Ro was glad to see that security hadn't overridden common sense: The TAV was directed to a 7,000-foot runway at the end of which were a turnaround crew and no unwanted onlookers. Off to one side was a dark limo with limp flags above her headlights. CIA's Forrestal and Ro's boss, Terrible Taylor, got out of it and walked toward *MEDUSA* as Ro was climbing down the ladder.

He had three hours of turnaround to wait out; he should have expected that the brass involved would make an appearance.

He hadn't. He'd been looking forward to hovering over *MEDUSA* while she was readied for the second leg of her flight to Ramstein.

Unaccountably, his mouth dried up as his heels hit the runway. Maybe it was that he'd had enough talk; maybe the sight of Taylor and Forrestal reminded him that a good deal of what was crucial about his mission would take place on the ground in Germany, where he was going to feel like a fish out of water, and not in the high sky up at Low Earth Orbit, where it would be just him, *MEDUSA*, and whatever Murphy's law threw at them.

Or maybe it was that when he was airborne, all his personal, earthly troubles fell away, and now, standing on the runway, he couldn't help thinking about his ex-wife and the squabble they'd gotten into over Amy Brecker's presence in the Blazer that night Ro had stopped by to pick up a few things.

What did he want his kids to think? Jenny had wanted to know. What kind of example did he want to set for his son? His daughter was in tears, didn't he know that? It was one thing to have girlfriends, another to throw them in his family's face.

He hadn't said anything then—not even reminded her that it was only "his" family when the term suited her purpose; the rest of the time, he had to negotiate for visiting privileges. He'd just gathered up what he needed and left.

Now, suddenly, it bothered him that he was leaving on such bad terms.

He shut down that train of thought quickly, not wanting to explore the logical end of his chain of reasoning: This time Ro wasn't entirely sure he'd have a chance to straighten things out when he got back. He resolved to give Jenny a call—at least say hello to his daughter—before he took off for Ramstein.

But he hadn't counted on Forrestal's obsessive security measures, or the thickness of the secondary briefing book he was handed, or the degree to which the two honchos were willing to take him into their confidence.

"Hayes." Forrestal spoke first, nodding curtly to Ro as the pilot took off his helmet. "Let's hurry this up. We've got to put you in the picture as far as the GDR is concerned, and fast."

Ro stowed his helmet under his arm and said laconically, "Hello, sir. General Taylor." He nodded to the air force man, trying to reestablish what he thought was the proper chain of command. He didn't like Forrestal, especially didn't like the way that walking skeleton talked to him as if Ro had been seconded to his command.

"Let's go, son," Taylor said, clapping Ro on the back. "We've got two days' work to do in three hours."

Walking toward the limo, still holding his helmet, his fingers nervously playing with a zipper on his flight suit, Ro Hayes forgot all about his ex-wife and the games she played. GDR was the German Democratic Republic—East Germany. Taylor had promised him there'd be no sorties east. They had run Amy Brecker through a combat course and a punch-out to make sure of it. But something had changed. It must have. Otherwise, Taylor would be willing to meet his eyes.

In East Berlin, on the western end of Unter den Linden, government buildings line the street; where it passes over the river Spree, it crosses onto Museum Island and runs into Marx-Engels-Platz, a dreary square housing the State Consul, the massive Palast der Republik, and the Ministry of Foreign Affairs.

In the ministry, under the shadow of the palace, Lutz sat before Marcus Wolfe's desk like a cornered rabbit: wide-eyed, still, and on the verge of trembling. Marx-Engels-Platz always had that effect on him, Lutz lied to himself. And, too, it could well be something he'd eaten, the way he'd been working round the clock, grabbing bites on the run.

But it was none of these that made his stomach queasy and his breath come short. Rather, it was the incipient smirk on the pleated lips of Marcus Wolfe now that Lutz had poured out his fears and suspicions in the matter of Amy Brecker and the Americans' counterintelligence strategy. "PKO must be protected," Lutz finished lamely, wishing his words had the ring of authority instead of the quaver of fear. "And so must the peace movement— and Reinhardt Dietrich. . . ." Lutz ran dry and spread his palms, his eyes beseeching understanding.

"From a woman? From one American girl?" Wolfe said with incredulity like a razor blade in his tone. And waited for Lutz to respond, his old, pale eyes fixing the short, stocky Lutz as firmly in place as manacles could have.

"From . . . errors," Lutz managed to whisper.

"From *your* errors, you mean." The German Democratic Republic's spymaster seemed to grow taller in his chair. Wolfe's face was a face of mystery, nondescript of feature and yet with eyes full of power. His nose was bold, but time had eroded it; his forehead was as high as his standing in the East German power structure; he wore a suit tailored in Italy and a gold Swiss watch, consciously flaunting his perquisites. His office was full of pictures of himself with Soviet and East German presidents and premiers; on one shelf was a shell casing inscribed to him, *With gratitude,* from a Chinaman named Mao. Wolfe was the most dangerous man in East Germany, and Lutz had made the mistake of looking like a cowardly fool, coming here with unsubstantiated fears and doubts.

Desperate to redeem himself, Lutz said, "But she's not just an American girl. She was—perhaps *is*—of their CIA. She's confusing Dietrich. She wants to see someone here, in the GDR, of high rank. She says she's ready to put aside her American allegiance and work for peace—"

"You're repeating yourself, Herr Lutz. And thus I will repeat *my*self. Let her come. Bring her east. Let her see the flowers at Checkpoint Charlie, and what lies beyond. And her gentleman friend, too, whoever he may be. Bring them here, to East Berlin, and I myself will meet with them. Your responsibility in the matter will then be ended." Wolfe's eyes were steady, deep pools with shards of ice in their recesses. *"Verstehen Sie?"*

"Ich verstehe." And Lutz did understand: Amy Brecker *was* important, too important to be left to a bungler like himself. He almost let an angry retort slip, but the anger in him was balanced by fear of the man before him, who had done so much to so many over so long. Instead he said meekly, "Bring her here, to your office? Officially?"

Wolfe shook his head slowly, almost pityingly, and said in a delicately disparaging voice, "Mein herr, you do *not* understand, evidently. Bring her into the East, to meet her peace workers. One of them will arrange a meeting for her with a certain man, a meeting whose particulars are no further business of yours. You must only see that she attends. The rest you will leave to others."

Others more competent, he means. Others who are not afraid of the Americans. Others who think with their heads, not their glands. Lutz's misery showed on his face.

Wolfe stood up, seeming taller than he was as Lutz scrambled to his feet in turn and held out a sweaty palm. The spymaster took Lutz's moist hand in his cool, dry one and stretched his lips, showing evenly yellowed teeth like those of a museum skull.

"Your service to the state will not be forgotten," Wolfe said, and the words had more than one meaning for Lutz, so that he never remembered leaving Wolfe's office or getting into his car, but just Wolfe's voice, which he heard over and over, saying those words that should have been calming but somehow sounded like an epitaph.

Alone but for *MEDUSA*'s AI copilot, airborne over the North Sea on his way to Ramstein, Ro listened with one ear to the chatter coming over his radio from the commercial traffic flying miles below, his eyes drifting from his weather radars to the distant, frozen sea, back to the midnight blue of the high sky that *MEDUSA* had claimed for her own. There was no one else flying up here; there wasn't another plane this high in the air to crowd the TAV, let alone give her a run for her money. He and the plane had the world to themselves, it seemed.

For the first time, Ro took a few minutes to get

the feel of the voice-actuation capability of the AI copilot, telling it to scan for surface ships and give him surveillance data on whatever it found. The TAV had the ability to give him pictures of the deck of a Soviet trawler fifty miles below—pictures so clear that he could identify a man smoking on the bridge.

He wished he'd been able to get as clear a picture of what Terrible Taylor and Forrestal had had in mind when they'd given him his final, unscheduled verbal briefing at Langley. It was disconcerting to have Forrestal tell him what a trigger-happy son of a bitch President Stewart was, not because the CIA man's assessment was a revelation but because someone like Ro Hayes didn't expect or want to be privy to the sort of confidences Forrestal was sharing.

"Remember, Mr. Hayes, your mission reduces to one single objective: Blow any hostile missile aimed at U.S. property out of the sky. My girl Brecker, the East German rendezvous, even the lives of our people aboard *Skylab Two*—none of them means shit in the larger context."

"Larger context?" Ro had questioned, not because he didn't understand but because he had to be sure he understood, sure he'd been specifically directed by CIA to leave its agent waving in the breeze and to sacrifice astronauts if necessary in order to perform the specified mission. And that was always hard with Agency types; they wanted to infer and imply, to leave an ambiguous margin in which they could implement "denial" procedures.

When he'd asked the question, impudent by his own standards, he'd seen Taylor smother a grin of appreciation and relief, and felt suddenly like he'd

slipped into some alternate universe where all the
rules he'd lived by were suddenly reversed—where
women, children, and civilians came last; where
all games were zero-sum; and where the best thing
he could do for his country was take aggressive,
preemptive action against the Soviet Union.

For just an instant, he'd seen Amy Brecker's
gamin face as it had been when she thought her
own service had pinged and discarded her, and he
was glad he hadn't given her some Boy Scout pep
talk about how her country would never do that to
her.

Because it would. At a moment's notice. For
reasons of national security. Or just to keep a lid
on things.

Forrestal had made that clear in the limo, while,
outside, a tanker truck pumped fuel into *MEDU-
SA*'s hungry belly. "In plain English, major, all we
want is an abort to the Soviet strike—before launch,
if possible, but anytime prior to impact will do.
Correlative casualties are beside the point. Not
your problem. Do you understand? You're to concern yourself with Brecker and the space-station
personnel only as circumstances allow. No one's
going to come back to you with after-action questions about cost in human terms, as long as that
cost's not based on your failure to stop that missile
before it impacts the American consciousness.
Clear?"

"I guess so, sir," Ro had said, watching Forrestal and Taylor but seeing Amy Brecker and thinking about the special weapons he was taking into
Germany, and whether he was willing to leave
Brecker swinging—or the space-station personnel—

simply because this CIA honcho with undertaker's eyes was telling him he could.

The final determination would be his own: "Circumstances" were always open to interpretation.

He found himself liking Amy Brecker better than he had previously, not because of anything she'd done but because she was so damned expendable. He'd had enough field experience to be unwilling to consider a fellow player expendable simply because it was convenient.

And Taylor had known what he was thinking, because old Terrible had leaned forward and said only, "Son, use your own judgment. Just remember, we don't want to let Stewart get his teeth into any kind of reasonable excuse for a 'limited' war."

Forrestal's face had frozen, and he'd opened the briefing book then, and the rest of the turnaround interval had been spent poring over dossiers of likely German players—Dietrich, Lutz, Marcus Wolfe.

Now, nearing the end of the transatlantic military radar handovers that made sure he was always tracked on course, with West Germany just minutes away, Ro began to consider his own cover, the hard part of his mission: playacting.

He hated deceptions. He had time to hope that somebody besides Lutz, the bearded German from BND who was to be their liaison and control agent, had been fully briefed, and then his AI, the damned computerized copilot he'd failed to return to standby, started talking to Ground Control for him, as if Ro were some kind of glorified passenger.

"Shut up, *MEDUSA*." He turned the AI off and got on the air, sweet-talking his way into Ramstein, a little bit of the U.S. Air Force abroad that he was more than glad to see.

Chapter Fifteen

Amy Brecker hopped up from her plastic seat in the sparsely crowded, civilian-accessible waiting room at Ramstein when Ro Hayes came through the institutional-green swinging doors, gear bag in hand.

Like the half-dozen other females around her, girlfriends of servicemen living on the economy, her name had been checked against a list on an MP's clipboard, her handbag searched for weapons or explosives, and then she'd been given a post pass.

She propelled herself across the linoleum and into the arms of the startled pilot with the five o'clock shadow who would have been content to wave and now, as she stood on tiptoe to plant a kiss firmly on his lips, was too slow in responding to suit Amy.

"Kiss me, you idiot," she whispered fiercely. "Put your arms around me like you mean it. We haven't seen each other for—"

Whatever else she might have said was muffled by Ro Hayes's belated but enthusiastic response.

When he withdrew his tongue from her mouth, she arched back and said softly, smiling, "You know, there's a part of you I really hate."

"Want to point to it?" he suggested, his arms still tight around her waist, one hand proprietarily flat against her haunches.

"Later," she promised. "Let's go, before—"

"Major Hayes?" came an intrusive voice from a loudspeaker set above the counter beside the swinging doors. "Munro Hayes to the information desk, please."

His eyes met hers questioningly as he let her go and shifted the gear bag he'd slung over his shoulder.

"Shit." She shook her head. "Let's both go," she suggested sotto voce. "Put your arm around my waist. That's it."

As they approached the counter, she saw only the uniformed American sergeant behind it. Then, from one of the plastic chairs, a man in civilian clothes rose and approached, reaching the counter as they did. The sergeant said, "Major, this is for you," and handed Ro an envelope with his name typed on it and the Federal Republic's "Official Business" notice in the upper left-hand corner.

Amy looked at it, dumbfounded and horror-struck, the civilian who'd come simultaneously to the counter forgotten. The last thing she needed was officious meddling. Not now. Not with Dietrich's secretary waiting for them in the car outside. Not with Dietrich himself convinced of her "genuine" status as a would-be defector—so convinced that he'd offered to pick up Ro himself so Amy wouldn't run the risk of having her civilian passport questioned at Ramstein's outer checkpoint.

And now this.

Ro took his hand from her waist to open the letter as the desk sergeant returned to his computer terminal. Amy leaned close as his fingernail slipped under the gummed flap, hoping against hope that nothing inside that envelope was going to ruin all her carefully made plans: Ro didn't know it yet, but the two of them were due at a rally in East Germany this evening.

As the pilot started to pull forth the folded sheet of paper, the civilian on Amy's right said quietly in German, "Major Hayes? Fräulein Brecker. If you'll accompany me, once you've read the verification you're holding—Herr Lutz awaits us in Munich."

Both Americans turned as if they were marionettes controlled by the same strings. Amy snatched the letter from Ro's fingers, scanned the terse lines, crumpled the paper and stuffed it in her pocket, then said, "You know, this is very inconvenient. Why don't you go back to your Mr. *Luft* and tell him that he's got the wrong people?" She spoke quietly, not knowing whether making a scene would help, or mire them more completely in this bureaucratic morass. Her eyes implored the pale, blond-browed ones of the civilian-suited man to read between the lines.

His opaque, answering look replied that thinking, let alone intuiting, was none of his job.

Amy considered screaming that BND had no right to order Americans around—it would suit her cover. But Hayes said smoothly, "Sure thing, friend. Thanks for the ride," and a touch on Amy's waist urged her to go along.

"This way, then?" The German strode off toward the doors, and the cars waiting beyond, in the featureless gray of the winter morning.

Munich. Great.

Hayes's hip brushed hers and he bent his head toward her. She was going to risk explaining to him how this was ruining everything, how bad it would look to Dietrich's waiting secretary if they were led to an official vehicle by the BND man, but he spoke too quickly.

"Lutz was part of my briefing, don't worry."

"Worry? What good would that do?" she murmured back, her mind racing, but trying to keep her face composed and appropriate for that of a woman just reunited with her lover. If Dietrich's secretary simply reported what she saw—the two Americans being hustled into a Mercedes with official plates—then the damage might be controllable. Amy could cook up some story—that she'd narrowly escaped being deported, that she was mistreated and mishandled by the muscular West German intelligence service, and that only Ro's presence had saved her from some sort of embarrassing incident. Yes, that was what she'd do—*if* Dietrich didn't jump to conclusions, if he was willing to listen, if Lutz hadn't just blown this whole operation to bits with one gigantic mistake, for which he'd better have a damned good explanation.

She wanted to ask for, to demand, answers. But Ro obviously didn't understand what was at stake. *Lutz was part of my briefing.* For Christ's sake, the pilot was a babe in the woods as far as tradecraft was concerned.

She slid into the car's back seat when the door was opened and watched through the rear window as the blond operative opened the trunk to receive Hayes's gear bag and the pilot stolidly refused to relinquish it.

After a short exchange of words Amy couldn't hear over the idling motor, an exchange punctuated by shakes of Ro's head and twitches of the German's mouth, which were clearer than any words, the pilot, bag in hand, got into the back seat beside her and closed the door.

While the German was sliding into the driver's seat, Amy got a glimpse of the car she'd arrived in as it pulled out of a space behind theirs and drove away. She hoped Dietrich's secretary would give a faithful report—the little altercation about the luggage would substantiate whatever story Amy fabricated.

The BND man must be low-level, or there would have been a second man, Amy knew, a putative chauffeur or an overt backup.

So no one was expecting trouble.

She smiled at the blond as their eyes met in the rearview mirror and he guided the big Mercedes away from the curb. "How about a little music?" she said in English.

"*Muzik?*" The man's brows knitted. Then: "*Ja. Muzik.*" He turned on the radio.

Amy still wasn't sure if the man spoke English, but the radio spat out pumped-up pop, and under it she said to Ro, who had his arm stretched out along the seat behind her head, "What was that about the luggage?"

"Luggage? Oh, my gear bag. I didn't get it here the hard way to find out it's locked away back there when I need it." His hand came down on her skirted thigh.

She stared at it for a moment, then at his face. There was laughter in his eyes.

"Don't you think you're carrying this a little too far?"

"What? I missed you, love. That's all." He leaned over, slowly and obviously, to kiss her again.

She placed both hands on the open front of his green flight jacket and pushed, muttering, "Okay, buddy, *okay*. You don't have to convince that guy up there. You were briefed, I wasn't. Tell me what you—"

"Sorry. Just trying to do my job." He redirected his gesture, contenting himself with nuzzling her hair.

Rage rose in her. He had no right to be so calm, or to have this much fun at her expense. And his hand was still on her thigh. She had an awful feeling that if she said anything about it, he'd tell her it was tradecraft.

She said, instead, "If you don't want to be on the receiving end of a major lovers' quarrel, you'll back the hell off, Hayes."

"Okay, okay. But we can't be sure of what—"

"Christ, don't talk about it here."

He shrugged, and now his hand did come away. "Fine. It's your show."

"Not anymore," she said ruefully, but he didn't hear her over the clanging of guitar strings and the wailing of a female singer.

Lutz was cold this morning, colder than the winter chill warranted.

He'd come to his office early, so early that only the night station personnel were on duty, so early that the night lights of Fasching were still burning over Munich.

He was here because of the magnetic cassette before him, which had been hand-delivered by a junior officer from the joint U.S.-NATO headquarters at Ramstein. The officer had insisted on waiting until Lutz arrived in order to give it to him personally.

The cassette was of a special type that destroyed its data as it was being viewed, and the courier insisted that he view it on the spot, so there would be no chance to copy or pirate its contents. Lutz, once he'd seen it, had no inclination to do either. He wanted only to run. Failing that, he wanted to find some way out of the mess he'd got himself into, an abyss on one side of which was the American CIA in the person of Deputy Director Forrestal, and on the other Marcus Wolfe of the GDR.

The data cassette prepared for him by CIA told Lutz precisely what the high-security aircraft designated *MEDUSA* was doing at Ramstein. It also told him who Amy Brecker's lover was, and what that lover had to do with the East-West power struggle, the Soviet PKO, and Lutz's own future.

Which, if he let Amy Brecker disappear into the East with boyfriend in tow, as Wolfe expected him to do, was nil.

Staring out at the reluctant, pollution-browned morning that faded Munich's lights, Lutz tried to think. He must decide on a course, and that course must be survivable. As much as he cared about the reunification of the Germanies, he must be alive to effect the changes he envisioned. A dead Lutz could do nothing for the Fatherland.

Without question, Wolfe would be furious if

Lutz did not deliver the American woman and her so-called lover into EastBloc's hands. But *furious* was a relative term. Wolfe did not yet know how important the woman was, nor the quality of information her companion possessed, nor anything more than Lutz's own suspicions. The Americans, on the other hand, knew enough to get Lutz killed: They knew whom to blame if Marcus Wolfe's people took more than the hint, meant to stop Moscow from launching a test missile—if Wolfe chose to take the American agents as his own.

Lutz knew Marcus Wolfe well enough to know that if Wolfe got his hands on Brecker and her partner, this Munro Hayes, an attempt to take possession of *MEDUSA* would soon follow. And whose fault would that be deemed by the Americans? Lutz's, that was whose.

So he came to his decision, a decision he'd known he'd have to face eventually, not in specifics but in generalities. He'd played a double game for years, and when one served two masters, inevitably the moment came when their interests collided. At that point it mattered only which side's interests were survivable.

To Lutz, this morning, the Americans and their NATO allies were the only viable choice.

He'd already sent a courier to intercept Brecker and Hayes at Ramstein, to bring them to him. When he met them, he would advise them as honestly as possible of the degree to which their mission had already been compromised, and on how to proceed. If possible, he would dissuade them from going east. In any case, he would give them good advice, which would prove to the Americans whose ally he was.

It was the only move that could save him. He hoped fervently that it was enough, and that he had made it soon enough.

The ride to Munich seemed to take forever, the hundred miles an hour they were traveling like a slow-motion dream to Hayes after his flight in *MEDUSA*.

Brecker was shaky, rattled, more than simply nonplussed. He didn't find out why until the driver pulled up in front of the Englischer Garten, a huge city park full of tourists and locals in Fasching costume, and said, "There. At the Chinesicher Turm. He waits. I wait here," and looked at them expectantly.

Obviously, they were supposed to get out of the car and find Lutz themselves.

"Chinesicher Turm?" Ro repeated, though Brecker already had her door open and was sliding out.

"The Chinese pagoda, Ro. Down there, see?"

He didn't, but she seemed content that she knew where they were going.

He got out, shouldered his gear bag, and proceeded to walk Brecker down paths crowded with beery folk, one hand on her elbow, his eyes searching unfamiliar terrain for anything out of the ordinary. But there was nothing ordinary, to his stranger's eyes, about these gardens during Fasching: people in ornate eighteenth-century dress, others in animal costumes, many with carnival favors, blaring radios, and sparklers in their hands.

He caught sight of the Chinese pagoda, a beer garden in front of it with long trestle tables on which revelers sat, despite the early hour and the cold. He pointed it out to her.

"Of course," she answered impatiently, her breath white in the chilly air, two spots of color high on her cheeks. "I told you I know this part of the game."

Game. Ro looked behind, the way they'd come. The Mercedes that had brought them still idled at the curb, blue diesel clouds belching from its exhaust pipes. He squeezed her elbow and she glanced at him, then went back to scanning the crowd ahead.

"Want to tell me what's bothering you?" he suggested. "While we have time to talk?"

"Bothering *me?*" she said, her facial expression, that of a woman on an outing with her lover, at odds with the harsh words coming through half-smiling lips. "Nothing's bothering me, except that I had all my prepositioning done. We had Dietrich's car waiting for us. We're due at an East German rally this evening—or we were. You've ruined everything, you realize. I'll probably have to start all over with Dietrich. He won't trust us any farther than he can throw us now that—"

"Hey, lady, you've got this all wrong. My part of it, at least. I don't want to go east. I'm doing what I'm told, yeah, but guys like me have passport restrictions for damned good reasons. I get in there and somebody decides they'd like a briefing on state-of-the-art American aircraft and maybe I don't get out again. And if all it takes to blow your operation wide open is a little improvisation on the part of the one West German our guys are willing to trust, that ain't real confidence-building about your ability to—"

She, in turn, interrupted him: "Hayes, this is my go, not yours. You fly the planes, all right? On the ground, you do what you're told. And lay off the touchy-feely, at least until we get to Dietrich's. If we do. Having to sleep in the same bed is something we'll just have to endure. Until I get you properly briefed and you've told me what they told you Stateside, you and I are going to—"

"I'm tough enough to survive a night with you or any other—" He broke off, looked at her, then in the direction she was staring. "What is it?" His voice was too loud, too brittle.

She touched his arm, squeezed it. "It's Lutz, that's all. You're right—you're tough enough. Don't let this cloak-and-dagger throw you. It's just that these Germans love to play 'espionage.' It's their favorite sport."

"Yeah, mine too," he said sourly, adjusting the weight of the gear bag on his shoulder. "But I'd rather do it in civilian clothes and without enough special weapons to land me in . . . wherever they put my type here. Some castle dungeon, probably."

He'd seen castlelike structures on the way here. Munich was filled with beautiful things—palaces and parks, rococo architecture and Renaissance statuary, baroque domes and glockenspiels. He didn't want a closer view of any of them, any more than he wanted a more than passing glimpse of the Landpolizei or Staatspolizei who sauntered by among the man-size rabbits and gorillas who went arm in arm with witches and clowns and bare-breasted women in hoop-skirted ball gowns.

The kit he was carrying was seeming heavier by the minute. He'd hate trying to explain what his reasons were for carrying his arsenal in here. There was no acceptable reason, except the truth, and spies tended to get unpleasant treatment before being handed over to the military of their own government—*if* they were.

For simply carrying what he was carrying—special weapons, side arms, ammunition with specs unacceptable to the Hague Convention, electronics gear—the local government could lock him up for a good long time. And he'd left *MEDUSA* in the tender care of another fighter jock who'd dearly have loved to be sitting in his seat, who wouldn't mind being the redundant component that replaced Ro Hayes if Hayes was, for any reason, unavailable to scramble.

Good old American paranoia: Forrestal had shipped over somebody of his own, in case the chips went down too hard, too fast. Or in case, the CIA pilot had explained, the "Ivans or their German shepherds come after the plane itself. It's possible, you know. And we don't like leaving anything to chance."

The CIA pilot had been sprung on Ro out of nowhere, when there was no way for him to complain or even inform Taylor that there was a replacement waiting in the wings. The inference that whatever Hayes was expected to walk into, groundside, might be something he wouldn't walk out of bothered him enough that he'd brought every piece of hardware in his kit along with him, not just one concealable pistol and a com unit disguised as a toothbrush.

So he was beginning to perspire, despite the cold, feeling the wetness under his arms and down his back as Brecker guided him through the thick-

ening, costumed crowd that swarmed around the
Chinese pagoda's beer hall.

He didn't recognize Lutz until they were almost
upon him: a single man, staring out at nothing in
particular, his back propped against a tree, his
beer before him on a trestle table at which there
was just enough room for Ro and Amy to squeeze
in, if they didn't mind being impolite.

They didn't—or she didn't—and so they jostled
a big fellow in a bear costume, who looked at them
through his bear's eyes, then got up and left the
table altogether.

It was loud in the crowd, there was music ev-
erywhere. Amy leaned over before she sat in the
seat the bear had just vacated, saying, "Herr Lutz?
You wanted to see us? Herr—"

She reached out and touched the man's shoulder, and still Lutz didn't look at them.

And then, very slowly, Lutz toppled from the
bench.

For Ro, everything slowed: The people around
him, Brecker especially, seemed to be acting in
slow motion.

There was a dark, wet stain on the back of
Lutz's neck, right below the hairline. As the body
hit the pavement and crumpled, Ro thought very
calmly that Amy was the last person to touch the
man, so obviously dead, lying now at her feet. He
reached down and grabbed her hand and jerked
her bodily from where she was beginning to kneel
over the corpse. If he'd read his briefing right, she
didn't have anywhere near the credentials she'd
need to make it through any ensuing investigation.
But he had enough firepower on him to put everybody watching them down beside Lutz.

It was just too much explaining. If nothing else, it would trash the operation beyond any hope of salvage.

To Amy, as he jerked her upright and away, he yelled only, "Come *on!* Let's find your friend Dietrich! Run!"

She yelled back, "Running's the worst thing we can . . ." But she was pacing him, and the crowd was beginning to mill, hysteria communicating itself.

Since others were running, they had a chance. And they took it, dodging toward the boating lake with its endless walks. Once, she stumbled. He still held her hand; he yanked hard, steadying her. But she stopped, among the trees, winded and panting. "We can't keep running. We've got to—"

"To what? You're here under a false passport. You were worried about your cover. We've just reestablished it."

She tore at the hair in her eyes with shaking fingers. "But Lutz . . . he wanted to see us. Somebody must know something—about us, I mean . . . that the meeting was set. Something!"

"Somebody knew enough to kill him just before we got there. Probably not a coincidence." In his mind's eye, he saw the big brown bear, who'd stared at him and given up his seat. Damned crazy country. "Can we get costumes? Everybody else has them. Can we rent them?"

She frowned, bit her lip, and then threw her arms about his neck and kissed him—a real kiss from cold, dry lips. "You're a genius! Yes, we can—"

"Just fond of living. Come on, let's go rent some." *A bear with a gear bag?* "Then we'll see about getting a car."

And they ran like lovers, hand in hand, through the walking paths, her fingers stronger in his, the gear bag thumping with its implacable weight against his shoulder blades, toward Dietrich, and away from the police sirens wailing toward the pagoda and the corpse they'd left behind.

Chapter Sixteen

Marcus Wolfe was on the hot line to the Soviet resident in East Germany who handled all Russian Line X (illegals and technology transfer) business in the Germanies.

The man was no more than a phone number; they'd never met. They never would. Wolfe might sit at table with general secretaries and highly placed officials of the various Soviet governing "organs," but he would never shake hands with the man whose job it was to monitor and verify the performance of Wolfe and Wolfe's operatives—and to operate independently on the USSR's behalf when Moscow deemed such action necessary.

Wolfe was concerned that no such determination be made in this case—that no new Soviet agents be dispatched to his territory because Wolfe's interests had been judged divergent from Moscow's. He wanted no KGB or GRU excursions into West Berlin in pursuit of Brecker and Hayes; he wanted no Bulgarians shot attempting to go over the wire at Ramstein; he wanted no international incidents on his watch.

146

And so, talking to the disembodied voice that represented the sickle that hung ever over his head, Marcus Wolfe, doodling on his desk's green blotter with his fountain pen as he talked, was very careful.

"Yes, it is done," he assured the Soviet resident. "The media have been given the descriptions of the Americans; the Munich police have been convinced by our 'eyewitnesses' that Brecker and Hayes are their prime suspects. They will be sought 'for questioning' in the matter of Lutz's untimely death, and—"

"And not found, of course, comrade," the gravelly, Russian-accented voice interrupted.

"And not found, of course," Wolfe agreed, stifling his irritation. Sometimes the Russians were purposely obtuse, sometimes simply crude. But they were never heavy-handed without a reason. Deception was their favorite form of recreation; displays of power came a close second. This Russian was reminding Wolfe that even the GDR's spymaster must answer, ultimately, to the ubiquitous KGB.

It was not a pleasant reminder. Wolfe took a deep breath and said slowly and with exaggerated patience, "Let me put your mind at rest, comrade. Once we determined that Lutz was striking out on his own when he interfered with the Americans' planned trip east by diverting them to Munich, we had to act. Although we'd long known that Lutz walked both sides of the street, there was no need to put an end to his usefulness until the pressure from his American allies became so strong he could not refuse them. Now we have turned all to our advantage: Hunted by the Federal Republic as murderers, the Americans have no choice but to come to us. Tonight, as planned, we will receive them with open arms. The rest—the presence of the spaceplane at Ramstein, the purpose or bona fides of the Americans themselves—will become clear once we can ask our questions of them at leisure."

There was a sucking sound from the other end of the line, as if the Russian were sipping hot tea. Then: "*Da, da*. But remember, this pilot, Hayes, is too valuable to lose. Because of this, we will have observers in place."

This was just exactly what Wolfe had feared. He had sacrificed Lutz to avoid it. He had made this call to preclude it. Now, faced with a flat statement of intent, he could say only, "Don't fill the woods around Ramstein with tree-climbing boys carrying expensive cameras, for God's sake. And don't get in my way, or you may lose—PKO may lose—what it covets most."

And he rang off, furious and unconcerned at the moment with protocol or the feelings of the mysterious Russian on the other end of the phone. Results, after all, were the only things that mattered. If the operation went well, Wolfe could claim many favors in return, including the reposting of the arrogant man who'd dared threaten him to Tonkin Bay or Afghanistan—or to Nicaragua, where the Americans were winning.

Here, the Americans could not be allowed to win. Here, Wolfe must win.

He sat back in his wooden chair, his fingers running along the cracked leather of its padded arms. If the American pilot became his, anything was possible, even the acquisition of the spaceplane called *MEDUSA*.

About *MEDUSA*, even the much-vaunted Soviet intelligence services had been ignorant. Everyone had been caught flat-footed when the hypertech weapons platform appeared out of nowhere. But now, it remained only to take advantage of the U.S.A.'s kind offer of a look, perhaps a hands-on examination if he played his cards right.

With *MEDUSA* in his pocket, there was no telling what Marcus Wolfe might accomplish—even the reunification of the Germanies in his lifetime. Even a new office chair, one with fresh, oiled leather and with springs that did not squeak; one with ergonomics and hydraulic lift capability and composite wheels.

Cheered, Wolfe turned and stared through his ancient venetian blinds at the massive Palast der Republik. When he'd been informed that Lutz had received a briefing by U.S. messenger before sunrise and straightaway sent a BND courier to Ramstein to intercept the American woman and her pilot/lover, Wolfe had felt no fury, no betrayal, only a sense of inevitability. Agents always put a foot wrong, no matter whose they were or how highly placed. Double agents, and doubled double agents, ran exponentially higher risks. Lutz was no exception.

It had to happen, eventually. Wolfe had been so prepared that it had taken only one word spoken into the phone to set a predetermined execution scenario in motion. Using that scenario to herd the Americans back into Dietrich's care, and from Dietrich's hands to his, had been the sort of pirouette that had kept Wolfe alive to bury so many of his underlings, compatriots, and enemies.

This gambit would be no different: though the Americans played, consistently, not to lose, Marcus Wolfe always played to win.

"Jesus God," Forrestal barked at Vice-Consul Aikins in West Berlin, half a world away from Langley, Virginia, where Forrestal was sweating bullets because Stewart wanted to see him in twenty minutes. "Can't you do something with those Federal Republic morons? This is so obviously a Soviet setup that even a vice-consul ought to be able to smell the stench. We can, I assure you, all the way across the Atlantic."

"What, exactly," came Aikins's frosty voice across the military-secure communications lines of the Defense Communications Agency and through Forrestal's STU-5—Secure Telephone Unit 5—where it was automatically unscrambled, "would you like me to do, Forrey? Stamp my feet on German TV and announce that as a representative of CIA, I can personally attest to the characters of two supposedly defecting Americans? Say that they may be naughty boys and girls, but not that naughty? Blow my own cover in the bargain?"

"No, no, of course not," Forrestal replied, his eyes closed, trying to infer facial expressions from the tonalities coming over the phone. Damned STUs took all the life out of the human voice, so nuances inestimably important to an intelligence officer tended to become lost.

"Then what, Forrey? I can't protect them without blowing them—and myself. As for the plane—"

"I don't want to *hear* a discouraging *word* about

MEDUSA's safety, Aikins. Anything happens to that weapons platform and you're going to go on German TV and explain the whole thing—I'd rather come clean on this one than lose that plane, or her pilot. Use your BND connections. Get them to override the land police, or whomever—if BND pulls Brecker and Hayes in, and holds them incommunicado, we've turned this mess into a win. Salvaged it. Get my drift? The Soviets will still buy their story, and I don't have to worry about that boy's ability to play superspy if the Russians start pumping drugs into him. Possible?"

"Possible," came the sigh bounced 22,000 miles into space and back to Langley, "but no guarantees. It's whoever gets to them first, after all. I'll do my best, but—"

"Not good enough. Use whatever means, but *get* those assets of ours out of play and safely into American custody, even if you have to produce their fake corpses to do it."

Forrestal paused to allow the vice-consul a stormy response. None was forthcoming. For a moment Forrestal thought Aikins might have broken their transatlantic connection, but then he heard the other fellow breathing.

"By whatever means, Aikins. Clear?" he insisted.

"I can only say I'll try, director. And I'd like to point out, for the record, that none of this was cleared with us, the field personnel directly involved, beforehand. Whatever you had in mind for the aircraft and its pilot, and for Amy Brecker, on whom I'm marginally better informed, the game's changed on you. We know it, and you'd best keep in mind that the Soviets probably know it, too. So let's call this what it is: a salvage run, damage limitation. And let's have our backup pilot fly that plane the hell out of here before you start trying to blame that on Berlin Station, too."

"No way. Not a chance. *MEDUSA* stays put. So does the relief pilot, until you hear otherwise from me. Just get Brecker and Hayes in out of that goddamned free-fire zone you laughingly call an 'area.' And now, if you'll excuse me, I've got to go let Stewart chew on my butt for a while."

The crew of *Salyut 10* developed the surveillance film they'd taken of the American *Skylab* and, simultaneously, the ground facility outside Moscow took the photo-return data and constructed computer-assisted facsimiles.

Then the crew waited, no more nervous than on any other shift of their 260-day rotation, unaware of the commotion they'd engendered far below.

Men hurried along corridors in the new KGB headquarters outside of Moscow. Women pored over code books. Secretaries entered offices and meetings were convened.

Finally, down from the senior levels of power concerned with anticosmic defense matters, came specific orders.

When the Soviet crew in *Salyut* received those orders, the mission commander asked for verification. When it came, he still didn't believe his instructions. But he had no choice—one didn't question orders; one carried them out.

Chapter Seventeen

At sunset, the rented Mercedes from Munich pulled up before the Stuttgart chalet Dietrich had rented and the March Hare and Alice in Wonderland got out.

Amy felt ludicrous in her costume, but the giant bunny beside her had been right—the disguises had made them seem normal, unremarkable, in Munich. Unremarkable to the car-rental agent, who didn't blink at the March Hare's counterfeit German papers, and rented Herr "Kline" the car of his choice with a smile.

Amy did blink. She'd felt resentful that Ro had been given all the help CIA had withheld from her: false ID, his picture on a British passport, an international driver's license, what seemed like a very large bankroll in cash, and platinum credit cards.

They'd sailed through the rental procedure without a hitch. Hayes was cool and self-possessed, the rabbit head he wore muffling his voice enough that his bad English accent and limited German went unremarked.

Obtaining the costumes hadn't been so easy, winded and wide-eyed with Hayes behind her, stuffing money into her shaking hand in the shop. And then they'd realized that his ears were too long and stiff to allow him to wear his rabbit head in the car, and they'd argued.

"I *wanted*," he'd reminded her, "the kangaroo." For his precious gear bag, he'd meant.

"You got," she'd rejoined, unable to stop herself, "better than you deserve, cowboy. What is all that stuff, any—" She'd reached for the gear bag as he was turning the Mercedes onto E-11, to take the autobahn northeast to Stuttgart.

His hand had left the wheel and grabbed her wrist in a blur of motion, grabbed it so hard that the pain made her cry out.

"Don't touch that," he'd warned, ignoring her exclamation, his grip still viciously tight. "Don't ever touch that."

"Fine. Let me go."

He'd let her go.

She'd said, after a time of looking at the increasingly mountainous terrain and his speedometer, which ramped up the kilometer scale into three figures without regard to safety, "If you don't slow down, we'll never live to fail on our mission."

He hadn't even cracked a smile. His eyes were on the cars ahead, judging holes through which he could wheel the flying Mercedes. She reminded herself that he was a pilot, but it didn't help. The cars he passed seemed like stationary obstacles until, closing on a Porsche, the other driver took Ro's speed as a challenge and she found herself in the middle of a road race that had her clutching the three-point belt across her chest.

"Don't you trust me to drive this groundhog? Don't sweat it, Brecker—we've got airbags."

"Not punch-out seats?" She tried to be flippant, but it came out sounding resentful.

He was too busy with his driving to answer. Pulling abreast of the Porsche, he raised one hand to his brow and looked away from the road, meeting the other driver's eyes for an instant. Then the road before her blurred and she might as well have been in one of his fighter jets.

She lapsed into silence punctuated only by her shallow breathing as the Porsche played games with Ro's Mercedes until its driver turned off for Augsburg. Then, furious once it was over and they'd survived it, she said, "You stupid bastard. Don't do that again. You could get us killed. I'm serious."

"I'm sure you are, Miss Brecker. That's part of the problem. But you look cute, so I'll ignore it."

She looked down and realized that Alice's décolletage was heaving. She blushed. "Look, Ro, we've got to get things worked out—brief each other before we get to Dietrich's."

"Okay. You first."

She sighed feelingly. "If not for your little stunt, deciding we should go with Lutz's courier, things would have been easier. Dietrich's secretary was waiting for us with a car, so we'll need a good explanation." She paused, but he didn't suggest one, just watched the road through his pale, sky-colored eyes. "So how about it?" she prodded finally. The man was maddening.

"So, Lutz asked for a meet—pulled us in for questioning; when we got there he was dead. It'll play, God knows."

"The truth?" She was aghast.

"Why not? We'll both be telling the same story. Just don't volunteer what he wanted to talk to us *about*—we never found out, anyhow."

"And we're good defector candidates, both of us, still. Dietrich has to buy that."

He shook his head minutely, the corner of his mouth she could see pulling tight. "I don't like that part, not at all. But I've told everybody involved in this I don't, and nobody gives a shit. So it's not your fault, by my count. We'll play it the way you set it up."

"Good. Great." She smiled and uncurled aching fingers from her shoulder belt.

"Not great, by a long shot. Necessary, at this point, though. You have enough German to tell if we're on the evening news?" He'd indicated the car radio.

"Sure, but don't worry. . . ."

His raised eyebrow was so eloquent that she trailed off and tuned in a station.

He was right—their names and descriptions were being broadcast. They were prime suspects. All Staatspolizei were looking for them.

She told him and then added savagely, "So drive carefully, all right?"

He tapped his console and his driving lights lit up the road. "Right. Now you see what I meant, though—we've got better reason now to 'defect' than we did before. Christ, we need some kind of help, that's for sure. Whoever wanted us tagged for Lutz's murder did a damned good job."

"But we didn't . . . surely no one will believe . . ."

"The bad girl Amy Brecker, here under a false

passport? Lutz was real visible when they pinged you at that party, or so I heard tell. You think it wouldn't read like revenge, when you're set up by professionals? What are you going to say, you and Dietrich, when they come to his house asking for—"

"It's not his house—at least not his regular house. He rented it for the holidays. And we'll be in East Berlin by midnight."

"You keep saying that and I keep trying not to hear it. Look, lover, I was telling you the truth when I said I ought not to be traveling east. This documentation I've got, the fake stuff, it's not fake enough by a long shot to pass muster. Do you understand? If EastBloc gets its hands on me, whatever credibility I've given you is gone"—he snapped his fingers—"like that."

"What are you saying, that you won't go? You've been *ordered* to go by—"

"That's right, I've been ordered to go." One hand came off the wheel again and he slid it along the seatback until he could take her chin in his fingers. Then he looked at her instead of at the road: "But if you're smart, you'll just find a way to leave me here—Stuttgart, West Berlin at worst. Somewhere I can scramble if I get buzzed." He took his hand away and tapped his waist, where a metal plate was clipped to the belt under his bunny suit.

"I can't change your orders, Major Hayes. And I can't disobey mine."

"That's that, then, I guess," he'd said in a tone that had made her know it wasn't.

Now, getting out of the Mercedes before the

warmly lit stucco-and-timber house with its Alpine porches and music coming from within, Amy was sure that the subject would come up again.

They had only a few hours to prepare for the East Berlin rally Dietrich had promised to take them to; maybe she could plead exhaustion, or convince Dietrich that Lutz's death had changed things too much to risk a border crossing, or simply muck up the schedule enough that they'd miss the last plane to East Berlin's Shönefeld airport. Hayes had suggested all of those things, diffidently, as if counseling moves in a chess game—somebody else's. His detachment, more than anything else, made Amy nervous. It wasn't natural, not when they were hunted criminals.

She said as much, as he took the keys from the ignition and his hare's head from the back seat: "Act scared, all right? You ought to be—we'll be in jail for a long, long time if they make this Lutz thing stick."

"I am. I don't like confined spaces if they're stationary," he replied. Then he settled his rabbit's head on his shoulders, slung his gear bag over one, and took her gallantly by the arm. "Shall we, fräulein?"

She had time enough to conjure a horrid fantasy of Dietrich's door opening to reveal armed police waiting for her before that door did open, to reveal Reinhardt Dietrich himself.

Their host had a smile pasted firmly on his handsome Teutonic face and a beer stein in hand. There was no flicker of warning, or doubt, in Dietrich's ice-blue eyes as he bowed just slightly. *"Guten Abend,* Amy. *Wie geht es Ihnen?"* Dietrich took one step over his threshold, embracing her coolly, pressing first one cheek against hers, then the other.

"I'm fine, Reinhardt, just fine, considering," she said as they disengaged. "This is my friend, Major Munro Hayes." Behind Dietrich, Amy spotted a few guests clustered in the front hall near the piano, glancing their way curiously. One of them was Jeremy Pratt. Her blood chilled.

Dietrich was shaking Ro's hand and welcoming the pilot to his home, not missing a beat, impeccably playing the gracious host. Could it be that Dietrich hadn't heard? Amy had to know, before she faced Jeremy.

Dietrich was saying, " 'Ro' it is, then," and motioning her inside.

"Wouldn't Herr Kline be better?" she asked harshly, and Hayes frowned at her.

Dietrich paused and inclined his head, looking at her squarely. "You're safe with me, Amy—and your friend, also. Don't worry."

This was too weird. In the foyer she leaned back against the doorpost, conscious once again of her costume. Dietrich and those beyond him in the great room were uniformly black-tie. But it wasn't the formal dress that bothered her. "You've heard, and that's all you can say? Don't you want to know what happened? Aren't you concerned that you're at risk, that we'll—I mean, aren't you going to ask us whether we—whether we . . ."

Hayes slapped her with a stare meant to calm a hysterical woman, his stubbled face otherwise impassive, as Dietrich filled in the blank Amy had left: "Whether you are murderers? No, I'm not going to ask. I'm not—how do you say?—the baby in the woods. Now, come. You need a drink."

Hayes sidled around Dietrich to take her arm. "Come on, honey. It's okay. I'm right here."

It was such outrageous bullshit, she almost yelled at Ro to take his hand off her. Instead, she took a step toward Dietrich, shaking off Ro's grip with an irritable jab of her elbow. "If everything's so god-damned great, what's Jeremy Pratt doing here? How do I know you're not going to hand us over to whoever wants us, and all this isn't just a way to keep us tractable until they get here? Come on, Ro, let's . . ."

It was a horrible chance to take, but she had to try it. The emotions she was feeling were genuine—the fear, the uncertainty, the distrust. Acting like nothing was wrong was impossible. Wondering who her friends were was natural. Finding out was a top priority.

Who the hell *was* Dietrich? Her former agent was altogether too cool. She remembered the stricken look on his face that night she'd been pinged at the embassy party. He was far too collected tonight. One of those two reactions had been a counterfeit. She need to know which. And she needed to know what Jeremy Pratt was doing here.

She stepped so close to Dietrich that her chest nearly bumped his. "Well?" she demanded.

Behind her, Ro was making tenderly worried excuses: "She's upset, Herr Dietrich. Understandably. Maybe we'd better leave. No use getting you involved in . . ."

Bastard. Ro wasn't missing any chance to screw

things up enough to avoid going east. But Amy hardly listened to him once Dietrich leaned close to whisper in her ear, on the pretext of giving her a kiss.

"I didn't invite Pratt; he just 'dropped by.' Don't worry, dear. I've got friends in East Berlin. Once we get you there, you'll be safe, you and your friend. My secretary told me what happened. I've heard the news. You've come to the right place." He straightened up, his expression protective, paternal, perfect.

She wanted to scratch out those eyes, resting on her so calmly. This man she'd thought was her agent, one she could manipulate for her government, was obviously entertaining the same sentiments and misconceptions about her. With hindsight's painful clarity, she saw that he had been using her the entire time she'd so carefully cultivated him. The old Dietrich had never frightened her, but this other creature, who didn't care if he harbored murderers as long as those murderers would willingly accompany him to East Germany, terrified her. Here was a master of betrayal. She shivered, and suddenly her fear bled away. There was no room in this game for frightened women. There was, however, time enough and opportunity enough for vengeance. Dietrich hadn't even bothered to ask if they *had* killed Lutz.

She was furious. But it was exactly what she should have wanted. Okay, she'd play, too. Jeremy Pratt was a real problem, and her professional self was demanding that she deal with it, insisting that she must.

She couldn't afford a misstep like the one she'd made when Azimov walked into her office.

"That doesn't explain what Jeremy's doing here, Reinhardt," she insisted softly. "Or what's going to happen when he tells—"

Dietrich cut in. "By the time anyone has reported anything, you'll be beyond America's reach. Come, my dear, at this juncture you've no choice but to trust someone."

"That's right, honey," Hayes, the concerned boyfriend, interjected from behind her, "and by default, our friend Dietrich's that someone—for now. This Pratt guy, who is he? What's the—"

"Later, major," Dietrich counseled, and exchanged a male-to-male look with Ro that made Amy even angrier.

She whirled on the pilot to tell him to butt out, that he didn't understand. But when she saw a giant rabbit suit, a hare's head staring out at her from under Hayes's arm as if it were a Carrollian flight helmet, she burst out laughing.

Hayes rolled his eyes skyward, said, "Come on, sweet thing. You need a drink," and maneuvered her into the party.

And then there was Jeremy, separating himself from the other men in the hall, coming toward her with a disapproving scowl that included Ro. He stopped before her as Dietrich suggested that Ro might want to change clothes, drolly attempting to avert a confrontation.

Amy said flatly, "Ro Hayes, this is Jeremy Pratt, your predecessor. If you'll excuse me, major, Jeremy and I have a little unfinished business."

Together, she and Jeremy walked past the staircase and stopped under a twelve-point stag's head that looked mournfully over the gathering.

"What do you think you're doing?" she demanded.

"That's your new boyfriend? The one everybody's talking about? Your partner in crime?"

"What difference does it make to you, anyway? Let's not get personal, okay? We managed to avoid it for years, living together. Why start now?" She turned to face him and saw a flush on the pinched countenance that she knew so well.

"Amy, I know what's going on. I didn't just show up here by accident, you must realize." As he spoke, Jeremy reached into his pocket and pulled out a Japanese FM radio no bigger than a matchbook, turned it on, and thumbed the dial until, between stations, it broadcast static that would make their conversation difficult to overhear or record.

Baby's playing spy, she thought. He wasn't up to it. She said, "Don't tell me you're here under orders. You don't do this sort of thing, remember?"

"I am, because of you, in this up to my neck."

"Jeremy . . ."—she pushed away from the wall and looked up at the stag as if she were admiring it—"go away. Go have a dinner party of your own.

"I can't, Lord knows I'd like to. We want you to come in, Amy. Come back with—"

" 'We'? Who's this 'we'?"

"You know who. And you know why." Desperation was leaking through the professional gloss of Jeremy's tone. "Aikins sent me here, on the off chance that I'd find you. That's how desperate they are. We can offer protective custody. I can, tonight. . . ."

She was shaking her head. "Dietrich will never

allow it. He's all revved up. Didn't even pretend he was worried about whether we'd killed Lutz."

"Did you?"

She closed her eyes, opened them, and said, "I guess I shouldn't have expected better from you. None of your damned business, is it, Jeremy? You're going to go back empty-handed, you know. You're just not the sort who inspires confidence. I didn't get any orders through channels I can trust. I don't know who Aikins is taking his orders from, and I don't care. If we blow this thing now, it's all a waste. And like I said, I don't think Dietrich would let us out at this stage if we wanted out—which I don't."

"You're not saying this." Jeremy's skin was now waxen. "You don't mean this. Amy . . ." He reached out delicate fingers to touch her. They hovered in the air, repulsed by the power of her gaze. Then he clenched his fist and withdrew.

"You're not worried about me," she said as if just discovering the fact; "you're worried about your career performance. Tough break, Mr. Pratt. They'll cut you some slack on this one—extenuating circumstances. You couldn't swear we wouldn't be turned over to the Germans, or become the focal point of extended diplomatic bickering while we sat in some American military holding facility. Not to me, you couldn't. I know the embassy merry-go-round too well. So you tried."

"Amy, they're going to think it was personal. Because of him." He jerked his thumb toward the great room, which Hayes was just then reentering, his bunny suit discarded, gear bag in one hand, and Dietrich by his side.

"Maybe it is, Jeremy." She couldn't resist it. "Major Hayes wouldn't leave me swinging in the breeze. He wouldn't ask me to compromise myself or my mission, not for the sake of America's West German diplomatic presence, or for his own sake. Think about that. Dips have to be capable of inspiring trust."

And she left him, wondering if she'd regret what she'd done. After all, Jeremy had gotten her the documentation, everything she'd asked for. He'd proved he was her friend. Then.

But this was now. Now she couldn't be sure who'd sent Jeremy after them. By now there must be one hell of an interagency flap about Brecker and Hayes. And she really believed what she'd said about Dietrich—he wasn't going to let them go without a fight.

And this was neither the time nor the place to have one.

She strode up to Munro Hayes with more confidence then she felt and put her arms around his neck, leaning into the kiss with more fervor than she'd managed previously. With Jeremy watching, it was very satisfying to play Ro's lover. And so was the confusion in the pilot's eyes when their lips parted.

Pumped so full of adrenaline that she no longer cared about life's mundane considerations, Amy Brecker was beginning to enjoy herself. This mad game of Forrestal's might be her last, but she was going to play it with flair, verve, and to the very best of her ability.

"Everything okay, sweet thing?" Hayes asked her.

"A-okay, fly-boy. Nominal," she quipped, and

saw the confusion fade from his eyes, to be replaced by an intense interest that suited their cover to a T.

Robinson had *Skylab*'s flight deck to himself. Canfield had the trots—he was in the head. Holly Gold had drifted in, shaken her pert white ass at him for a few minutes, and drifted back to her sleep quarters when she'd gotten no results.

It was one of those charmed moments when Robinson felt almost at ease up here, with the spectacular earth below and space like a star-studded blanket wrapped around him.

If he got through this mission without blowing it, he'd never ask for orbital duty again, he promised himself. He'd promised his wife the same thing, but that was different. He'd thought he could make it, handle the stress, handle the height, handle the vertigo and the terror that overcame him periodically. The NASA psychologists had pronounced him fit for this mission, which proved how much a man could do with determination and designer drugs.

The stuff he'd brought up here, forbidden but not yet illegal, was almost gone now, because it was so damned hard to float between the stars, like it was hard to be the Perfect Black Overachiever that everyone back home wanted him to be. From here on in, it was going to be damned near impossible to be cool. He had some allergy medication that had tranquilizing side effects, but it wasn't enough. He knew it wasn't enough. Last night he'd awakened soaked in sweat, dreaming he was falling forever.

Another two weeks . . . it really was an impossible situation. But he had a son at Yale, and it was impossible to disappoint the boy, or his sister. And it was impossible to wash out of the program, because if he did, he washed out too many other blacks' dreams.

It was just bad luck that space scared him half to death. And militarized space, with its tiny, deadly pinpricks of light, each capable of mass destruction, was preying on his mind more and more. Probably would be better if all that stuff—the laser battle stations, the rail guns, the high-orbit military communications satellites, the Low Earth Orbit KH series of photo-return satellites, the positioning mirrors, and the C3I stations—were all blasted the hell out of here, swept away so that there was nothing in the sky but the moon and the stars. . . .

Do it now, before it was too late, before somebody turned that arsenal on the beautiful, sleepy planet below and then it *was* too late. . . .

Robinson shook his head to clear it. Designer drugs could be tricky. He'd doubled his doses because he was nervous and irritable; now he was coming down fast and hard. Rubbing his eyes fiercely, he told himself he'd better get back to work before Can came floating in.

And, looking at one of his monitors, he saw a telltale that told him he'd better shape up. The telltale was from an island in the Sea of Japan, and the data he pulled up minutes later said a very big, very nasty missile was being emplaced on a launch pad there.

He was just about to alert Can, or exercise his prerogative of calling the data in and putting the entire U.S. Space Command on alert, when he began having trouble with one of his consoles. It beeped and bleated and began throwing up garbage on its screen.

As he sweated over the frozen system, another started malfunctioning, and another.

Simultaneously, the real-time surveillance cameras stopped feeding exterior views and the flight-deck lights went out.

Chapter Eighteen

Munro Hayes had lots more in his gear bag than his rabbit suit; he had personal weapons he didn't want to lose. Carrying it around Dietrich's Stuttgart chalet didn't help him blend into the crowd of penguin-suited men with their sequined *frauen;* neither did his flight jacket or his casual clothes.

But he didn't want to lose Amy Brecker, either, especially because he'd been told by the brass he could consider her expendable. As far as Hayes was concerned, she wasn't—not until his buzzer vibrated the skin next to his hipbone, and possibly not even then.

He'd taken a good look at Jeremy Pratt, the embassy staffer somebody'd sent after them, and he hadn't liked what he saw. He didn't like Dietrich much, either, but that was to be expected: No matter what Amy thought, Dietrich was clearly part of the opposition.

That revelation made his time in the chalet a recon mission. Recon was something Ro Hayes did very well.

He slid around and through the crowd, noting faces, memorizing names, always keeping Amy in sight when she wasn't by his side. She was looking better to him by the minute: game, plucky, and a whole lot tougher than he'd expected, without being unfeminine.

They all looked good until you got to know them, he cautioned himself. And reacting protectively to Brecker in a situation like this was more a function of training than attraction: Way back in basic, men like Hayes were taught that women were part of what they were fighting for. The marines called them Suzies, short for Suzy Rotten-crotch, but even among the rowdy leathernecks, the message was clear, graven deep, and as American as a '59 T-bird: You took care of the women.

Brecker didn't seem to realize that she needed protection, parading around with Dietrich, whom Ro had seen on rec-room TVs around the world, in her Alice in Wonderland outfit, playing her espionage game for all she was worth, flirting and shaking her pert little ass. Like a comet, she orbited back to him every now and again, long enough to critique his performance ("Come *on*, Ro, mingle. Work the room") before she disappeared among the literati and politicos. He knew she'd been wrong when she'd muttered under her breath, "You're blowing it, lover—you can't just stand in the corner looking like you can't wait to get out of here."

He could, and did, do as much of that as possible: One of them had to look worried enough that Dietrich wouldn't start wondering if they seemed to understand what was happening to them.

Ro chose corners with good views of doors; he

kept his back away from open windows; he didn't
drink anything but coffee and he ate enough smoked
meats from the buffet to satisfy his protein re-
quirement for the next forty-eight hours.

And he watched Brecker work, telling himself
she deserved whatever she got. She was a player,
not somebody's wife or sweetheart.

So when she came over to him again and took
his arm, saying, "The plane's a private jet, leaving
from someplace near here for Shönefeld in an
hour, Dietrich says. You, me, him, and a private
pilot, okay?" he didn't argue. She wanted to go to
a rally in East Berlin. It was stupid, but she equated
it with success. In this deep, in some high roller's
chalet, with heavily muscled "waiters" and "wait-
resses" who could have doubled for MPs, it was
too late to argue.

He waited, letting his mind roll and his priorities shake out. Pilots did plenty of waiting. The
low-level adrenaline feed of standby was welcome;
it helped him think about what was going to happen when Brecker realized that everything he'd
told her about going east with him was true.

A private plane beat the hell out of a commercial flight. He was just about reoriented, his mind
made up about everything but Amy Brecker, when
Jeremy Pratt, sheepskin coat over his arm, made a
beeline toward him.

"Thought I'd say goodbye." Pratt smiled cheerfully and held out his hand.

Hayes didn't take it. "Goodbye, Pratt. My re-
gards to your station chief."

"That's all?" Pratt's scowl was laced with challenge, making Hayes realize that Pratt thought Ro

actually *was* romantically involved with Amy Brecker.

"Far as I know. Why? Is there supposed to be something more?" If this Pratt had something up his sleeve, now was the time to flash it. Amy, Ro remembered, hadn't thought too much of Pratt's offer.

"More?" Pratt repeated. "Not unless you can make her listen to reason—I never could. Just remember, Porsches—nothing else even comes close."

"Right, I hear you." He'd thought the Porsche he'd been playing with on E-11 had been a little too tenacious; it was nice to know that the driver was from his side, not the opposition. "I'll keep it in mind."

There were too many Porsches in Germany to make any assumptions, but it was a fallback somebody had kindly put in place: Somewhere, somehow, if he was in enough trouble, he'd see that car again, and the crew-cut driver who'd given him a solemn-faced salute. It wasn't much, but Taylor and Forrestal were trying to give him something—some hope, some help. It made him feel better, facing EastBloc and every military pilot's nightmare.

Then he looked Pratt squarely in the eye and saw the resentment and hostility there: This career dip didn't like him one little bit.

And he realized that the feeling was mutual. Damn Brecker—women didn't belong on this kind of mission; it made everything too confusing. He wondered how Pratt, still gazing at him as if he were a dangerous spider under glass, would feel if he knew that Munro Hayes had spent the last hour letting his own conscience and his sense of duty wrestle over whether he'd let Amy Brecker sashay into an East Berlin rally all by her lonesome; that he'd thought out a way to do it without blowing her cover—at least not right away.

He met Pratt's stare with an opaque, unblinking, and perfectly neutral look that forced Pratt to disengage, glance at his feet, and move away toward Amy and then the door.

Pratt was a fool to try for personal points that way. Munro Hayes had won staring wars against his nation's Joint Chiefs of Staff. It had to do with knowing you were right and not caring what the other guy thought. Like with Dietrich: Dietrich, whether Amy recognized it or not, wanted to get into her pants. One way or the other, the famous Teutonic firebrand might get there yet.

Watching Amy, who managed not to look silly in her costume and around whom Dietrich and his kind fluttered like moths near a flame, Ro wondered if she understood how much she was risking. Playing defector was playing for keeps. Once she went behind enemy lines, there was no way to get her out again, short of trading valuable spies for her. EastBloc could claim she'd defected voluntarily. They would make her give a statement to that effect. And then Dietrich and his kind would have all the time in the world with her.

He knew she was Agency, and that he shouldn't be worried for her safety, but he couldn't shake it. It wasn't that he didn't take her seriously as a player, he told himself, or that he didn't want to credit her with all the questionable virtues of intelligence types. It was that he knew exactly what he was going to do when he got airborne in that private jet, and he really didn't need anybody else's ass to worry about while he was doing it.

But there was hers, pert and cute and staring him in the face as she made nice to Dietrich. He should thank her for playing diversion, giving him the time he needed to think things out. And the time to foray into Dietrich's powder room, once she'd told him the flight was by private plane, to deploy some of the weapons from his kit. There'd be a cursory search at whatever little field the private jet left from, of course, but it was unlikely that there'd be X-ray or metal-detecting arches, and what he had would pass unnoticed through all but the most stringent searches.

In a cross-draw holster under his jacket, he was wearing a composite pistol made from the same material as chopper rotors and with dual-feed magazines filled with very illegal ammunition, the sort NATO had outlawed in specifics long after the Hague convention's low-tech standards had been outmoded. The 8mm automatic held two vertical magazines with thin grip plates between, so the butt was no bulkier than that of a Browning Hi-Power, which the custom pistol mimicked.

There all resemblance to commercial handguns ended. The ambidextrous selector chose the magazine and automatically switched when the designated box was empty: In one, he was carrying eight special APDS (armor-piercing discardable sabot) bullets that left no telltale rifling on the depleted uranium slugs; and in the other, four high-penetration DU-shot rounds that achieved a twelve-foot spread of mercury-centered particles, followed by four ceramic-airfoil expanding rounds for point-blank killing with minimum penetration—

the sort of thing you wanted in a pressurized aircraft, or in a spacecraft.

Right now he'd selected the shotgunlike mercury rounds, but a flick of the switch would make him as ready to deal with SWAT teams in armored cars as he currently was to put down every civilian at Dietrich's party.

Ready, and waiting for his buzzer to go off. Only there was this girl named Brecker to worry about. . . .

He shifted his gear bag, automatically checking the hidden compartment where a spring-loaded knife and another pistol nestled. The central compartment was filled with electronics and various explosive ordnance in disguise.

Full kit, Taylor had said, back at the very beginning. He wondered how much Taylor knew—had known, from the outset—then thrust the suspicion away. Too much that was random had shaped events; not even Forrestal could have foreseen everything.

But they'd told him she was expendable, and as she came toward him then, he knew she wasn't.

Which canceled the simplest plan he had, the one he liked the best, because it meant letting them take Brecker east while he stayed behind. He could have played it out if he had the intestinal fortitude: The boyfriend loses his nerve at the last minute; it was natural.

Hell, it was half true.

She said, reaching him, as Dietrich hung back and watched, "Ro, darling, it's time to go." And, as she came closer and he held out a hand to her, "Come on, you're pushing this strong-silent-type business too far. You ought to be asking some questions; I know I am."

"I trust you," he said distinctly, for Dietrich's benefit. "Let's go, if we're going."

"Just like that?"

"I can't think why not. Unless Dietrich'll give us an hour in his bedroom first. . . ?" The wicked grin he gave her wasn't feigned.

He was prepared to grab her wrist before she slapped his face, but she caught herself and laughed instead. "I'd ask him, but we both know the answer."

Dietrich was edging up behind her. Ro hoped she had eyes in the back of her head. He held his breath because she was obviously going to keep talking.

And she did. "Once we're safe in East Berlin, we'll have plenty of time to work things out between the sheets."

Dietrich cleared his throat and joined the conversation. "Ready, yes? It's not terribly polite behavior, but my friends are familiar with my grueling schedule. Our car is waiting. If you'll get Fräulein Brecker's coat . . ."

"You bet," Ro said, realizing that he really detested this smooth-talking German and he wasn't going to feel at all bad about doing what he had in mind.

The Soviet crew of *Salyut 10* surveilled the American *Skylab* they had crippled. In their monitors, they could see the results of their jamming and of their physical assault on the external cameras of *Skylab*. Scanners showed low, emergency-power readings; people's movements could be followed, so those aboard were still alive, giving off readable heat signatures.

The jamming techniques included wideband noise, tone jamming, frequency following, and countermeasures for the antijamming techniques of pseudonoise, frequency hopping, and spectrum spreading. Processors on board *Skylab* had been overloaded; a pulse blast had sent molecules oscillating at right angles along sensitive silicon microprocessor pathways.

Skylab had been hardened against nuclear attack, but she had not been adequately hardened against Soviet beam technology; thermal effects and wave effects had taken their toll.

So had the carefully aimed projectiles that spewed opaque material onto her external cameras.

Eventually, *Skylab* could recover. Soviet planners and the personnel of *Salyut* understood, even expected, this. But for a crucial time, a window of vulnerability, of opportunity, had been created. Eventually her crew would realize that even with their auxiliary power supply, they could put *Skylab* back on line by implementing procedures meant to allow operation in a nuclear environment: the beam effects on wave propagation, absorption, amplitude, and phase scintillation could be countered. Rayleigh channel decorrelation time and frequency-selective bandwidths could be adjusted to end the virtual isolation *Skylab* was currently experiencing.

And down below, American space managers would realize, as did the Soviets, that the men and women on *Skylab* were alive and well, and working to reestablish communication through standard mitigation techniques and frequency-hopping schemes.

If the Soviet planners had not been certain that
the heat signatures of those aboard *Skylab* would
be as clear to America's Space Command as to the
crew of *Salyut*, they never would have ordered
the impairment procedures implemented. It was
hardly an act of war. It was, in fact, nearly deniable. Even the dye, by now frozen onto camera
lenses, could be explained, or denied. But it was
crucial that Americans not be able to use Skylab to
monitor the final preparations for the "test" launch
of the Soviet missile meant to destroy it.

Human beings—panicking, helpless people desperately in need of aid from the huge American
defense establishment of which they were a part—
might be ignored or quantified if they were silent;
if *Skylab*'s crew was allowed to scream for help,
the American president might lose his head, lose
control, and lose perspective.

No one, especially the Soviet war planners,
wanted that.

"You *what?*" Stewart demanded of Taylor. "You
lost contact with *Skylab?*" he repeated incredu-
lously. "If this is the start of that Russian gambit,
I'm going to shove every missile we *didn't* launch
at them up your ass—yours and Forrey's. It's going
to be very unpleasant, and it's going to take a very
long time—as much time as we've got left." Stewart had been holding a WHITE HOUSE pencil between his clenched fists. He snapped it in two,
threw the pieces to his desktop, and got up, pacing.

The speakerphone was capable of picking up his
voice wherever he was in the Oval Office. It would
have given him visual contact with Taylor if he'd
wanted it.

Stewart didn't want it.

"It's just a power outage, we think, sir. Sun-spots, some kind of complicated interference. We don't think it's Soviet jamming. . . . We have good intelligence that there's no Soviet missile launch. At least not yet."

" 'At least not yet,' " Stewart mimicked savagely. "How soon?"

"There's something happening that might be preparations, sir. Island in the Sea of Japan. We'll have to wait until one of the polar-orbit recons passes over, with *Skylab* out of commission. Or maybe *Big Bird*—"

"Fuck *Big Bird*. I want to talk to those boys up in that space station, and I want to talk to them by dinnertime, or you're going to spend the rest of your days in a lockbox. Clear?"

Taylor's terse "Yes, Mr. President" didn't mollify his commander in chief.

"And I want two missile experts in here—the general in charge of the Hippo Herd silos, and his best technical expert. We're going to prepare a little surprise for our Russian friends."

"Yes, sir," said Taylor as if Stewart had just ordered a ham and cheese on rye.

"And I want Forrey and you to put your heads together and tell me what the hell it means that we can't recall these Classic Thunder agents of his. Diplomatic channels tell me that girl of his said no to a direct order to come in. If I find out either of you are responsible . . ." Stewart trailed off. He couldn't think of a suitable threat, what with the end of the world dominating his calendar for the next few days.

Taylor's quiet "Yes, sir. If that's all, sir, I'll get

right on it" sounded like a mosquito buzzing around his ears. He strode to his desk and slapped a button that cut the connection, not bothering to answer the air force man. Bunch of idiots, all of them. He wasn't a career soldier, or an intelligence officer, but it didn't take a genius to realize that *Skylab*'s sudden silence and the PKO scenario and the missile being readied at some damned island in the Sea of Japan were related.

It would take NSA, CIA, Air Force Intelligence, and thirty-one other components of the intelligence community at least twenty-four hours to process that raw data, collate, cross-check, conference, query, convene the IC staff, and render him a bulletin, however. Then he'd get some nice single paragraph on the CIA director's letterhead that gave him "best assessment" or, if things were considered really urgent, a National Intelligence estimate on the matter. Most likely the "finished intelligence" wouldn't reach his desk until tomorrow morning's *Intelligence Daily* came out.

By which time, the shit would have hit the proverbial fan, or not, and whose name was on what piece of paper might not matter a tinker's damn.

The worst thing about trying to guide the behemoth known as the U.S. was that you could never, ever, get anyone to do anything fast enough or unequivocally enough. Sometimes he wanted to declare himself king and dissolve the whole damned bureaucracy. Today he'd have settled for wiping out CIA, which was putting him in the ridiculous position of having agents out in the field who were uncontrollable, and of having to justify that fact to his German ambassador, who was afraid that the whole matter was going to go public, and to every other scandalized component of the intelligence community who'd found out that some junior clerk named Pratt had had Brecker and Hayes in his grasp and let them slip away.

Nobody had authorized the murder of any BND men; nobody had authorized any assassinations whatsoever. But somebody had brought him Ro Hayes's supersecret, red-stamped, blue-bordered file and asked taciturnly, "What did you expect, sir?"

What Stewart expected now was some action, on all fronts. No matter what kind of stonewalling tactics his various agencies tried, CIA was and always would be the president's personal intelligence service.

There was another pilot on the ground at Ramstein with *MEDUSA*—another CIA pilot. If Stewart didn't get satisfactory answers from his missile boys, and from Forrestal, and from Taylor, he was going to issue an executive order and implement Classic Thunder: send *MEDUSA* up to *Skylab*.

And on the way, if *MEDUSA* happened to fry a few Soviet satellites, why then, those were the fortunes of war—especially undeclared war in space.

BOOK THREE

Chapter Nineteen

When Dietrich's limo had pulled up before the little, lighted airport terminal, Ro's eyes had been fixed beyond, where a small business jet waited on the apron while a man wiped its nearer wing's forward edge.

"What's that, what's he doing?" Amy had asked, although she really wanted to know how private this airport was, how lax its security, and whether there would be any problem about her papers.

"That?" Hayes answered, squinting through the red, green, and blue-white lights that defined the runways. "It's a Eureka propfan, manufactured by Dassault, maybe a ninety-five. Front strakes, the engines faired into them; that long canard, the tail fan on a nonstandard tail to increase the angle of attack at stall—nothing else looks like that. Cruise at Mach three, no sweat; the pilot's wiping debris off the leading edge of the wing, which means that it's got natural laminar flow, probably with a compatible deicing system of pulsable magnets to momentarily deform the wing when a capacitor's discharged. Pretty high-tech stuff, even these days. Right, Dietrich?"

"I bow to your expertise, Major Hayes," said Dietrich with a smile. "I just buy them, I don't fly them. It's fast, yes, and safe, at least so far. I'm told it needs very little takeoff room, which is why, of course, we keep it here when we're in Stuttgart."

Dietrich was sitting behind his driver, on Amy's left; Ro was on her right. The quarters were close, and she'd been ignoring the heat passing between Dietrich's thigh and her own for the last forty minutes.

"I wouldn't want less than five thousand feet," Ro said, "if *I* had to put her down. Mind if I skip the formalities and hop the fence? I'd like to see that wing deicing close up." He held out his "Kline" passport to Dietrich, brushing Amy's breasts with his arm as he did so. "Little one-horse outfit like this, they're not going to mind if I don't present my papers personally."

Dietrich hesitated, then took Ro's Brit passport. "Yes, you're right. That would be best. Even here, unnecessary chances must not be taken."

Hayes already had his door open and was jack-knifing out onto the tarmac before the limo had entirely stopped. Amy slid over into the space he had vacated, toward the door he'd left ajar.

"A smart fellow, your Major . . . Kline," Dietrich mused. "Both of you, together, might jog someone's memory." He leaned close. "But he should not worry. I have many good friends, and my patronage is important here."

Amy was watching Ro, a lithe figure in cords and flight jacket, gear bag in hand, as he vaulted the low fence and sauntered up to the man wiping the little jet's wing and the two shook hands.

She said in a tight voice, "It's hard not to. Worry, I mean. They're saying we killed Lutz. And we didn't, we—"

"Amy, Amy my dear." Dietrich's fingers found her knee and squeezed. "Don't you trust me? Your friend, I think, is more worried about getting that bag of his through any security check unmolested. He's not once let it out of his sight. What has he got in there, do you think?" Dietrich's voice was serious, but his eyes sparkled with humor.

She moved her knee just slightly, a prelude to leaving the car. The chauffeur was already unloading the overnighter she'd had at Dietrich's from the trunk. She'd changed out of her Alice outfit into a pair of wool pants, hiking shoes, and a sweater before they'd left the house, though Dietrich had protested she'd have plenty of time to change on the plane.

"In his bag? I'm sure I don't know. Maybe his security blanket," she quipped without much enthusiasm—she had a right to play nervous Nellie, thank God. For she *was* nervous. And Jeremy's appearance and surprise offer, plus Ro's infuriating boyfriend act, hadn't helped one bit.

"Reinhardt," she blurted, once out of the car, leaning down to speak across the seat to him with the wind clawing her body beneath the waist where her jacket ended and only one layer of wool stood between her and Stuttgart's winter cold, "are you sure this is going to work? What *about* security? Not just here, at Shönefeld? How can you be sure we'll—"

"Here, I call home away from home. There, a very influential personage will meet us at the airport—one, as you requested, who can make decisions regarding your future. He will see to our welfare. There will be no problem in East Germany he cannot solve. It is not like the West—"

"He?" Still bent over, her stomach rolled. She could see her breath, white clouds puffing fast as her breathing accelerated. "Who? I thought we were going to a rally, meeting peace activ—"

"This, too, we will do. As you requested. Amy, this is no time for questions. It is understandable that you are concerned, but I, too, am in some danger, because of you and your . . . friend. And I am not asking you questions, but behaving as a good comrade should. Learn to accept the inevitable. If you had a choice formerly, you do not have one now, unless it is to surrender to the FRG authorities, and that is obviously unacceptable, if not to you, then to your friend. Am I right?"

"I—"

Not waiting for her answer, Dietrich slid out the far door and closed it. Striding to the rear of the limo, he took her bag from the chauffeur, then motioned to her. "Come, fräulein, your new life waits."

New life? "Wait a minute." She had to trot to catch up with him. "I'm just going to meet some people. There's nothing certain. . . ."

Dietrich's cheeks were reddening from cold. "Come now, dear," he said, putting an arm through hers, "you've not thought this through. Previously, perhaps, you had a choice. Now you do not, unless it is American censure or Federal Republic justice. And you say you have been falsely accused. So what is there for you to be uncertain about?"

"But they'll think we're guilty, for running away."

"Then you should not have run. You should have turned yourself in to the authorities immediately. We will send a denial, if you like—if you decide. There are ways. You are a diplomat. When you can negotiate from a position of strength, perhaps you will choose to do so. From East Berlin. From the Harz Mountains. From elsewhere." As he spoke, he was hurrying her up a rubber-coated entryway flanked by heavy-gauge wire fencing.

Glass doors parted for them as she said, satisfied with both her questions and his answers (it wouldn't do to appear too anxious to make this trip), "All right . . . I guess. But promise that you'll stay with me. You won't leave me alone there. Not with this 'someone,' at least. Not until I've figured out what to do."

"Alone? What of your friend Hayes, for whom you waited so anxiously?" Again, a lecherous flicker.

She brushed her hair out of her eyes impatiently as behind her the glass doors closed with a sigh. Ahead she saw a counter with the inevitable mosaic-tile motif, a blonde female ticket agent, and a man with a broom sweeping a spotless floor into which two dozen empty plastic seats were set along parallel rows of steel pipe. The place seemed deserted but for the blonde ticket agent, a similarly dressed aviation official with a clipboard, and three maintenance men.

The section of counter to which Dietrich steered her abutted glass-and-steel doors to an open passenger-debarkation area beyond, by which a mechanized luggage cart waited. One rented planes here, Amy realized, and autos as well.

The blonde woman, who had been at the center of the counter, met them when they reached the end of it. Dietrich greeted her familiarly, handed his papers and Ro's to her, and asked for Amy's. Amy fumbled them out of her handbag, wondering at the laxity of the formalities as Dietrich and the blonde woman discussed flying weather and made jokes while the woman riffled pages and stamped papers and handed Dietrich a sheaf of them from her clipboard.

And that was that—their flight plan had been filed, the weather was good, and there was nothing to worry about, Dietrich chided her as he guided her through the second set of doors into the cold night. Luggage in hand, they climbed onto the open baggage truck, which would take them to the jet, whose engines were beginning to scream.

For a moment, when a German in a parka and a military-type cap came out and strode toward them, Amy teetered on the verge of panic: Was this the Staatspolizei, come to arrest them? Where was Ro? She didn't see him anywhere, and the plane was obviously ready to depart.

Then the man in the cap greeted Dietrich politely, saying, "Taxi, anyone?" in a jocular voice, and slid behind the wheel to start the baggage cart's motor.

She'd never been driven to the ladder of a private jet before. It was all so confusing. She still had the handgun in her pocketbook if she needed it. She was so frazzled, she hadn't even considered what would happen if the girl behind the counter had asked to search her bags.

But she hadn't. Everything was going smoothly, as Dietrich promised.

If only Ro were in sight, her heart might stop pounding. As Dietrich leaned forward, talking to the driver in words the wind whipped away, she told herself she could always take out her pistol and refuse to leave the ground if he was pulling anything—if Ro wasn't alive and well and aboard the little jet.

It had four windows that she could see. In one the pilot was visible. Behind that were three smaller windows, probably those of the passenger compartment.

As the cart pulled to a halt and Dietrich jumped out, holding up both hands to encircle her waist and help her down, she saw a silhouette peering out at them: Munro Hayes. Even backlit, his form was unmistakable.

Relief flooded her and she nearly went limp in Dietrich's grasp. For better or worse, they were on their way east.

For someone who was so afraid of the upcoming flight and the adventure at the other end of it, Hayes was doing a fine job of playacting. Amy cautioned herself that she must do as well.

When Dietrich set her on her feet on the tarmac and said, with a sweeping bow, "Your carriage awaits, my dear," a thought struck her with paralyzing force.

She said, rooted in place, "I want you to tell me who's meeting us at Shönefeld, Dietrich. I have a right to know."

"Someone has said you do not? Mysteries, Amy, are your province, not mine." Firmly, he urged her toward the plane's open door and the steps up to it.

As she relinquished control and put one booted foot on the first metal stair, she tried again: "So, who is it? Anyone I know?"

"By reputation, perhaps," said the voice behind her as they climbed the stairs. "Watch your head there . . . that's good."

She'd just ducked into the cabin and seen Hayes, stretched out in a leather recliner, alone amid more opulence than she'd been prepared to expect, when Dietrich finally answered her question.

"Someone you might know by reputation," Dietrich said calmly as outside the baggage handler stowed their gear and Dietrich himself pulled the door shut and levered the locks. "But not personally, I think: Marcus Wolfe."

"*Marcus Wolfe!*" she repeated so loudly that Hayes could not fail to hear.

And waited for his response—some explosion, a leap from his seat, a scramble in his gear bag for whatever weapons he'd smuggled aboard. Waited in vain.

Hayes stretched slowly, one hand behind his head, and began uncrossing his legs. "If you two don't mind, the pilot said I could ride up front with him."

Cool as could be, he was. Amy nearly stumbled as she sank into one of the leather seats, shaking. She hoped Dietrich hadn't noticed. *Up front!* And leave her alone back here with Dietrich? She was going to kill Munro Hayes, she decided, at the first opportunity.

"Of course, major," Dietrich answered smoothly. "Whatever you like."

"I don't like sitting back here, where I can't tell what's happening. So yeah, thanks. Y'all have a nice flight now," said Hayes as he got up, ubiquitous gear bag in hand. Beside Amy he paused, bent, and planted a long kiss on her lips, whispering, "It'll be okay, sweet thing, just count on me."

And she found herself responding, her arms going up of their own accord to embrace him while she told herself it was acceptable, perhaps even necessary, to seek a little comfort from her supposed lover.

The thing was that, after he'd given her a soulful look and sauntered forward into the cockpit, she really did feel better. And it wasn't because of the drink that Dietrich poured for her from his well-stocked bar, or the rush of gravity when the plane finally took wing.

It was because she'd believed Munro Hayes when he'd told her she could count on him.

The air corridor that commercial traffic must fly from the West to Shönefeld is one mile wide. Divert from it and shoot-down becomes a real possibility. There is no alternate route, no argument, no margin for error.

There is, however, a great deal of traffic on that single route from West to East, the Luftkorridor, which passes first by Frankfurt.

Sitting with the pilot, giving himself a crash course on the Eureka-style instrumentation, Hayes considered vectoring to Frankfurt as they came up on it. It was a simple, safe move to make: Stick his pistol in the pilot's face and suggest that they'd better radio "Erfurt" that they needed emergency clearance to land. It was the best legal vector out of this nastier-by-the-minute situation.

Marcus Wolfe. At least Taylor and Forrestal had done their homework: Wolfe had been part of Ro's last-minute briefing at Langley.

But the stakes were higher than anybody had predicted, if Wolfe was going to meet them at the airport personally. That single fact told Ro Hayes he hadn't been overestimating the problem. Possibly Wolfe had stepped in only when it became known that Brecker and Hayes were now committed defectors; more likely Wolfe had made sure they would be: Lutz's murder made this scenario run, and Hayes was unwilling to give the credit to coincidence.

And he was too long in the field to think that Dietrich was benign, acting independently, or capable of improvisation. The lack of muscle on board—no backup, not even the chaffeur—had to mean that Dietrich was under orders from Wolfe not to spook them, no matter the risk. However badly American intelligence was wired in the Germanies, Wolfe ran his shop like a gallium-arsenide circuit board: top-secret, high-tech, and very, very capable.

So the plane was Ro's hole card, plus the fact that since he and Brecker were working seat-of-the-pants, totally improvisationally, they were less predictable than Wolfe might have liked.

Hence, the personal meeting. And hence, also, a chance to get the ball in America's court before Ro had to say goodbye to Amy Brecker and wish for the rest of his days that he'd been chauvinistic enough to object while objections still could have done her some good.

So he said, "Hey, Hoffman," to the pilot, who spoke good English. "Give me some tune-up on this buggy. We've got nothin' better to do, and that way I can spell you if I have to."

Dietrich's pilot was willing to oblige, after the standard disclaimer that Ro wouldn't have to "spell" him because nothing was going to go wrong.

Once the copilot's controls were in his hands and he was feeling out the craft designed by a spin-off group of the European space consortium as a commercial venture, Hayes was feeling lots better. It was always a matter of knowing what it was you had to work with, and then letting nature take its course. As long as that course wasn't to some East German holding facility, Ro was willing to play along.

And Plan B, the one that didn't entail letting Amy fall into the hands of any EastBloc agents, was looking more and more feasible.

Sometimes you got lucky. Sometimes you made your luck. Ro didn't care which; he just wanted to make sure he could handle a touch-and-go out of Shönefeld if he had to. And that he could get on the horn to Taylor while he was at it, so that he didn't get their tails shot off.

Dietrich's plane had just touched down in East Berlin at Shönefeld and taxied to the apron when Munro Hayes stuck his head around the partition and said with a pleasant smile, "You want to come forward a minute, Herr Dietrich? Tower wants to talk to you."

"Me? *Was ist dies?*" Dietrich cast a sidelong look at Amy. The American fräulein was curled up in the facing seat, staring glumly out the window at the lights of East Berlin. There was no flicker of treachery in her eyes, no tension in her slumped form. She merely turned slowly in her seat, numb like a prisoner of war, and glanced questioningly at Dietrich, then at her lover, shifting her hand-bag in her lap.

Major Hayes didn't answer him, just shrugged the shoulder that Dietrich could see. Infuriating American cowboy.

Getting to his feet, Dietrich tried to pretend it was all routine. His orders had been to preserve whatever semblance of normalcy, of trust, that he could. He still thought he might convince Wolfe that Amy Brecker would be more valuable to the peace effort—and thus to EastBloc intelligence—as a willing participant than as a captured spy. She would have come to East Berlin without all this subterfuge. Without Lutz's death. As Lutz had been wasted, Amy Brecker was in danger of being wasted. But it was not, Dietrich knew, entirely up to Wolfe. Wolfe was as much a puppet as was Dietrich, both of them jerked hither and thither by Soviet puppeteers.

And Wolfe had seemed to be responsive to Dietrich's suggestions, at least up to now.

Thinking that there must be some trouble with debarkation clearance, trouble having to do with Lutz, dead in Munich, trouble that Wolfe's people should have been able to suppress, if not forestall, he hurried forward. As he passed Amy, he gave a comforting pat to the crown of her head, telling her in English, "Don't worry."

When he reached the partition around which Munro Hayes was peering, he found himself staring into the muzzle of a gun.

And stopped, his attention fixed on the pistol with its bulky, silenced muzzle. "My pilot! Hoffman!"

"He's tied up at the moment, Dietrich. Want to come this way? I wasn't kidding. Hoffman and I can't seem to convince the Shönefeld tower that your Herr Wolfe is going to have to come aboard."

"Hijacker!" Dietrich snarled, his fists balling of their own accord. "Cowboy!"

"Now, now," said Hayes. "I was nice. I was polite. I just told 'em the truth: I've got no intention of setting foot on East German soil—none of leaving this plane. I've got you, an unharmed hostage, and I've planted enough of the right kind of explosives aboard this aircraft to make sure that if it goes, it's going to wreak havoc on this runway. So they ought to be kind enough to relay the damned message, don't you think?"

"Jesus God, Ro!" came Amy's pained voice from behind Dietrich. "Why'd you have to go and do that?"

"Because there's no such thing as a 'peace rally' in a ComBloc country, honey. There're controlled demonstrations for the benefit of gullible Westerners like yourself, but that's all."

Dietrich finally managed to tear his attention away from the cavernous hole in the gun's silencer, a deep and frightening channel that might at any instant suck away his life. Somewhere he'd read that one was never, ever, to allow oneself to stare into the muzzle of a gun pointed one's way.

With his eyes fixed firmly on the American major's face, he regained the power of speech. "This is outrageous. Verboten. Another thing 'they' don't have in EastBloc, major, are hijackings. Terrorists are not permitted here. They are eradicated like vermin. You think they will take orders from you? For my sake? You're wrong. They will exterminate you, and myself and your innocent lady friend also, without thought."

"Not with the kind of mess this plane's going to make if it blows. The ordnance I've got gives new meaning to the term *area denial*. You get on the horn to your Commie buddies, tell 'em nobody's been hurt—yet—and tell 'em what I tell you to. They'll listen."

"You're a fool, major," Dietrich said to the gun that Hayes held.

Behind him, Amy called from her seat, "Ro, for my sake, don't do this. He's right. They'll kill us. There're more armed guards and commandos at this airport than—"

"Sweet thing, shut up," Hayes said quietly, and waved Dietrich forward with the gun in his hand. "Let's go, hotshot. We'll see what kind of sand your Wolfe has got in his craw. I want him on board, alone, in the next ten minutes, or you're going to find out what you're really worth to your Soviet masters when I fly this baby out of here."

Wordless, but with a deep, all-suffering sigh, Dietrich took half a dozen steps into the cockpit.

And saw his own pilot, Hoffman, neatly trussed with wide white strips of adhesive tape over his mouth and plastic strips binding his wrists and ankles.

Hayes was handing him the cockpit mike, punch-

ing presets without looking at the radio, his eyes
as level as the gun pointed steadily at Dietrich's
midsection.

Dietrich took the mike in his hand, pushed the
button, and began to speak to the unhappy ground
controller, assuring the tower of his welfare and
demanding to speak to Marcus Wolfe personally.
As he spoke, he could see his entire career crum-
bling before his eyes like the ice being fluxed
mechanically from the little jet's wings in preparation for a hasty departure. Nothing but firepower
or negotiation could preclude one if Hayes chose
to cut and run. The plane's tanks were at least
half-full—Dietrich had paid for the fill-up before
they left the West.

And Dietrich didn't doubt the American's threat
to blow up the plane: The gear bag Hayes had
carried aboard was open, half-empty. On the floor
of the plane, between the seats, a curved American munition was affixed, its red ARMED light blinking steadily. To Hoffman's right was another. How
many the American had secreted in the fuselage
before Dietrich had come aboard was a matter for
conjecture, but the gear bag nestled by Hayes's
foot looked very empty.

The tower asked him to hold, then to hold again
for "the authorities," then came back on line and
began reassuring him that Marcus Wolfe had been
"informed of the situation and is now in transit.
Do you understand? He cannot talk to you now,
but he is on his way."

Dietrich squeezed his eyes shut, expecting a
jarring concussion, a sear of fiery light against his
lids: A bullet from the American major's gun, or

the end of this incident in an explosion set off by East German guards—it would make no difference.

If he died, so very much that was good died with him. Still holding the mike in a sweating hand, Dietrich bowed his head and tears squeezed their way out from between his tight-shut eyelids.

Chapter Twenty

It was 2150 hours, Berlin time, when Marcus Wolfe's car pulled out onto the Shönefeld runway where two Americans held Reinhardt Dietrich, darling of the German peace movement, hostage and the whole of East Germany at bay.

For the moment.

Wolfe had laughed aloud in his Mercedes 600's empty rear seat when he'd heard of the American pilot's audacious move. Insolent, aggressive, worthy of the best of his own men; Wolfe had silently saluted Forrestal, his archenemy, and the operative that he commanded.

Now, with a motorcycle escort and after endless shielded communications from his car phone to the various agencies of the German Democratic Republic whose resources he could command, Wolfe's mood was beginning to darken.

It always did when he was forced to consult his Soviet compatriots. He preferred to consider himself autonomous, and to act in Germany's behalf without Soviet pressure.

He would have boarded the little jet without

prompting; he resented being treated like a lackey.
And yet, the man with whom he had spoken was
concerned with matters in earth orbit, matters
about which, in the normal course of things, Wolfe
would never have been apprised. Thus, he'd gained
a fresh perspective, new information on the immi-
nence of the PKO gambit, and been able to assess
the degree to which the Russians longed to get
this Major Hayes in their grasp.

MEDUSA, Soviet Intelligence insisted, would
be no threat without her pilot. Wolfe learned with
some surprise that the aircraft had been preoccu-
pying KGB, worrying the PKO boys to distraction.

If there was any chance, even at this late date,
of cajoling or coercing Hayes into returning to
Ramstein, boarding his advanced tactical fighter,
and flying it east—if there was even the slightest
chance that Major Munro Hayes was concerned
only for the safety of himself and his woman, that
he wanted guarantees, under which his defection
could proceed—Wolfe was empowered to promise
whatever was necessary. The flight would be a
matter of mere minutes, Wolfe had been assured;
a matter of no danger to pilot or aircraft, or so he'd
been briefed—*MEDUSA* had sufficient countermeasures to avert or elude attempts to shoot or
force it down should Hayes consent to fly it into
the waiting arms of a slavering Soviet government.

If Hayes could be persuaded to bring *MEDUSA*
with him, under whatever guise, even that of Wolfe
returning as a "captive" with him to Ramstein,
Wolfe was empowered—no, implored—to go along.

Personally, Marcus Wolfe thought that the Soviet KGB was simultaneously underestimating and
overestimating the American players, both the pu-

tative defectors and CIA Deputy Director Forrestal. It was much more likely that Hayes had lost his nerve, had a fight with his girlfriend, or had never intended to defect in the first place, than that the convoluted scenario KGB suggested was being played out.

Soviets forgot that other nations did not put the premium on lies and deception that the USSR did. In other nations it was possible to assume that the waiter bringing your bill at a restaurant was not actively attempting to overcharge you; in a market, it was not necessary to doubt the scales on which your meat was being weighed; in international affairs not involving the Soviet Union, it was not certain that a position put forth was necessarily different from that actually pursued.

But KGB assumed everyone else to be as circuitous in motive and as Byzantine in logic as they themselves were. In the case of Forrestal, it was possible they were right. But Hayes was a different breed of cat. Hayes was a single man in the field with one very exceptional piece of hardware and his life on the line.

Wolfe had run too many agents in too many different venues not to assume that whatever Langley wanted, whatever America's reasons for sending *MEDUSA* to Ramstein, Hayes was trying to save his own skin within whatever latitude he perceived in his orders.

Obviously (though not to the Soviets), *MEDUSA* was a warning shot across the USSR's collective bow. Her presence at Ramstein, and Hayes's on Dietrich's jet, now visible outside the window of Wolfe's Mercedes, might be simply a deterrent.

Or might have been, before the pilot had taken
Dietrich hostage.

Now the situation could turn ugly—would, unless Wolfe could take control. Already he was having to insist that if he were to board Dietrich's
plane, any attempt to send KGB agents over the
wire at Ramstein be scuttled before he put one
foot on the little jet's stairs. He wasn't about to
participate in a stunt of such consummate foolishness as trying to steal the plane from under America's nose.

If Hayes could be coerced or persuaded to fly it
out, however . . .

The desperate plan appealed to him more and
more, partly because of its inherent foolishness
and partly because if the hints his KGB contact
had dropped of what was going on above the earth
were true, it would be well to distract the superpowers with earthly events. The superpowers were
playing with fire this time. That the U.S. would sit
by while its crippled *Skylab* was destroyed was as
unlikely as the Soviets' failure to launch because
America had opened its collective coat and displayed its secret weapon, *MEDUSA*, to the USSR.

Space war would lead to ground war; and in a
ground war, noncombatants would suffer horribly,
Europe most of all.

It might be possible to stop this rapidly escalating madness either by prevailing on Hayes to defect with MEDUSA or by sacrificing himself in an
attempt to do so. Marcus Wolfe was willing to take
the chance.

That was why he hadn't brought along a young
hostage negotiator fresh from the Muslim world,
or asked for special squads to guard his person.

This was a battle of wits, one that experience, not merely training, would win or lose.

As his car pulled to a stop beside the little jet, Wolfe could no longer see the black-clad men hunkered down behind artfully placed trucks and on rooftops with laser-sighted rifles in their hands and night-vision goggles on their heads. The whole runway was at risk, according to the communiqué from the hijacker. Area-denial munitions. Difficult to ignore or cover up such damage if the American pilot blew the plane.

With a sudden satisfied feeling that Wolfe long ago had come to associate with making exactly the right decision, he opened his door and stepped toward the plane, hands spread from his overcoated body, open and clearly empty. He was wearing a wire, of course; it was necessary to keep his own channels of communication open, for the sake of the hostage takers as well as his own. But he had come unarmed, unaccompanied, and ready to negotiate.

He hoped it would be enough. Whatever happened here on the ground, American satellite over-flights would at any moment register the jamming and electromagnetic shielding of point defense over the Soviet missile launch site on the Sea of Japan. One could only trust that heads in Washington were sufficiently cool, that no one would "jump the gun," as the Americans said. Wolfe took some small comfort in knowing that there were men like himself and Forrestal involved, men capable of avoiding hasty action.

Forrestal would be automatically informed of events here at Shönefeld in only two cases: if the Defensive Condition alert status of the American defense establishment escalated; if the plane on the runway was destroyed.

Otherwise, it was Marcus Wolfe's show. And he was determined to make it a good one.

Amy Brecker had fished the gun Forrestal had left for her in the locker at Tegel out of her purse and was holding the tiny Walther steadily on Dietrich, whose wrath had bled away to be replaced by bottomless Teutonic angst.

It was Hayes she was arguing with, not Dietrich: "You bastard, here comes Wolfe, for Christ's sake. Now what do we do?" She couldn't forgive Ro for blowing her operation. She glared at him.

The pilot had been lounging against the partition separating the cockpit from the passenger area, watching shadowy motions in the dark that had significance only to him, occasionally telling her, "Well, their snipers are in place," or "Here comes the cavalry."

Now he just watched the Mercedes and the man climbing the boarding ramp, his gun pointed ceiling-ward, flat against the bulkhead behind the door, ignoring her.

"Well, *darling*," she insisted, "aren't you going to answer me? I hope you're satisfied. We'll never get out of here alive." She was still desultorily playing her part, in case something could be salvaged. There was no need to let Dietrich know that Ro Hayes had been so afraid of setting foot in East Germany that he'd decided to go down with his ship rather than risk losing the precious intelligence he carried around in his head.

"I'll be satisfied when I've talked to this Wolfe guy and he's convinced me of the GDR's benign interest in our welfare—honey. Meantime," Hayes added, his voice lowering as the legendary Marcus Wolfe mounted the stairs, "you just be cool and keep your gun on Dietrich. If I'm wrong, I'll apologize later."

Later. There wasn't going to *be* any "later." Not if the GDR dealt with them as their policy on hijackers mandated. She kept kicking herself mentally for not realizing that her fellow American didn't have what it took to pull this off. If they ever did get out of this, she was going to write a report that would ground Munro Hayes for the rest of his natural life.

She'd been careful not to let on to Dietrich that she was other than she'd pretended, even while she and Ro were bickering. Maybe she could still do what she'd been ordered to do, although whether there was any use in carrying through this charade was arguable.

Major Munro Hayes, USAF, had pulled out his handgun and changed all the rules.

The snipers he was talking about were as real as the sophisticated munitions he'd planted aboard the aircraft. She could have forgiven the gun, but she couldn't forgive the way he was cavalierly playing with her life. She didn't want to be spattered all over Shönefeld like so many crushed insect fragments.

And poor Dietrich just sat there, staring at Marcus Wolfe as if he were seeing a ghost while the tall German spymaster stooped through the hatchway into the plane.

Wolfe's eyes were like a gust of Alpine air as they swept the passenger compartment to settle on Ro, who stepped out from behind him with the gun.

Wolfe's hands were well away from his body as he extended one. "Major Hayes, I assume?"

"See anybody else who fits the description? Step away from the door, Wolfe. And toss your ID over to the lady there as soon as you've sat in that seat." Ro's gun pointed to the first leather recliner.

Wolfe did as he was told without a word. Amy took the black leather billfold and flipped it open, though she didn't need to check the picture against the gray-whiskered face to know Marcus Wolfe when she saw him. Oh, God, she thought, we're really screwing this up. Once she had the papers, she didn't know what to do with them. She stood up to give them back to Wolfe, but Ro's loud "Amy, stay where you are. Cover Dietrich" made her feel like she was trapped in a nightmare as Ro shut and latched the jet's door and moved a few feet to sit in the seat opposite Wolfe.

For long seconds, the American air force major and the GDR spymaster stared at one another.

"Thanks for coming," Hayes said finally. "For not siccing that artillery on us."

"You're welcome," said Wolfe in flawless English. "And if that is all you need—to be assured that you and your fräulein are welcome in my country, I am more than happy to provide that assurance personally. We understand that the circumstances of your arrival here—the circumstances under which you fled the West—may have made you doubt your reception. If that is it, I can assure you, we will do our best to protect you, if you will grant us your trust. Concessions, of course—"

"Do your best? What's that mean?" Hayes, even

to Brecker, seemed too taut, too nervous, too intent. "You're going to refuse extradition procedures? You're going to give us political asylum? What?"

"We'll talk about that later. Until you landed . . ." Wolfe said, slowly reaching into his coat pocket so that Hayes stiffened and his gun came up, to point at Wolfe's belly. "A smoke, a cigarette—with your permission, major?"

"Yeah, if you give me one."

Slowly, Wolfe drew out a pack of Sobranies, lit two with an old-fashioned flip-top lighter, and held one out to Hayes.

Ro took it.

Amy wanted to scream, to cry, to shoot the gun in her sweaty hand; its plastic grips kept sliding in her grasp. Cigarettes? Next they'd be asking her for coffee.

"As I was saying," Wolfe resumed smoothly, "until you landed, you had committed no crime against the Democratic Republic. Now . . ."

"Yeah, now. Now you've got half the German Army out there and I've got you in here. Pretty even odds."

Amy realized that she hadn't known anything about Munro Hayes, that the man with the flat voice and the spring-wound posture was not the same one she'd been mentally castigating for cowardice. But she was more worried than relieved: This was the Munro Hayes whose file she'd been given a peek at, the man who'd been grounded as disciplinary action for overstepping his authority over the Gulf of Sidra and shooting down four Libyan fighter planes.

Wolfe sighed deeply, exhaling blue smoke. "No

one has been hurt so far, Major Hayes. No one has
to be hurt. I have worked with many agents of
your type over the years. I do not take it amiss
that you have doubts, or that you have taken decisions and made threats to protect your welfare. It
just shows that you and I are the same kind of
men—that we can do business. Now, if you'll just
tell me what you want, why you have come to my
country, then we shall see how I can help you."

"What I want? I came to your country, buddy,
because somebody decided to try and pin a murder on me."

"Ro!" Amy objected.

"Yeah, yeah, all right. We probably would have
come anyhow. She thinks you guys are a bunch of
real motivated peaceniks. But we've got our differences, you understand. Maybe all I want is free
passage out of here, with this little plane's tanks
topped off, to the third country of my choice.
Maybe she wants to stay here. I don't know yet.
Why don't you tell me what *you* want, Wolfe.
What you wanted enough to kill Lutz just to make
sure we'd be having this little talk."

"I? I want nothing. You demanded to see me,
not I you."

"Bullshit," Amy hissed from her seat, watching
Hayes with a complex of distrust and admiration.
Where was the pilot taking this? And why? Just to
save her from the horror he imagined East Germany to be? She couldn't believe it of him, but it
was flattering. It would have been more flattering
if she weren't sitting in a mined aircraft holding a
gun on Dietrich, her onetime friend.

Dietrich at the same time said harshly, "Herr
Wolfe, it is no good. They *know* you were sched-

uled to meet the plane in any case. About the defection of—"

"Amy Brecker, yes," Wolfe said calmly, and turned those diamond-hard eyes on her. "You, fräulein, have caused everyone a great deal of trouble. We went to great lengths to accommodate you. Now you have the opportunity to return the favor. We never asked what you had to offer us, nor did we doubt you when word came to us through channels that you had tired of the posturing of your Western government and were ready to work seriously for peace. Tell your fiancé how you were mistreated, if he does not already know, by your own government. You, after all, are at the heart of this. Major Hayes and I, as well as Dietrich, are here because of wheels you set in motion." Gaze locked with hers, Wolfe waited expectantly.

"I . . . Ro, you wanted assurances, let's get them. Herr Wolfe has said there'll be no trouble if we go along quietly—"

"The hell he has," Ro interrupted.

Dietrich groaned and covered his face with his hands.

"I would say that, if it is what you want to hear, Major Hayes," said Marcus Wolfe. "I certainly have implied it. Disarm the explosives you have planted, put away your firearms, and come with me." Wolfe, once again facing Hayes, shrugged and smiled paternally. "You may keep your personal weapons, as an article of faith."

"Gee, thanks," Ro said.

Amy got to her feet abruptly. "Ro Hayes, you stop this. I don't want to die here. I just want—"

"Amy, you sit back down." Ro's gun swung to cover her, Dietrich, and Wolfe as best he could.

"*Now*. Unless you want to be part of the problem. Keep your gun on Dietrich. Dietrich, don't be a hero."

She sat back down very slowly. If Hayes was faking this, he was doing a damned good job. Hopes of continuing with her mission were draining out of her, leaving a leaden horror in their wake.

Hayes once again concentrated on Wolfe. "You were telling me what *you* want out of this—you and your GDR. That's what's really bothering me. I don't want to spend the next twenty years talking about the last twenty while various teams take notes."

"Ah." Wolfe nodded, exhaling the last puff of his cigarette. "I see. What we want, Major Hayes, is *MEDUSA*, of course—let me finish explaining, please—if not the physical plane, then your expertise in regard to it. That is all. And in return we'll give you a comfortable—"

"Aw, shit," Hayes said softly. He dropped his cigarette butt, ground it underfoot, and reached with his left hand, eyes still on Wolfe, toward his hip pocket.

Dear God, Amy prayed, *don't let it be that. Not now*.

But it *was* that: Ro's buzzer, the silently vibrating piece of metal clipped to his belt that summoned him back to base.

He looked at her, said, "We're scrambled, sweet thing," in an almost inaudible voice, and then continued, louder: "You and I are going up front, Herr Wolfe, and you're going to clear us for take-off to Ramstein. You want to see *MEDUSA* first-hand, maybe I'll oblige you."

Wolfe's head swiveled. For a moment a look of confusion, so obviously alien that it was blatantly visible, crossed his features. Then he said, "How do you expect to implement such audacity? If I can get clearance out of here, how will you get the landing permission for Ramstein?"

"We'll play it by ear, you and me. Hijackers tend to fly around a lot, don't they? Well, tell 'em to top off our tanks or we'll go with what we've got—it's that or your ass blows with ours. Over Ramstein, I've got you to offer, till I get on the ground, anyway. Then maybe you tell the Western authorities we didn't kill Lutz, maybe somethin' else—whatever it takes. And maybe, if you and I have a deal, I'll worry about getting *MEDUSA* through no-man's-land. All you have to worry about is waiting things out—your people won't let you sit five minutes in NATO hands."

For a moment Amy was aghast. "God, Ro, you can't. You'll . . ."

Both men ignored her, and looking between them, she was no longer sure that Hayes was playacting.

"Yes, yes. . . ." Wolfe was nodding, but his brow was furrowed. "You know, I do not trust you, Herr Hayes."

"I don't trust you, either, Wolfe. And that makes us even. One way or another, I don't see you've got another choice you'll live through. Get up."

Wolfe did, slowly, rumination showing in every careful movement of his long limbs, and Ro put a hand on the German's shoulder before he looked back at Amy and winked: "Go up front, sweet thing, while I watch both of these. Untie Hoffman's feet, bring him back here. I can fly this tub solo. Keep your gun on him the whole time, okay?"

There was nothing of the urgency Amy knew must be there in Hayes's tone. "Okay," she said, "darling."

Together, they just might pull this off, whatever "this" was; get home in one piece, anyway.

And then it hit her: Ro had just been scrambled. Alleged murderer or not, he'd been called back because *MEDUSA* was needed—because the infernal space war was about to start.

Chapter Twenty-One

Aboard *Skylab*, under the flickering amber lights of emergency power, Canfield was on the flight deck trying to pull his crew back together.

It wasn't going to be easy. There was something about floating helpless, blind, in space that generated hysteria like nothing else in Canfield's acquaintance.

Robinson, who should have been helping Canfield deal with the civilian mission specialists, was sweating buckets, barely responsive to direct orders, curled into what Canfield hoped wasn't a fetal position as the black man drifted free among the dead eyes of powered-down electronics.

They'd turned off everything they could, to extend the life-support capabilities of the command module. Most of it was nearly useless anyway—or had been by the time the lights went out. Robinson had been yelling then, babbling about Soviet jamming and something he'd seen in his monitors. Only God and Robinson knew whether any of the gibberish he'd blurted had reached Houston on the hot line before communication with Earth abruptly ended.

Now Canfield's first officer wouldn't say a word in his own defense. Canfield had tried getting Robinson to talk about it, admit that whatever he'd seen in the Sea of Japan might have been a function of the breakdown of the equipment, electronic phenomena related to its failure. But Robinson would only say "Jamming," when he said anything at all.

He was responsive to direct orders, thank the stars, especially when those orders sent him back into the science module, which had its own power supply and whose toilets still worked. But whatever his last communication had been with Ground Control, Robinson wouldn't, or couldn't, say. Disciplinary action was a real possibility, Canfield told himself, if he ever got out of this to write up a report.

"Go aft, Robinson," Canfield said slowly and clearly, with a lazy tone he reserved for his wife and kids when he was telling them something he knew they wouldn't want to hear. "Send Gold and Alpert forward when you get into the science module."

But even there, all eyes to the outside world were blind, all ears deaf, all mouths closed. Still, Canfield knew morale to be among his most pressing problems.

As Robinson, mouthing something inaudible that Canfield hoped to hell was "Yes, sir," or even "Yeah, whitey," unwound himself to obey Canfield's order, the mission commander thought, *That's it; that's the way to do it. Simple stuff, easy wins, give 'em all something to do until I figure out what the hell's going on.*

By the book, he'd have kept the civilians out of this. But the book assumed competence of military personnel—*all* military personnel. And the book never assumed failure so obvious as the entire satellite hanging deaf, dumb, and blind, virtually inert and indubitably helpless, so many miles above the earth.

If he just could have convinced himself that Robinson had really come unglued, that nothing like Soviet jamming was at the root of his problems, or even that it didn't matter which was the case, he'd have been able to get a handle on the problem quicker. But he couldn't. He was too busy suppressing his own reactions. Why the hell couldn't they *see* out there? There'd been nothing wrong with the real-time cameras—nothing he could find, at least—when he'd diverted power to them.

There was something wrong with Canfield, and he knew it: He was scared half to death. Panic tended to freeze everything—your body, your mind, your reactions—so he was trying to take comfort in the fact that he wasn't panicked. Yet.

He wanted, more than anything, to shut down the lights in here and power up the log recorder long enough to run Robinson's last communiqué to Houston. But he'd have to be alone and uninterrupted to do it. And that meant that he'd have to find something for the mission specialists to do.

So he waited, letting himself float in the eerie quiet that should have been filled with the nearly subaudible hum of functioning equipment, for the two civilians to arrive.

When they pulled themselves through the lock,

Holly Gold in the lead, he said to the woman and the crippled man behind her, "Well, folks, we've got to send somebody outside to look for external damage, and Robinson's needed aboard. Both of you've got the training. Who wants the job?"

The woman, her face smoothed by the low, amber light, looked like a teenage girl. She was pretty enough that he'd thought she might be his biggest problem on this mission.

She said calmly, "Look, Can, you don't have to sugarcoat this for us. We know it's bad. Level with us."

Alpert, behind her shoulder, looked like a moon rising, his round, small-mouth face full of concern.

"What I'm telling you is that I don't know yet. If there's a reason you two can't deploy the OMV from the science module, say so. Otherwise, tell me who's going along for the ride and who's going to do the remote piloting?"

"Remote piloting takes power," the crippled Alpert pointed out. "Can we spare it when we don't know how long we've got to last up here?"

"If there's enough power to solve the problem, then we won't have to 'last' up here longer than it takes to get everything up and running, mister."

Canfield hated the civilian mentality of decision making by committee. This wasn't a goddamned debating society. These two should realize that—and realize that the OMV was their one hole card. If necessary, they could cannibalize its power supplies. If they were lucky, whatever had crippled the command module's sensors hadn't affected the OMV's. It was possible, since the science module seemed to have taken incrementally less damage, that the OMV might have operational surveillance capability.

If, of course, they'd been the victims of some weird space phenomenon and not, as Robinson insisted, purposeful Soviet attack.

In that case the OMV would be little help unless it could be maneuvered out of jamming range. But that would prove something: that the damage wasn't systemic; that it could be countered; that human ingenuity could solve the problem without a warehouse full of spare parts.

And there was a chance that the OMV could communicate with Ground Control—one-way, of course, but communicate, nonetheless, that everyone in Canfield's command was alive and well. They had the power to waste on that: Distress signals were uppermost in Canfield's mind.

He wanted to go out there himself, wanted to go so badly he could taste it, like a metallic pall in his mouth, as if he'd been sucking copper wire, but he couldn't leave these civilians alone in this multimission module. He'd have sent Robinson in his stead, but he just didn't dare.

So it was between the woman and the frail, arthritic Alpert, and he wished to hell they wouldn't argue among themselves about it.

But they did, as if they were on Earth—about the "feasibility" of the science-module remote being able to "complete" the mission; about which of them should go and which stay behind; about relative risk, as if they weren't as close to dead as you could get and still not be willing to recognize it.

If they didn't reestablish communication with Earth, they'd be out of power and frozen stiff well before somebody sent up a shuttle to see what had happened. If they were written off below, they were history—very unfortunate history.

Watching the woman whose hair swayed around her face and the moonfaced arthritic with his glassy, academic eyes discuss their relative priorities, Canfield was nearly ready to put his money on Robinson, who at least was a soldier. Robinson might be a little shook, but he knew the meaning of duty and the meaning of emergency in ways these two coddled academics never could. Just then, however, Holly Gold gave him a winsome, puff-faced smile and said, "Okay, Can. We'll give it a go. I'll try to pilot the remote from the science module until you give me a shutdown notice—we don't want to end up wasting all our juice."

"Then," Alpert took up in his reedy voice, "we'll use the onboard maneuvering rockets to head the OMV toward the docking platform." The look on Alpert's face wasn't confidence-building. The last time he'd taken a space ride, the crippled scientist had been proving something to himself. This time, there was no safety net.

"We've got to clear those external cameras," Canfield said implacably. "You've been trained in the OMV. I haven't." *And my place, damn you, is with my ship.* "I want data on what's going on out there—what happened to us; whether it's ongoing or residual; and if it's ongoing, just what the hell it is, where it's coming from, and what we can do about it."

"You realize, of course," Alpert replied with a savage undertone, "that the science module probably won't be capable of pilotry by remote means for more than a very few minutes, if at all. We have no idea what kind of interference—if that's what it is—we're dealing with, but we do know what kind of power consumption we're dealing with. There is a large, and exponentially increasing, factor of risk."

"Riskier than staying here?" Robinson interjected in his velvet voice from behind them. His chocolate eyes were round in their sockets, floating in a sea of white that seemed almost fluorescent in the emergency illumination. "I'm wondering how come you didn't ask me, Can," Robinson said in a tone Canfield had never heard his old friend use in all the years they'd known each other. "I'm wondering if you don't trust me, now that the chips are down."

And the big black man pushed off from the hatchway, floating toward Canfield like some sub-Saharan avenging angel, a long socket wrench in his right hand.

Twenty-Two

It was 1620 EST when Terrible Taylor authorized the scramble of Ro Hayes and *MEDUSA*.

Less than five minutes later, Forrey was screaming into his ear over the STU in the Pentagon's Tank, where Taylor was waiting to be called on the carpet by the Joint Chiefs of Staff.

The anteroom was institutional gray-green, low-stress decorated, peppered with aides who sat in chairs against the wall—young men from disparate components of the DOD whose job it was to monitor proceedings for their various bosses; who never said a word beyond introducing themselves and declaring their affiliations; who wouldn't have a cup of coffee or smoke a cigarette but were always present at any event remotely important, whether it was a luncheon in a Senate or Congress chamber, or a four-star butt-chewing in the Tank.

Taylor turned his back on them, closing his eyes, fingers massaging the bridge of his nose as he concentrated on the words coming across the secure line from Langley.

"I know you've got a backup pilot, Forrey. I

know he's ready to go. But I also know he's not sufficiently familiar with the aircraft in question to make me authorize the substitution."

He waited out Forrestal's explosion, and then said, "Well, the president wants to see me, too. Five o'clock, I'm told. So I'll meet you over there, okay? We'll give Hayes until then to appear—"

"Idiot," Forrestal interrupted. "When last seen, your Major Hayes was winging his way toward oblivion—to East Germany, to be more exact— wanted for murder. If you think he's ready *or able* to scramble, you're dreaming."

"And you don't know Hayes. He'll be there. Maybe not in the next five minutes, but as fast as he can. If he's anywhere near anything with wings and a couple of props, you can bet on it. Or we'll hear why not, from him, and then I'll okay your substitution. Whatever's wrong up there, it'll still be wrong an hour from now, you can bet on it."

"And you're going to tell Stewart so," came the dry, overly controlled voice of the CIA man through the earpiece of the Tank's STU, "in person, Taylor. Because he's got some sort of stunt up his sleeve, something involving Hippo Herd that's going to go on line, *and I quote*, 'by dinnertime,' or he'll need a damned good reason why not. So have one ready, or *I* will, and you can consider your *MEDUSA* commandeered by the Agency for national security reasons that you and yours have proved unfit to need to know."

"Christ Almighty, Forrey, calm the hell down," Taylor advised before he realized he was talking to a dead phone.

By the time he'd cradled it, an aide to the Joint Chiefs was standing a polite distance behind him,

ready to escort him into the amphitheater where
the lions waited.

It was tough being the only Christian on the
menu.

On the runway at Shönefeld, everything was
deceptively quiet.

The little jet sat still, closed up tight, gleaming
in the apron lights. Off to one side was a tank
truck, its motor idling. Behind it and other vehicles, on rooftops and at windows, East German
riot police and specially trained commandos waited
for orders.

Ro Hayes could see them in his mind's eye as
clearly as if he'd been given a deployment breakdown, though from the cockpit nothing untoward
was visible. Nothing untoward, if he discounted
Marcus Wolfe, beside him in the copilot's seat,
talking slowly and precisely into the hand mike on
an open channel Ro monitored through his headset.

"Wolfe, tell them we'll let Dietrich and Hoffman go in exchange for the fuel and safe passage
out of here," Ro said, palming the bead mike that
extended from his headset. He didn't need the
fuel, but he didn't want them to know that. He
was perfectly willing to put the little plane down
on its belly in a swath of fire-retardant foam if he
had to. Without the weight of Hoffman and
Dietrich, he could probably make it to Ramstein
on what fuel he had, providing they knew what
kind of corners he was cutting and cleared the
traffic for him.

He hadn't expected so much hassle—but then,
he'd never hijacked a plane before. He didn't think
Wolfe was stalling, or playing out some predeter-

mined fallback scenario; it made no sense for the East Germans to delay the inevitable.

Unless somebody in the East German government was arguing that the loss of Wolfe, even temporarily, was unacceptable no matter the cost. Because Ro Hayes wasn't worth all this back-and-forth to anybody, not unless EastBloc knew he'd been scrambled, and why. And he didn't see how that could have happened.

But there was no use wondering about it, like there'd been no use searching Wolfe for a listening device: It was there, somewhere on his person, but Ro was willing to give odds that he couldn't have found it if he'd stripped Wolfe naked and burned the spymaster's clothes. For all he knew, Wolfe's bug was surgically implanted somewhere beneath the old guy's skin, or sitting in his stomach in a gelatin capsule, or up his ass.

Hayes wasn't sweating that: He wanted the GDR informed; he wanted them to be able to make an informed decision. He just hadn't counted on the opposition's bureaucracy being as unwieldly as his own. It made him feel better, in a way, to find out that in a crisis the Commies were no better than any other government at getting the lead out.

But he was going to be in big trouble if he didn't get his own ass in gear posthaste.

Wolfe was saying, ". . . Repeat, they will release Hoffman and Dietrich in exchange for fuel. I urge you to comply without tricks or attempts at rescue. I say again: Do not attempt to board this aircraft; they will blow it up. Simply follow my instructions. Over."

Wolfe slapped the hand mike back into its cradle and stretched cautiously in his seat before looking at Hayes. "Young man, you have succeeded in, as they say, 'gumming up the works' quite thoroughly. Trust me, you will have your fuel. I have guaranteed that there will be no publicity, you heard me. This is what concerns them: A hijacking of this sort, broadcast to your Western media, will do our security no little harm."

"Yeah, yeah, I *said* okay. Nobody wants to put you on TV, friend. We just want to play it the way you and I agreed. But it's beginning to really bother me that you can't keep up your end of the deal. Maybe they don't care as much about you as they do about losing face, ever think of that? Because if they try anything, I'm going to splatter your brains all over this cockpit and jack out of here, even if it's just long enough and high enough to get myself shot down over no-man's-land. You copy?"

"No-man's-land" was what Western pilots called the swath indicated on their air sectionals as the terrain between the hard, straight air boundary and the convoluted land border of the German Democratic Republic.

"Yes, Major Hayes," said the German carefully, as if he were dealing with a fuse, "I do indeed. Trust me, I implore you. We will have your take-off clearances, and your fuel, momentarily."

"You were saying that ten minutes ago, Wolfe. Prove it to me."

"How can I do that? You have heard . . ." In the cockpit lights, Wolfe's face was gray, tired, and obviously arranged to try to transmit patience to the young man holding a gun on him.

"That's what's bothering me, what I heard. What I want is a clear com line out of here, no jamming, no listening. I want to talk to Ramstein, and I'm going to need a little help from Shönefeld tower to do it. Can you set it up?"

"I can try, Major Hayes," Wolfe replied. "I can try."

"Fine. Try." Ro wanted to kick things over so bad he could feel his every heartbeat. Since he'd been scrambled, his apparent time and clock time had begun to diverge: Wolfe and his GDR players were all acting in slow motion. It was an experience common to fighter pilots, but it usually kicked in while you were taxiing down the runway in something with a lot more speed and teeth than the little personal jet he was stuck in, when his better self was already back at the secluded Ramstein hangar where *MEDUSA* waited, ready to roar at the stars.

It was bitching him something fierce that things were going so slowly. The specter of the CIA pilot who'd been strutting around *MEDUSA* hovered in his mind's eye, giving every second of delay sharp edges.

He wanted, more than anything, to talk to Taylor. It didn't exactly fit with the "no publicity" pact he was willing to make, but if he didn't respond to his scramble soon, he was going to be standing on the ground squinting up at the sky like everybody else while some guy who'd never tuned up with *MEDUSA*'s AI did his job for him.

And he really didn't want that.

He listened with one ear to Wolfe, the other pad of his headset angled back against his skull, leaving his other ear free to hear Amy in case she called to him from the passenger compartment.

The first gambit from whoever was up there in

Shönefeld tower had been to ask that Brecker and Dietrich be sent out together. He'd been surprised at his own vehemence when he'd refused. He didn't want them taking this out on her. Wolfe had looked at him funny, thinking he'd found a weak spot. Hayes was telling himself that it fit with his cover—he was supposed to be Amy's lover, after all. But he kept seeing the faces of Forrestal and Taylor when they'd been telling him Amy Brecker was expendable. Right now he wasn't sure that she'd be safe anywhere but with him.

"All right," Wolfe said with satisfaction.

"Huh? Oh, yeah? Dietrich and Hoffman for a topped-off tank? Great. Let's go."

Reaching up, Ro switched off the cockpit lights before he let Wolfe stand up—no point in presenting an easy target to those snipers. Then he motioned with his gun hand to Wolfe and the German spymaster preceded him into the body of the plane, where Amy sat, her gun steadily on the trussed-up pilot and Dietrich. Her head was resting against the padded, curving windowsill instead of her seatback.

"Stay away from the windows, Amy, okay?" She just didn't think like a soldier, although she sure as hell thought like what she was—an intelligence type. Not once during all of this had she let her cover slip. He'd tell somebody, if he could find anybody interested enough to listen, once he got her home.

If he got her home, he amended. He wasn't out of the German woods by a long shot. Anything could happen: They could use the fuel truck to bring up commandos, who'd pry them out of the plane or start shooting through the windows; they could sugar the fuel so the little jet crashed; they could decide that they really didn't care as much about their runway and their spymaster as they did about losing face by letting a hijacker make it out of East German airspace alive.

And then there was Ramstein. They were both still wanted for murder; Amy was probably as hot a target for his own side as she'd be for the swarm of GDR and KGB agents who'd be waiting in the wings if he managed to put down in the West with Wolfe aboard. If he knew his government like he thought he did, there wasn't a damned place Amy Brecker was going to be safe until this whole thing was over—unless it was with him.

He didn't need her to worry about. He should have agreed to let her off with Dietrich and Hoffman. He could have persuaded Taylor to get Forrestal to trade for her. Maybe. It hadn't been good enough then, when the Shönefeld tower controller was asking; it wasn't good enough now.

And she was so plucky, her face pale and her lips tight as she said, "Right, you're right about the window," and crouched in her seat as she moved from it to his side.

He said, "Wolfe, sit where Amy was," and put an arm around her, still watching his prisoners. "You okay, sweet thing?"

"A bit tired, that's all. What's happening out there?"

He kissed the top of her head, telling himself it was for the audience, and the smell of her hair was an unexpected distraction. He took his arm from her shoulders and moved away. "We're going to give them Hoffman and Dietrich, and they're going to give us enough fuel to get straight to Ramstein, as the crow flies, not in the traffic lanes. Right, Wolfe?"

Wolfe started to tell Amy not to worry, and that gave Ro a chance to look at Dietrich's bonds. Amy had done as good a job securing the Teutonic firebrand with the plastic strips Ro had given her as he'd done with Hoffman. Over the surgical tape across his mouth, Dietrich's eyes were wide. Ro winked at him. "You'll be safe soon, buddy, unless I've got my wires crossed and these GDR guys aren't real good friends of yours."

Dietrich's head shook and he said something Ro wasn't interested enough to free his mouth to hear.

"Ro," Amy said from off to one side, "I'm going to make coffee. I—"

"You're kidding," Hayes said admiringly. "You'd do that? Do I dare ask for—"

"Cut it out, major, or you won't get any. I'm tired, that's all. My gun hand's cramp—" She cut off in midword and turned toward the cockpit. "Somebody wants to talk to you."

He'd heard it, too. He was brushing past her when he heard her sharp "Stay put, Herr Wolfe. If he wants you up front, he'll tell you."

As long as she was pointed in the right direction, she was one very competent woman, that was for sure, but saying so would probably make her mad.

And anyway, Shönefeld control was telling him that the tanker was going to pull up to the plane, and that if he dialed a specific frequency they'd patch him into Ramstein's military channel. Not a peep about how come they could do that, at will and despite coding procedures, and at just the same time that the fuel tanker was going to be pulling up to his plane and guys would be crawling all over it. . . .

"Amy, tie Wolfe good, and watch that tanker as it comes up," he said before he answered the Shönefeld controller. "If more than two men get out of that truck—if you even see a third pair of feet or a glint of extraneous metal—you're going to have to shoot Dietrich." He had the TRANSMIT button down while he talked, in case Wolfe's wire was too far from him to pick up what he was saying.

Amy's response was loud enough to carry to the hand mike, in any case: "Whatever you say, major."

Then he went on line with the tower, agreeing to the procedure, saying, "When we're full up and the tanker's well away from the plane, we'll let Dietrich and Hoffman out. You're going to have to trust us that far. Over."

And Shönefeld agreed without an argument, which meant either they had something up their sleeve or they'd decided to play ball, Ro couldn't waste time worrying which. Instead he cleared his throat, then facilitated the patch and started trying to get Taylor on a line that couldn't support even the pretense of being secure.

He watched the second hand sweep around the analogue portion of his diver's watch as the East Germans broke through millions of dollars' worth of electronic security and cut him into a priority NATO-Ramstein channel.

"What the fuck?" was the first thing he heard from the startled American noncom unlucky enough to take his call.

All he wanted was a transatlantic patch to Taylor, but there were lots of problems: It was against regulations; guys were running around in the background yelling at each other about whose ass was going to fry over this one; Taylor wasn't at Vandenberg.

For four and one-half minutes—as Ro's request made its way up through channels, and as higher brass with the requisite security clearances were interrupted and invoked, and as the fuel truck at Shönefeld began to pump—Munro Hayes waited, with a rueful smile tensing the corners of his mouth. There was just no disguising all this fuss, no matter how the poor bastards on either side tried. From here on in, this operation was about as secret as the air force's annual budget.

But secrecy wasn't what Forrestal and Taylor had wanted. And now, whatever they *had* wanted previously, they sure as hell wanted action.

Just his luck that Taylor was out somewhere with his girlfriend, Ro was thinking as somebody identifying himself as "Classic Thunder Control" offered to give Taylor Ro's message. Then the man interrupted his own flow of words, saying, "Wait a sec. Okay, we've got General Taylor. We're patching you through, major. Please hold."

"Have I got a choice?" Ro said into the mike.

But then it was Taylor on the other end, saying, "What's the password, major?"

Ro gave it, adding, "I just wanted you to know I'm on my way, Terrible. So nobody gives my ride to some other guy. And I'm bringing you a present—an East German named Wolfe. Use him to hold the Agency at bay till I get there, okay? Over."

"Hrrmph," Taylor snorted. "I told them, son— you'd check in."

Pride was there, and relief. And something else, something Ro didn't like: Taylor hadn't answered him, not directly. "So you'll hold my ride for me, sir?"

"I'll do my best, major, but you'd better scream back here. We've got Forrestal politicking for his pilot and a Hippo Herd in the wings. Over."

"I copy. I'm on my way," Ro promised. "Over."

His thumb relaxed on the mike button, and after he'd replaced it in the cradle, he rubbed his forehead. His hand came away moist with perspiration. At least Taylor hadn't told him that it was too late. Hippo Herd. Christ, he hoped that didn't mean what he thought it did. He rubbed his eyes, smelled coffee, and there was Amy, gun in one hand, plastic cup of steaming brew in the other.

"Will you marry me?" he joked gratefully as he took the cup from her.

"Ask me later," she shot back. "I've got to get back there. So far nothing strange, and both men are back in the fuel truck. When you're ready, we'll off-load Dietrich and Hoffman."

"Good enough." He took a sip of the coffee and, refreshed, grinned at her. "I got Taylor."

"I heard, some of it. Is it going to be okay?"

He sipped again, decided he could handle the heat, and tossed off the cupful in three gulps. "This is no time to start asking those kinds of questions, sweet thing. Don't you trust me?" He handed her back the cup and began to get out of his seat.

"You? It's the rest of them that worry me."

"We're going to do the best we can up there in space, you and me, okay?" There was no better time to tell her what he'd decided, and no time to explain why.

Amy just looked at him levelly and raised one eyebrow, turning his empty cup in her hands. He was grateful then that she was an intelligence type, as conscious as he of the possibility of electronic eavesdropping—if not from Wolfe's person, then from any number of exterior sources, by now.

But it took him a moment to comprehend what was happening when she said, her eyes fixed on the view beyond the windscreen, "Are they going to have a crash here, or what?"

Then he turned and sat back down in his seat, his hands automatically readying the plane for take-off as his eyes counted the lights of four approaching aircraft. He divided them by several ground vehicles with blue flashers headed toward his runway, and came up with his solution: "Sit down. Strap in. Quick."

She did, saying, "But what about Dietrich and Hoffman? We said we'd—"

"That was before they decided to sic MiGs on us. All deals are off."

And then he couldn't hear her over his own screaming engines and the chatter, then threats, then staccato German that began pouring out of his tower channel. But there was no use talking: He had to get airborne before the dark shapes speeding across the runway toward him, their emergency lights doused now, opened fire and the dark, longer shape of a huge gasoline truck he could barely see pulled up in front of him, blocking his runway.

As busy as he'd ever been in an aircraft before it left the ground, he yelled to Amy, "Put that head-

set on," did the same himself, and punched into
the tower channel, saying laconically to the controller that he was taking off with or without clearance and instructions, and that "if you block me
with that mobile incendiary, I'm going to go over
or through it. As for those fighters, you get 'em
the hell out of my way or you're going to lose at
least one of 'em."

He just ignored the comeback.

If Shönefeld tower was telling him the truth and
the Soviet-made jets were only his escort out of
East German airspace, then he wouldn't have to
purposely crash into one of them.

He didn't mind being "expelled"—he'd escorted
plenty of enemy planes through restricted areas.
But he wasn't armed; this business jet was far from
dangerous, unless you wanted to consider its mass
as a weapon.

And he had to do that: If even one warning shot
came across his bow, Ro Hayes was going to make
a great big fiery mess in the sky—over downtown
East Berlin, if possible—that not even a totalitar-
ian government could suppress.

He felt as if he were manually lifting Dietrich's
private jet as he pulled her nose up, leaving the
ground at a rate and angle she wasn't built for. He
could feel the wings shudder, and the engines
he was pushing keened with strain. But then came
that wondrous feeling of being airborne, and he
hit his emergency landing-gear retractor switch
just in time to keep from grazing the approaching
gasoline tanker coming to a halt on the runway.

He kept pulling up, forcing the plane into as
close to a vertical climb as she could manage,
thanking his luck and Saint Murphy that the Eureka-

built composite frame was as strong as it was. If he had to, he was going to find out whether that modified tail would let him pull a stall, a straight-down head-on dive that might well crash the escort MiGs now coming up on him in tight-four formation.

He had time, as he leveled off with all that Soviet-made air power squared off around him, to glance at Amy. She had her knuckles pressed against her teeth, but she was far from paralyzed with fear. She caught his eye and said, "Want me to do anything? Answer these tower guys—my German's better than yours—or tell you what they're saying?"

She knew what those escort planes could mean; she merely ignored it.

He was liking her better and better, he decided as he said, "Just sit back and enjoy the ride. Our passengers will keep, tied up like that. Maybe they'll even keep us alive. It won't be long, one way or the other."

And it wouldn't: He'd be talking to Erfurt control in minutes—unless the MiGs shot at him or tried to force him down first. And if that happened, some CIA bastard was going to get the chance to fly *MEDUSA*, because Ro Hayes wouldn't be in any position to argue.

He took a good look around him, at the MiGs and at the stars beyond, wishing there were punch-out seats in business jets.

But there weren't.

Chapter Twenty-Three

President Stewart had a formal dinner at seven; Forrestal and Taylor were merely appetizers.

But Stewart's wife wanted him to shower and try on his new tux and she refused to comprehend that he was in the middle of a crisis and didn't give a tinker's damn about how the Women's Crusade for International Famine Relief was going to feel if he was late to a sit-down, seven-course meal that, dollars being worth what they were, had cost enough to feed the entire human population of the Horn of Africa for a week.

Susan Stewart never let such dichotomies bother her. She was the perfect Washington hostess, doing her job of extending Stewart's power base to the distaff side of Those Who Mattered in D.C. She could talk arms control with the Soviet premier's wife at breakfast and then show the American-born queen of Jordan weaponry after lunch with equal enthusiasm.

In fact, Susan never let anything bother her. So when she blithely sailed into the Oval Office as her husband was chewing out Forrestal and Tay-

237

lor, she was genuinely surprised when Stewart lost his temper and yelled at her. She blinked, and he saw in that suddenly composed face a harbinger of what he was going to pay, later tonight, for his loss of temper.

She said, "Dear, I'll leave you to your work, of course. Deputy Director Forrestal, General Taylor." She nodded huffily. "Don't keep my poor husband too long. It's just another crisis, after all." And she flounced out, all Chanel pleats and perfectly coiffed curls.

" 'Just another crisis'?" Stewart repeated her words after the door had closed behind her, mentally thanking the woman with whom he shared his life for once again putting things in perspective. He hoped. "Is she right, gentlemen? Can either of you promise me that Classic Thunder will get off the frigging ground in time to do us any good?"

"Sir?" Forrestal queried mildly.

That infuriating CIA unwillingness to ever answer a goddamned direct question made Stewart want to demand that Forrey come to verbal grips with the problem, so that Stewart could get back the head of steam that his wife had magically vented.

But Taylor fixed his commander in chief with a level stare and said, "Sir, my boy is airborne, just minutes from Ramstein. As I promised he would be. We've got a good chance of—"

"You've got four East German escort fighter planes on that pilot's tail is what you've got, Taylor," Forrestal interrupted. "You've got trouble—"

"How do you know that?" Taylor demanded,

and Stewart sat back, willing to let the two men spill whatever their tempers would allow.

"Oversight, friend," Forrey shot back. "You've heard of it? CIA has its methods—"

"I don't mean the trouble, in general. I mean the four MiGs."

There was a pause in which Forrestal intended that President Stewart realize Taylor had been withholding information: The incriminating term *MiGs* had slipped out of the air force's mouth, proving that CIA's analysis, at least in part, was accurate.

Stewart looked from one man to the other, then said, steepling his hands and tapping them against his lips, "You know, you two ought to remember that I don't care which service does what—that this isn't the Tank, and when I called you two in here, it was the *unified* Space Command hats you both wear that I thought I was inviting in to hang on my hat rack. Get it? I want results, not assessments, not excuses, not interservice haggling. You boys are old friends, old hands at this sort of thing. For future reference, and to save a lot of time, I don't *care* whose pilot flies *MEDUSA*—I'm beginning not to care about *MEDUSA*, or at least using it in this context. I've got my own backup plan, you know: Hippo Wallow."

Forrestal squeezed his eyes shut. Taylor said quietly, "We don't want it to come to that, sir. Anything involving Hippo Herd people and hard assets is, we think, an overreaction."

Now Forrestal opened his eyes. "A serious overreaction. Sir, I must formally protest."

"I second that," Taylor added. "Sir, do you realize what Hippo Herd means? A nuclear exchange is quite a few notches more serious than—"

"Than," Stewart interrupted, "taking one Soviet missile in our soft underbelly? Letting them have a free throw at us? Read my lips, gentlemen: There are no free shots, no free throws. As far as I'm concerned, we're already about to raise the Defensive Condition alert status, as soon as I can verify that whatever happened to *Skylab Two* isn't the fucking sunspots your people keep talking about, Forrey." Stewart repositioned his glare from Taylor to Forrestal.

Forrestal said only, "Yes, sir," very quietly.

Taylor looked at his hands.

Into that silence the president said, "All right, gentlemen. Taylor, you've got an hour's extension. At the end of that hour, if your pilot hasn't shown up, Forrey's pilot takes over. Don't come back to me about it, just do it.

"Forrestal," said the president with as presidential a sigh as he could manage, "your part in this looks just as much like a fumble on the fifty-yard line. What good is CIA if it can't predict even the behavior of Americans, let alone the opposition? I expect a full analysis of the repercussions, if any, attendant to Hayes and Brecker hijacking that German plane. And I want a précis on Wolfe—what we can do with him, if we're really going to get a crack at him. I want it by ten o'clock. That goddamned dinner ought to be over by then."

He got two Yessirs for his trouble, and both Forrestal and Taylor were sitting forward, anticipating being released to their tasks.

"And, gentlemen, one thing more: If the next time we meet we're in the Situation Room and wearing radiation badges, I'm going to fire you both on the spot. You're supposed to be in the prevention and preemption business. Get to it— get out of here. Prevent the loss of your god-damned jobs."

And the country, the whole blessed shooting match, Stewart thought but did not say as the two bureaucrats made polite noises; extended their dry, aging hands; and filed out.

Stewart blew out a noisy breath, alone for a moment in the Oval Office and wishing, for one fleeting instant, he were someone else—anyone else.

But he didn't really mean it. If there were somebody else sitting here, Stewart would be scared to death, not merely angry and determined. He knew and trusted his own abilities to perform in a crisis; he wasn't sure he could name another soul he'd say that about, right now.

And he had one more meeting to squeeze in before dinner: the Hippo Herd specialists, the man who'd spearhead Hippo Wallow if it became an operation, and a scientist who was supposed to explain to Stewart all about the "electromagnetic shield" that the eggheads thought might actually be closer to functional than they'd let on.

So far, what he'd heard about the shield, which was meant to place an umbrella no one thought was feasible over U.S. cities and counterstrike si-los, wasn't comforting. There was no way to test its protective capability except in a "nuclear envi-ronment." There was no way to simulate the "sat-uration levels" all that expensive equipment might be subject to in an all-out or even limited exchange.

But the Hippo Herd men didn't understand that

Stewart didn't want to go all out. He wasn't a madman. He had a doctrine, however, that demanded that he respond in kind.

If the Soviets had crippled, and were going to kill, one of his satellites—manned or unmanned—Stewart was obliged to strike back. He wasn't talking about overkill. He was talking about a straight, or parallel, kill ratio: one American satellite for a Russian satellite, or maybe a single warhead lobbed at Moscow.

That was what he wanted, but even a president couldn't always get what he wanted. If he took action unilaterally, he might be impeached—assuming there wasn't an unequal, opposite reaction in Moscow that made impeachment unfeasible because you don't impeach your president in the middle of a nuclear war.

He didn't want to *be* in the middle of a nuclear war. But he didn't want to let the Soviets win this one; they were too likely to take inaction as a sign of inability to act. Ground had been lost that way: Afghanistan, Poland, Czechoslovakia.

Stewart had run on the platform of "Give no ground; give no quarter; give no advantage." He had to stick to it, for his sake and the country's sake.

He wasn't sure if Susan was right. He wasn't sure if this was "just one more crisis." It could easily be the last one he, as president, had any say about. But giving up space, in this technological era, was worse than giving up ground—he'd rather cede the Sahara with its mineral deposits, or even Alaska, than let the Soviets think they could scare America out of space. He had to respond vigorously to an attack on an American satellite.

That it was a manned satellite hardly seemed to matter to anyone but him. It wouldn't matter to the Hippo Herd people who'd come traipsing in as soon as he gave the word. They were bound to think in terms of massive kills and massive retaliation.

All Stewart wanted was an honest assessment, a few engineering alterations on a single piece of the national armory, and one man whose loyalty was above reproach to do the work. Then, if the Soviets launched—which was looking increasingly likely from NSA's data and CIA's assessment—Stewart would launch his own, personal, customized calling card.

He really liked his plan the more he thought about it. He knew nobody else would, but it was nobody else's business. The Hippo Herd expert waiting in the anteroom had been chosen from a number of candidates; they'd met before and discussed generalities. This meeting with the electromagnetic shielding maven was a formality: Stewart had no intention of letting things go that far.

But, like Forrestal's Classic Thunder, operations could begin escalating on their own.

If the worst that came of this mess was that CIA and the air force ended up the culprits in an international hijacking, Stewart was willing and even happy to take the blame. But if he was looking at four Americans dead in space, and if the Russians really launched a missile at *Skylab*, and hit it, destroying any evidence of previous foul play and claiming a no-fault, a technical error . . . that was different. It was the United States, who had spent billions on SDI, that would suffer international humiliation.

One way or another, Stewart wasn't going to be the president who scuttled SDI because he was afraid to test it.

He had *MEDUSA* and Classic Thunder.

He had Hippo Herd and now Hippo Wallow.

One way or another, the U.S. was going to come out of this a winner, even if Stewart went the way of Richard Nixon.

His desk intercom beeped politely.

"Yes, send them— Oh, hello, dear," said the president. Then, meekly, "Yes, Susan, I know I promised. Give me another fifteen minutes to wrap up my last meeting and I'll be right there."

Fifteen minutes, to make the most important preparations and decisions of his entire term—no, of his entire life. He wished to hell they could just reestablish communication with *Skylab*.

Stewart found that his fingers were clammy as he toggled the intercom and told his secretary to send in the missile experts from the program called Hippo Herd.

Chapter Twenty-Four

An eerie quiet had settled over the *Skylab 2* command module where Canfield floated, alone in the amber-shot dark.

Too eerie. Canfield couldn't shake the uneasiness he felt and was taking himself to task for what he had to consider a loss of nerve. He'd been in tight spots before. There was no excuse for the way he was responding to this crisis.

He told himself that his gut was reacting to merely physical cues: to floating in zero-g semi-darkness; to the lack of instrument noise; to the lack of something he, personally, could do to alter the situation he and his crew were facing. But it was more than that, or else he'd have felt better when he went aft to the science module, where the lights were brighter and Holly Gold was spacewalking the OMV and Alpert, inside it, through their paces.

He'd been back there twice. It hadn't helped. So he'd come forward, partly out of habit, to the command module, where a mission commander was supposed to be. As if there were anything to do up here, with all his equipment down, dead-eyed and silent. As if the juice from the solar panels was going to come back on any minute, the monitors flare to life, the red and green status lights start chasing one another across his rack-mounted control boxes.

Alone, he slapped a console hard enough that the palm of his hand stung from the impact. Alone, he had all the reason in the world to do so.

He kept trying to make sense out of what had happened to his control capability—to his craft. He always thought of *Skylab* as a craft.

It had to be jamming, he'd admitted glumly to himself—some sort of electronic countermeasure that pulsed his semiconductor-driven instrumentation out of working order, or else something as unlikely as a solar flare. He'd considered diverting all his battery power to the com system for one last call to Houston: a big fat SOS. But he had to be sure of the cause, sure enough that he wasn't crying wolf the way Robinson had.

Canfield heard a sound, metal striking metal, behind him.

And turned to see nothing at all: an empty hatchway, open, spilling the better light coming from the science module. Nothing there, then. Nerves. He was getting as flaky as Robinson. And Robinson was really getting flaky. That in itself was enough trouble for any single mission—one guy teetering on the brink, one man struggling for self-control, tottering over an abyss yawning like the free fall to Earth, 250 miles below all their feet.

He hadn't said anything about it, not to Holly Gold or Alpert, not to Robinson himself. He was ignoring it, giving Robinson a chance to get his act together.

There had been a moment, as Robinson had floated toward him with that big wrench in hand, when Canfield's body hair stood on end and his mind threw up lurid fast-forward fantasies of struggling with Robinson, contesting for the wrench—fantasies that ended with Robinson smashing every console in the control module.

But it hadn't happened. Robinson had slid by him, muttering about opening up one of the consoles to take a look at the interior where the backup power supplies were bolted down under a bulkhead plate.

Robinson was one of his best friends. Had been for years. It was a damned shame to have thoughts like that about a friend.

Probably a result of the helplessness Canfield felt in this particularly demoralizing crisis. It was the situation itself, the mission commander kept telling himself, that was at fault. Like in the science module, where two men hovering over Holly Gold's shoulder did nothing except make the poor woman nervous. She had plenty to be nervous about, as it was. So he'd left Robinson there; Robinson would come tell him as soon as there was anything worth reporting.

Robinson was watching the power supplies. Everything they did took juice, even opening the cargo-bay doors. They were all becoming concerned about the strain on the life-support systems. If this extravehicular activity didn't turn up a quick solution to the power outage, they were going to tape and send a general distress signal, shut down everything they could, and start sitting still a lot:

The less kinetic energy they used, the better, if they were going to try to sit things out until Houston or Vandenberg could send a shuttle up after them.

But a shuttle had just been up here, and turnaround time wasn't better than a week even in an emergency, as far as he knew. There was a chance, of course, that a shuttle could be ready sooner. There was even a chance that if he sent that distress call and there wasn't any foul play involved, somebody would decide to ask the Soviet *Salyut* station to send a rescue party. It wasn't likely, but it was possible.

Canfield was now wrestling with the possibility of dying up here—of losing control not only of his mission but of the ultimate fate of everyone aboard. He was looking Murphy in the face, and he didn't like what he saw.

He pushed off from the observation window, out of which he could see the OMV, like a Tinkertoy as it rotated slowly among the stars. They'd be getting an initial report on the aft cameras soon— Robinson would be bringing him the word because they didn't want to waste juice, not even on the intercom. Right now, battery power was the breath of life. And he could see that breath—how much they'd used, how much they had left— metered out for him neatly under each red light that told him a backup supply was engaged and being drained. It was the single loudest noise in the command module, a 10K hum that set his teeth on edge.

But when that humming stopped, he wouldn't be hearing anything: He'd be in his space suit, down to hours of life remaining, or taking his turn in the OMV, which then would be their only operational craft. The trouble with the OMV was that it could support only one human—there was no room inside it for more. . . .

Canfield shook his head to clear it. No use thinking about that. No use in defeatism. Ever. He kept seeing his wife's face, his kids as they'd been on New Year's Eve: faces defined by the 900-odd lines of his ground-link monitor. Digitized. Black-and-white. Unreal.

And he'd better keep them that way, or he was going to be more of a problem to the salvage of this mission than Robinson.

Damage control. Damage limitation. Survival. In a dark corner of his mind, he'd already discounted the "women and children first" adage of the early twentieth century. If it came to the point where someone tried to reach the Soviets on *Salyut*, if it was a matter of sending somebody over in the OMV, that person was going to be Canfield.

The part of him that remained ethical had good reasons: He was the highest-ranking officer, the only man capable of making an on-the-spot decision with regard to the termination of his mission and the lives of his crew; he was a fluent Russian-speaker, the only one on board; and, damn it, he *knew* he could make it—could stretch the OMV's capabilities and pilot her right up to *Salyut*'s space dock.

Hiya, comrades. Just stopped by to borrow a cup of air and a quart of juice.

Robinson probably could have handled the piloting job, but Robinson was just too hair-triggered lately. And Robinson didn't speak Russian.

Truth be known, Canfield wasn't about to put

his life in anybody's else's hands. Not when the OMV was using up whatever safety margin anyone aboard it might have had, trying to find out what the trouble was and put it to rights. Not when—

"Can," came Robinson's voice from behind the mission commander's shoulder.

"Yeah, I—" Canfield turned with a practiced push against a padded console bumper, and found himself nose-to-nose with his first officer.

And Robinson was still carrying that wrench, like some sort of talisman.

This close, Canfield could see Robinson's nostrils flaring, the other man's tight-drawn lips. Whatever news Robinson had brought him, Canfield knew it wasn't good.

But he continued in a carefully even voice: "—I was just about to come aft. What's the situation out there?"

Robinson's big left hand was sliding up and down the wrench's handle, stroking, stroking. . . . "Well, whitey, there's something on the camera lenses. Something opaque—something black." Robinson's startlingly bright grin came slowly over his face; his teeth seemed pinkish-yellow in the emergency lighting.

"Something *on* the lenses? What do you mean? What kind of something?"

Robinson shrugged. "Something. Space fungus, maybe. Alien shit. Who the fuck knows? Alpert doesn't. He thinks it's paint—spray paint. But I think it's alien fungus, creatures from . . ."

For the first few seconds, Canfield thought Robinson was making a macho joke, trying to lessen the tension. He was about to retort that space fungus was out of season when Robinson's left hand flashed out and grabbed him by the shoulder, while his right hand raised the long, heavy wrench high.

"Oh, God . . . look, Robin—"

In the middle of the word, red flashed across Canfield's vision as something hit the top of his head with an impact that shut out the entire phenomenal world. And then he was struggling blindly with something too big and too hard and too hostile to be beaten by someone who couldn't control his own limbs, who couldn't see or move, who was full of pain, until finally he couldn't feel anything at all and the red pall before him turned to a soft, white, magnetic light toward which he floated.

The light was warm and it wanted him and it didn't care about the mess all over the *Skylab* control module or the limp corpse of Canfield, floating amid its own bodily fluids, that he'd left behind.

It didn't even care about Robinson, who was humming as he pushed off toward the science module, trusty wrench in hand.

Chapter Twenty-Five

Amy Brecker had never before been escorted by fighter planes of a hostile nation out of enemy airspace. She'd never been party to a hijacking of a high East German official. She'd never even had to tie anyone up before.

But she couldn't show weakness and she couldn't ask questions.

Ro Hayes's neat, intent, all-American profile became her beacon—at least what she could see of it. As long as Hayes was calm, she told herself, she would be calm.

He kept chatting with "Erfurt"—Frankfurt—Control, and ignoring the MiGs all around them, until, as he'd arranged with Erfurt, four American F-18s came up out of the dark. Just like that. Then, as Ro had predicted, the MiGs peeled off and away.

But she saw his narrowed eyes, his tense frown that didn't relax until the F-18s enfolded them and the American pilot of the lead fighter said, with an audible sigh, "Okay, Good Bogey, I guess it's welcome to Western airspace—they're turning tail."

Hayes leaned his head back against the head-rest, puffed out his cheeks, and expelled a long, noisy breath.

Then she realized that all the pilots—Ro, his F-18 escorts, and even those aboard the MiGs—had been anticipating an order from Moscow via East Berlin to shoot down the personal jet despite, if not because of, the fact that Marcus Wolfe was aboard.

An international incident had just been averted and all Amy could say was "Ro, do you think there's an airsickness bag up here?"

"No, go aft, sweet thing; we're out of the woods—time's past for a dogfight."

Sweet thing. Dogfight. Macho bullshit.

She found that the toilet was closer than the first passenger seat, and emptied her stomach. Then she saw to Dietrich, Hoffman, and Wolfe. They were all still bound fast, but it was the pleading look Dietrich gave her that made her bring him a white coffee and say, "I guess this'll hurt a little, Reinhardt, but then we'll have coffee," and pull the tape from his mouth.

Immediately she regretted what she'd done: A stream of invective accusing her of horrible treacheries she'd never meant came from between Dietrich's bloodless lips, to which strings of adhesive still stuck.

She said, "Look, Reinhardt, I'm sorry, but it's better than being left behind in East Berlin. . . . Isn't it?"

The handsome face that had mesmerized millions of Westerners hungry for peace reformed itself: Dietrich's color returned to normal, his sharp eyes softened, his mouth attempted a smile as he said, "Sorry? Yes, I see that you are. Amy, Amy, why did you do this to us? For him?" Dietrich's eyes slid toward the cockpit, then returned to her face. "He is not worth it. He is an American cowboy, part of the capitalist war machine you and I both—"

"Reinhardt, do you want this coffee or not? I'm not untying your hands, so get ready to take a sip."

She was firm, knowing the persuasiveness, the duplicity of this man. She didn't trust him; he'd made a fool of her. The way he was treating her now, the obvious attempt to play her, to confuse her, confirmed that she had been right: Dietrich was definitely Marcus Wolfe's fair-haired boy. She didn't understand how he'd managed, not by words but by implication, to make her feel dirty, guilty. She stifled the urge to explain, to apologize once more. This blond champion of peace had been working for—or with—the GDR all along. Reinhardt Dietrich had been their agent even when he'd been pretending to be hers.

She remembered crying in his arms and squeezed her eyes shut as she held the coffee cup to his lips. A lurch of the plane caused by turbulence resulted in coffee spilling down his chin and over his shirtfront.

He didn't reproach her—merely stared at her as she got a towel and cleaned him up.

Now the other two were staring, too. She supposed that she was showing favoritism, but it was Dietrich who'd hidden her from the FRG police, Dietrich who'd . . .

Who'd what? It had been agent manipulation, a game, a ruse to get Ro into East Germany. And before that, they'd been playing her for the consummate fool. If it had continued—if she'd been allowed to stay at her Berlin embassy desk—Dietrich probably would have been the mechanism by which Wolfe tried to turn her. Eventually her career would have been ruined—she'd have been faced with blackmail, a double agent's misery. They'd been after her, probably for years. Azimov was probably a dangle, a way to inveigle her into the clutches of the opposition. For all she knew, she was still playing right into the hands of EastBloc Intelligence.

She put a palm to her forehead, and Dietrich said with paternal concern, "You are thinking of your next move, yes? Of the dangers that await you at Ramstein—which is, of course, where they will take us now, the USAFCE portion of the base: American ground. And then what, for you? An interrogation cell, my dear, I'm afraid. A murderess, they think you are. NATO politics will demand that you be tried by the FRG. Your embassy and CIA friends will not be able or willing to protect you."

"Reinhardt . . ."

The handsome German inclined his head, a ruminative gesture she remembered from so many symposia, invoked to silence an imprudent question or an ill-thought argument.

"Now, I answer your question: Yes, I would rather have been left at Shönefeld. I have friends in East Berlin. I am not a traitor. I am not a spy. I have no fear of my brothers in East Berlin; I have no fear of anyone in Eastern Europe, with the notable exception of your American CIA. Do you think they—how do you say?—'framed' you for the murder of Lutz?" He let the question hang.

She said, "Of course not," with too much vehemence for someone telling the truth.

"Do you think that if it was necessary to go to so much trouble, they have now changed their minds? You are meant to be put somewhere safe, where you will do no harm to your own nation's diplomats. This they will do to you, whether in the guise of protective custody or more openly. Oh, Amy, my dear, if only you had realized that your lover is not your friend, that he is a patriot. Misguided, but a patriot. He has sacrificed your love for his country. It is not a terrible thing, to such a man, to sacrifice one woman's freedom for 'national security.' "

She said, "Reinhardt, I'm putting your gag back on now," in a cold and resentful voice. If Ro had really been her lover, she probably would have been devastated by Dietrich's words. Even as it was, her confidence was shaken.

She got fresh tape and scissored it before Dietrich's eyes with savage satisfaction: The used tape would have sufficed, and been more comfortable for him. Once she'd plastered it to his mouth, she stood up, a hand to the small of her back.

And saw Wolfe's icy eyes watching her. She stifled an impulse to stick out her tongue at the German spymaster. These bastards weren't going to be so damned cocky when the intelligence contingent at Ramstein got through with them.

She tried to push away her doubts, the fears that Dietrich's spiel had evoked. But she couldn't. The murder of Lutz was a very real difficulty. At the least it would take some explaining.

She remembered Ro's declaration of intent to take her with him into space—to take her in the TAV. She hurried forward, the words spilling out of her mouth before she'd slipped into the copilot's seat: "Ro, we've got to talk. About space. About Lutz. About Ramstein."

"Not with the cockpit recorder on, we don't. Not more than to agree that we'll tell the truth—we didn't kill Lutz and we don't have time to argue about it. Now, you can stay up here, but we're going to be landing soon and I've got plenty to do as it is without you deciding it's time to debrief. Okay?"

The look and the quick touch of his hand on hers that accompanied those words made them comforting, not harsh.

"Okay," she said with forced insouciance. But he appreciated that sort of bravado. She only hoped that he was right, that telling the truth was going to be enough for the authorities at Ramstein.

She was still hoping when they began final approach procedures: Ramstein was not only the air force's main base in Central Europe but also a NATO facility. And Ro was already invoking Taylor's name, and Forrestal's, and giving instructions about the "prisoners" on board, and other instructions related to the TAV called *MEDUSA*, although the private jet hadn't yet touched down.

When it did, and Ro pulled up to the apron, they were swarmed by airport officials and military and FRG police, all talking at once. Amy could see limos through the window—one with American Embassy flags, and one with GDR plates.

"Now remember," Ro cautioned her, putting one arm around her shoulders, "don't answer any questions and stick right with me—let me handle this and we'll be fine. You copy?"

There were still MPs in the plane, although Wolfe, Dietrich, and Hoffman had already been hustled away.

"Affirmative," she said with all the pluck she could manage, and stuffed her shaking hands in her pockets as he left her to begin a sotto voce, heads-together conversation with the highest-ranking of the American MPs.

Chapter Twenty-Six

Alpert, alone in the OMV, said again, "Holly? Holly, can you hear me?"

He'd asked her for an attitude correction and gotten no response. Inside the cramped quarters of the orbital maneuvering vehicle, he'd begun to sweat.

Oh, there were emergency controls—he could get back into the cargo bay, with luck—although nothing as sophisticated as the remote pilotry system, because the OMV was never intended to be piloted by an onboard human being.

And if something else had gone wrong on *Skylab* . . .

The stars didn't seem romantic now; they seemed cruel and hard, so distant and so very, very uncaring.

Alpert fairly yelled into his helmet mike: "*Holly! Dear God, Holly, answer me!*"—all communications protocol forgotten.

Out here, alone in the OMV, with obvious evidence of sabotage right before his eyes! Alpert had begun regretting that he'd volunteered minutes ago. Now he was near tears. His throat was tight. It was hard to swallow. He was nauseated. If he cried or vomited in his helmet, he'd have to live with the consequences; he couldn't wipe the results away if he fouled himself.

And he was as near to that as he'd ever been.

Somewhere beyond the bulk of *Skylab* was the *Salyut* station—the only place the opaque material spattered on the exterior of the American space station, occluding the cameras and smearing the exterior around them, could have come from. The Soviets were probably watching him right now. He was a prime target, he and the OMV.

His hands were in the waldoes that could direct the remote manipulator arm; he was about to squander power trying to wipe away the black stuff and he'd have to be very careful not to scratch the camera lens.

Where *was* she? Why wasn't she answering? Dear God, Alpert thought, don't let us die up here.

And then there was a crackle in his ears and through the transceiver in his helmet came Holly Gold's voice, tense with strain. "I'm right here, Alpert," she assured him. "Right here."

"Is something wrong in there? Where were you?"

"I—uh, everything's fine, just fine. Now, what is it you want?"

"What is it I *want*?" Alpert was relieved, and simultaneously enraged. "What do you think I want, a date? There's some sort of goop all over the cameras out here, remember? It's as if somebody filled a balloon with paint and threw it against the hull or whatever you call it. Didn't you hear me before? I want to scrape it off, damn you.

That's what we all want, isn't it? That's what I'm out here for, isn't it?"

"All right, let's see . . ." Holly Gold replied, and Alpert was sure her voice was shaking.

But then, evidence of sabotage was something more than a suspicion of sabotage. He didn't dare be any more explicit than he'd been, in case *they* were listening.

"They," in this case, were the Soviets. And that bothered Alpert almost as much as Holly Gold's distracted, tense voice in his ear. These damned warmongers were going to ruin everything, destroy the world on the very brink of a new era in which science could have created a veritable Utopia.

But that train of thought wasn't going to get him anywhere. Right now he had to get Holly's attention back on the task at hand. He should have known she couldn't take the pressure of this kind of job. He should have run the remote and sent her out here, where he could override if she froze up. If she froze in there, with him out here, it was going to be very hard to get the job done.

"Well," he said testily, " 'all right' what? Are you going to take over the manipulator arm or not?"

And the woman's voice came back huskily: "Alpert, never mind the camera. Just come back in. Please."

Two hundred and fifty miles below, President Stewart had finished explaining to the scandalized Hippo Herd officer and his science expert exactly what he wanted done with a single, modified missile, and when.

Now, with his retaliatory policy hammered into

strategy, and that strategy refined to a tactical level, and those tactics on an automatic implementation basis, Stewart was dealing with a different sort of crisis: He was having trouble fastening his gray satin cummerbund, and his wife had just broken her best strand of pearls.

He wondered what Susan's excuse was. He knew his own fingers were clumsy because he'd just issued an executive order that would literally rock the world. She couldn't know what he'd just done—it was Top Top Secret and it was simply too damned soon for the thing to have leaked.

Lincoln's bedroom was seeming unreal, almost two-dimensional, as Stewart waited for the phone to ring. Taylor and Forrestal had only about fifteen minutes left to get Classic Thunder on line; Hippo Wallow was already, ineluctably, in motion. The shit had, in essence, hit the proverbial fan—all that remained was the time lag between Stewart's awareness and the world's.

He couldn't remember another crisis when he'd been the only one who knew about events of this magnitude. He was considering explaining things to Susan. She deserved to know. She deserved a break. He wanted her to hear the truth from his own lips—before truth was dispensed with on all sides and replaced by propaganda and PR.

He was opening his mouth to begin when, at last, the red phone by his bed rang.

He actually flinched, and Susan saw him. By the time he'd grasped the receiver, she was heading toward the bathroom: She knew him too well; she was going to let him tell her what he wanted, when he wanted. She never intruded. She was all he'd ever needed. . . .

Moist-eyed, Stewart cleared his throat. "Yes?" he said, hoping he wasn't going to regret Hippo Wallow for the rest of his life; hoping the electromagnetic shield that would be raised over D.C. and various other crucial sites after Hippo 1's launch would hold; hoping he'd live to be impeached. . . .

"Mr. President, Forrestal here with a situation report. I'd, uh, like to come up there, sir, for three minutes. That's all the time I need, but I'd rather not do this on the phone. You understand, sir."

"Get over here fast, then. Where are you?" Stewart understood, all right. The new Soviet Embassy in Washington was on high ground, bristling with antennae of every sort, and even STUs weren't perfectly secure, despite the acronym.

"Right downstairs, sir. I thought you'd want to know as soon as possible—"

"Yes, of course, Forrey. Don't apologize—it doesn't sound like either of us has the time."

"Be right up, then," Forrestal said, and hung up.

"Susan," Stewart called toward the closed bathroom door, "I've got one last, five-minute meeting and I've got to have it in here."

Any other wife would have balked. And for a moment, when only silence answered him, Stewart thought Susan had finally reached the end of her rope. But then she came out of the bathroom carrying a cosmetic bag, her hairbrush, and a jewelry roll. "Of course, dear. I'll see you downstairs."

He intercepted her on her way to the door, put his arms around her jeweled waist, and kissed her fervently, with a passion he hadn't displayed in far too long.

She pulled back in his embrace and studied him soberly, then said in an even voice, "I hope this doesn't turn out to be as bad as you think it's going to be, Stew. For all our sakes."

"You're too perceptive," he growled, releasing her.

"I know." She smiled, and left him alone.

He sat on the edge of the bed, staring at his wing tips, until Forrestal knocked and entered.

Deputy Director Forrestal was pale and his eyes were glittering as he said, "Classic Thunder goes with Taylor's pilot in . . ."—he consulted his wrist chronograph—"fourteen minutes, unless you abort or alter now."

Forrestal waited a decent interval, during which Stewart only shook his head.

"All right, sir. Same game plan, then." There was subtle disapproval in the CIA man's tone.

Stewart didn't care what Forrestal thought; he wasn't going to ask the tall, thin man what the trouble was. Forrestal knew how to give a briefing. And Stewart didn't want to discuss Hippo Wallow, not with anyone. It was entirely possible that CIA had gotten wind of Stewart's plan, but until it was broached by the president, there was a "flag on the jacket," as intelligence types said. And if Forrestal was here to make a final plea for his own pilot, he was wasting his time.

"Same game plan," Stewart said with finality.

"There's a matter of West German red tape . . . the murder of Lutz . . . they'd like to talk to Hayes and Brecker, sir."

"They can talk to Brecker all they want. They can talk to Hayes later, if there *is* a later." Ostentatiously, Stewart glanced at his own watch.

"No, sir, they can't. Hayes is insisting on taking Brecker with him—he says he needs her. I told you he was an insolent, uncontrollable—"

"Cowboy, I know. Exactly what America needs right now, Forrey. I don't give a damn about some dead German, to tell you the truth. If Hayes wants Brecker, that's his business. I don't tell people how to do their jobs, especially when their lives are on the line. You can tell the West Germans for me that when we get those two back, we have prior claim: We might want to start our own disciplinary proceedings against them. But for now, Classic Thunder takes priority and Hayes gets whatever he wants. Clear?"

Forrestal nodded woodenly, and Stewart found himself wondering whether General Terrible Taylor was aware that his opposite number, Forrestal, was in here trying to play dirty pool. Forrestal seemed preoccupied: He didn't bring up additional items; he didn't argue; he seemed to have no agenda. He simply stood in the middle of the carpet, gazing around the room as if he were taking inventory.

"Anything else, Forrey? I've got a formal dinner. . . ."

"Yes, sir. You're not going to like this, sir. We've intercepted a space-to-space communication between *Skylab* and the OMV—orbital maneuvering vehicle."

"Thank God!" Stewart burst out. "They're alive! What do you mean I won't like it? It's the best news I've had all—"

"No, sir, you're not going to like it. The communication in question makes it reasonably clear that Soviet sabotage is at the heart of the *Skylab* problem. . . ."

Forrestal took a step backward on the Aubusson carpet, anticipating the blowup to come.

It came. And Stewart forgot all about the dinner he was dressed for, as Forrestal began to explain the particulars and made a startling proposal:

"Sir, we think it would be prudent to use Marcus Wolfe, since Hayes and Brecker delivered him to us so conveniently, to open a back channel to the Soviets on this one. . . ."

Stewart didn't even comment that it had been Forrestal's bright idea to send Hayes on a wild-goose chase to East Germany in the first place, or that flashing *MEDUSA* at the Soviets by basing it at Ramstein hadn't done a gnat's ass worth of good that Stewart could see. He didn't bother reminding Forrestal that at a Soviet military reservation on an island in the Sea of Japan, a Russian missile was absolutely and positively, according to NSA, being readied for "imminent" launch.

If Forrestal wanted to play "hot line" with the politburo, that was fine with Stewart. If Forrestal wanted to use Marcus Wolfe as an intermediary in off-the-record discussions with Moscow, that was fine, too. Stewart had Hippo Wallow. As long as nobody expected him to get on the line and beg some Soviet bastard not to launch that firecracker, so that Stewart didn't have to lie and wasn't tempted to threaten, whatever Forrestal wanted to try was fine with him.

With Classic Thunder ready to go and Hippo Wallow as his secret weapon, Stewart was holding a pat hand in the most important poker game of his life.

Let the others bluff. Let Forrestal dither himself into an old ladies' home. Stewart had known that the shit was going to fly well before the Hippo Herd boys walked out of his office shaking their heads.

The overt sabotage of *Skylab* meant only one thing: The Soviets were so sure of themselves—so sure that they were going to blow *Skylab* into teeny-tiny bits of space junk—that they were willing to leave tracks, certain that those tracks would be obliterated when their missile hit its target.

Stewart hoped Classic Thunder worked out. He was a humanitarian. The fact that there were live Americans, not simply American corpses, in *Skylab* made *MEDUSA* worth every cent she'd cost. He wished Hayes and Brecker the best of luck. When Forrestal ran out of wind, he was going to order the CIA director to make Classic Thunder's second priority the evacuation of all American personnel from the threatened *Skylab*.

He could do no less. But Classic Thunder's primary objective remained unchanged: Blow that Soviet missile out of space before it reached its target.

And Hippo Wallow's retaliatory mission was tied to the moment that the Soviet missile lifted off. As soon as the Soviet launch was confirmed, America was going to evince a knee-jerk response: One U.S. missile would speed toward Moscow sixty seconds after confirmation of a launch from the Soviet site on the Sea of Japan. Subsequently, America was going to be way too busy saving *Skylab* to manage to abort or destroy its single retaliatory missile—it would be loudly proclaimed to be exactly the same sort of "accident" that the Soviet "accident" was.

Their "accident" would trigger an "accidental" response—just a single missile launch, nothing too damaging. The Russians must be taught that any aggression would be met with no less than equal and opposite aggression.

It would be interesting to see whether the Soviets' antimissile defense around Moscow could succeed in destroying one American incoming. And it would be equally interesting to see if America's apology for its launch would be any more or less acceptable than Russia's. Most interesting of all, to the intelligence communities worldwide, would be the data gained as two superpower systems went on line.

Most interesting to Stewart would be the aftermath—whether, when all was said and done, he still had a job.

Chapter Twenty-Seven

Ro had his hands full on the Ramstein apron, keeping Amy in sight so that none of the slavering West German intelligence types dogging them got a crack at her while he was running interference for Marcus Wolfe.

They'd found a bulletproof limo for him when he hauled out his custom sidearm and began "explaining" to all and sundry that it was part of his mission to give Wolfe a tour of *MEDUSA* before turning the East German honcho over to American Intelligence.

Now the whole base was in an uproar, at least all the intelligence types were. Everybody wanted Marcus Wolfe, and Ro just kept saying "Terrible Taylor" and using the air force intelligence officer on duty as a buffer.

And it was working: The air force man was having visions of faster-than-light promotion and loving every minute of this once-in-a-lifetime opportunity to pull off a jumbo coup while CIA stood around playing pocket pool with a wistful look on its collective face. It wasn't going to last, Hayes knew. The air force colonel with the shit-eating grin knew it, too. But for now, they used Taylor's name like a battering ram and used their limo to break through lines of protocol and cars from every interested nation and service.

Eventually, "intelligence sharing" would be invoked, first by CIA, then by a string of acronyms representing a host of NATO allies. But that wasn't the business of Munro Hayes. His business was to get Amy Brecker suited up and on board the TAV, get himself clear of the FRG *polizei*, and get *MEDUSA* airborne.

Showing Wolfe the transatmospheric vehicle was really a diversion. But it couldn't hurt. If Wolfe was sufficiently impressed, and could be persuaded to call home—if CIA could stand to let that happen—then maybe Wolfe could convince Moscow it ought not to launch its damned missile after all.

Getting out of the limo in which Ro, Amy, Wolfe, and the air force colonel had been riding, Ro took a minute to survey the troops fallen in behind—and tsk'd to Amy: "Look at that. I wouldn't want to be in Hoffman's shoes, or Dietrich's, let alone Wolfe's."

It looked like a presidential motorcade back there, so many cars were strung out down the line, their little flags whipping in the cold night air.

Brecker said, "Ro, are you sure about this? Space, I mean?"

Her, she meant. "Yeah," he said. "I'm sure. They'll turn you into a Pentothal pickle otherwise. Trust me, you'll do just fine."

He turned away to finalize details with his new buddy, the air force colonel.

Amy's suit was the most real difficulty: She was too small for a standard helmet and suit, and pressurizing could compensate for only so much. Ro remembered that the CIA pilot was nearly a midget, so they were trying to get the guy's suit. But pilots don't give up things like custom-fitted pressure suits without a fight. Since Ro was giving the air force Marcus Wolfe in exchange, he was reasonably sure that his team would come through.

The other major difficulty was showing *MEDUSA* to Marcus Wolfe without showing her to half of NATO. Secrecy, Ro reminded both himself and the colonel beside him (a sharp-dressed, short-haired, square-cut fellow who'd probably been on a recruiting poster in his youth), wasn't important on this mission—not anymore, not when Classic Thunder was about to go operational. The colonel agreed, but said, "All right, major. You and your lady friend go ahead; I'll bring Wolfe along after I've broken up this traffic jam." The man grimaced at the festival of headlights raying the Ramstein dark. "Taylor and Forrestal'll be over here themselves, I bet, fast as they can scramble transport, so Wolfe will have all the best people as his party."

"No good. I want to take him into the hangar with me, now. And Amy's suit—where is it?"

"In there," said the colonel. "I don't mind telling you there's going to be hell to pay over that one."

"Not if we win big enough," Ro said, one eye on Amy, who was in turn keeping an eye on Marcus Wolfe as the East German spymaster surveyed the local sights—hangar, runways, lights, and towers—as if he had cameras implanted behind his eyes.

"Yeah," said the colonel grudgingly, "not if we

win big enough. Okay, major, take your superspy with you and I'll be right along. If you can't keep him under control with that arsenal of yours, I couldn't help you anyhow."

Ro still had his gear bag, and it was chock-full again: He'd disarmed everything he'd emplaced on Dietrich's jet and retrieved what he'd hidden there. It felt good to be ready for anything, although he doubted that he'd need much of what he had in orbital space.

Amy brought Wolfe up on Ro's signal; they came arm in arm like a father and daughter. If Hayes hadn't known that Amy had her gun pointed through her coat pocket, its muzzle pressed firmly against Wolfe's ribs, he'd have worried. But he'd found that worrying about her was a waste of time: As long as he explained what he wanted and it made sense to her, Brecker was an adjunct to whatever he had in mind.

She'd given him pause only once, when Dietrich was being handed to the MPs. But they'd been friends, maybe lovers. It wasn't Ro's business to judge whom she kissed or why. Still, it bothered the hell out of him that she had kissed Reinhardt Dietrich goodbye.

Women were so damned inscrutable; he'd long ago stopped trying to scope them. But Brecker, except for that one instance with Dietrich, didn't act like any woman he'd ever known. He wasn't worried about her ability to cover Wolfe; he led the way into the hangar without a backward glance.

And then there was *MEDUSA*, his one true love for the immediate future, hunkered down under the rafters like the wrath of God.

He'd forgotten how the sight of her tended to take his breath away.

He slapped her nosewheel with bold familiarity and the ladder came down. Then he bowed sweepingly and said, "Herr Wolfe, you're about to get the guided tour, and if it doesn't persuade you to tell your people to back the fuck off, then you don't understand what you're looking at."

As he was talking to Wolfe, he saw the pressure suit that must be Amy's, because it was barely half the size of the one next to it, both hanging from a punched girder to one side of the plane.

"Amy, I'll give Wolfe the once-over. You put that on. And the helmet. Take your shoes off first. Pull the right-hand sleeve tab and it'll inflate some— enough to snug it up on you. If the helmet's big, don't sweat it—we can fudge-factor the seals."

The suit had to be airtight, because of possible orbital applications. If they were going to try rescuing the *Skylab* crew, as the colonel who'd read him Taylor's message had instructed, there was no way to tell whether there'd be any atmosphere left inside the station modules. Brecker must be capable of assisting him, or else she was extra baggage. And she was too competent to waste that way, even if Hayes could have justified it.

There was no way he'd leave her here to deal with that cavalcade of brass just looking for somebody to tear to shreds because too many high-ranking toes had been stepped on. Toe-tromping was one of Hayes's specialties; it had gotten him grounded the last time out. He could handle it; he was always prepared for it; he rather enjoyed it. But Brecker shouldn't be left to take his heat while he was off playing hero.

"Come on, Wolfe," he said, and started pointing out in layman's language *MEDUSA*'s strong points: her Stealth technology, her electronic countermeasures, her chemical laser batteries, her kinetic-kill weaponry.

But his mind was on Brecker, a small figure struggling valiantly with the black pressure suit and helmet. Maybe he should have let her decide whether she wanted to risk her life up there with him or face criminal charges down here. Maybe his motives weren't as pure as he'd thought. He could buy the farm on this one and take her with him. Then what kind of favor had he done her?

He shook off second thoughts: If she really hadn't wanted to come, she'd have told him in no uncertain terms. It was her mission, too. He had to treat her as he'd like somebody to treat him. She detested anything less.

But under the shadow of this war machine, like nothing else he'd ever flown, an untested beast meant to rend and kill in Low Earth Orbit and beyond, he couldn't shake the feeling that he ought to have explained to her how much she might be risking.

So when Wolfe and he came around to *MEDUSA*'s pointed snout again, he said, "Wolfe, there's your pickup—my friend from the air force, remember? He's *your* only friend until the top brass comes to get you. So be nice to him," and held out his hand.

He'd intended to bring Wolfe on board, into the cockpit, but somehow it didn't seem important now.

Amy did.

Wolfe said, "Thank you, Major Hayes. I'm sorry

we couldn't do more . . . substantial business." A covert look. "If in later years we might, you know how to reach me."

Cocky son of a bitch was sure he'd be traded by breakfast.

Ro said without rancor, "Yeah, I know. Look, let's have a world to screw around with, okay? You try to get on the horn to your people and scream for an abort; I'll do what I can to get back to Earth alive. Then we'll see. Copy?"

"Loud and clear, major," said Wolfe as the air force colonel came up to take him by the elbow.

The colonel said only, "Everything nominal?"

"You bet," Ro responded. "Clear the runway for me. No onlookers. We're out of here in five minutes, unless you've got new orders?"

"No new orders," said the colonel, who understood what was happening, regretfully.

"Right, then." Ro flicked him a thumbs-up and strode over to see how Amy was doing.

She looked like a doll in a doll suit. He pulled her tab for her and she giggled as the suit hissed and plumped. Then he slipped into his own, saying, "Okay, do what I do," and went through the rest of the suiting-up procedure with her aping him.

When they walked over to *MEDUSA*, helmets under their arms, the hangar doors were opening and a tow truck was backing in, ready to haul the TAV out into the night where Ro could start her engines. He put one hand on the lowest ladder rung and said, "This is a dumb time to ask, but I've got to: You game for this? Would you rather stay here and take your chances with the FRG police and your friends from CIA? You can, you know."

"No I can't," she said, wrinkling up her nose. "I have no idea how to get out of this monkey suit. And anyway, I want to be the first woman to ride in one of these." She tapped MEDUSA with the flat of her hand.

"You got it." Ro grinned at her, and added, "Climb in, then. Ladies first."

BOOK FOUR

Chapter Twenty-Eight

Marcus Wolfe was hustled by the American air force colonel into a waiting limousine with a Porsche idling ominously behind it. From there he was driven among enough long, low buildings to have constituted a small German town, always with the Porsche's lights following, low to the ground and baleful.

The colonel said very little to him from the front seat. Wolfe was alone in the rear, between doors locked automatically from the driver's console.

Intermittently, the colonel talked on his car phone.

Intermittently, Marcus Wolfe thought about his predicament. He'd gambled and lost . . . or had he?

True, he was in Western hands, temporarily. He had no doubt that he'd be quickly returned to the East. He knew too much, and though there would be fears that he had masterminded this whole comedy of errors to arrange for some future defection, a serene retirement on the Côte d'Azur in exchange for playing a double game for the next few months or years, EastBloc Intelligence could not afford to lose him. He was as close to indispensable as a man could be.

And his KGB contact was as culpable as Wolfe himself for the mishandling of the Hayes and Brecker affair. This, too, could work in Wolfe's favor.

But mostly he thought about Munro Hayes—what the pilot had said, what the American had shown him: *MEDUSA*.

Hayes was right in his basic assumption that Wolfe—that any sane man—wanted nothing more than to avoid a nuclear confrontation between the superpowers. The pilot had made perfect sense as he escorted Wolfe around the TAV, trying with indisputable candor to convince Wolfe that *MEDUSA* was more than a match for "anybody's guided missile."

For there to be a nonconfrontational resolution to the problem begun by Russia's PKO, there must be some "fancy footwork" by those who understood the possible consequences.

Wolfe was not averse to aiding the Americans in order to avert a nuclear war, or even an embarrassing international incident. He doubted that it would be simple, but he was willing to try. He had been ever since he'd seen *MEDUSA* and the set of Munro Hayes's jaw. Wolfe was no space planner, but he was a consummate judge of men. Hayes was absolutely sure of his ability to fly *MEDUSA* into Low Earth Orbit and interdict PKO's missile gambit—to create a no-win situation.

Wolfe had underestimated Hayes once—when he'd gone aboard Dietrich's jet at Shönefeld. He would not do so again. He felt a twinge of acquisi-

tive jealousy toward the Americans: If Hayes and
MEDUSA had been his, if Wolfe had managed
somehow to acquire the operative, if not the hardware, what he could have done with such an
asset . . .

But something had been missing from Wolfe's
data base—Hayes and Brecker had not been what
they seemed.

Marcus Wolfe felt only the most subliminal concern for his safety as the limo pulled up to one
long, low building and MPs came to escort him
inside. The Porsche was still there, behind them,
and out of it stepped the driver—doubtless, one of
Wolfe's interrogators.

He wasn't fooling himself: The Americans would
keep him as long as possible; he knew more than
any single man since Gehlen about German, Bul-
garian, and Soviet intelligence operations. If he
decided to defect, he could name his price, write
his own ticket.

And when he left here, he would never again be
fully trusted by KGB.

But defection was a possibility subsumed by
permanence: There must be an East and West to
be able to leave one in favor of the other. Wolfe
hoped that the American air force colonel and his
superiors shared Munro Hayes's opinion as to what
must be done. Wolfe was perfectly willing, even
anxious, to call his KGB contact and relay data as
to *MEDUSA*'s capabilities and U.S. preparedness.
He wanted to do so on his terms, however.

As the air force colonel came around and the
rear doors of the limo were opened, Wolfe had
time to wonder whether the American intelligence

component was not too constipated to allow such a phone call to be made.

Then the colonel held out his hand, as if Wolfe were a woman, to help him out of the limo and said, "We've got a secure line for you inside, Herr Wolfe. As long as one of our people can listen in, you're welcome to use it—for everybody's good. Now. Before the higher brass shows up and decides we can't take this sort of risk . . ."

Their eyes met and Wolfe knew, looking into the other man's soul, that both their careers, if not their lives, were on the line. The colonel was a true patriot of his nation—he was willing to act unilaterally to protect it, even if that action caused him to be tried for espionage or treason.

"Risk?" Wolfe echoed, levering himself out of the low-slung, American-built car. "The risk, colonel, is in inaction, not action."

"Yeah, that's what Forrestal thinks—I got a message from him to go ahead with this, off the record. So it's hush-hush, okay? Just you, me, that CIA guy with the Porsche, and the highest-ups in KGB that you can access. We'll worry about trading favors later." He motioned toward the one-story building and the man from the Porsche, waiting for them in an overcoat by the door.

"If there is a later, you mean, colonel," Wolfe replied.

Whatever the air force man said then was drowned out by a deafening roar overhead as *MEDUSA* leaped into the midnight sky and, seconds later, the sound barrier shattered with a rolling *crack*.

When speech was possible again, Wolfe was introduced to the CIA man, "Smith," who asked without preamble, "Think there's any chance they'll listen to you? Considering your circumstances and where you're calling from, I mean?"

"Herr Smith," Wolfe sighed as they crossed the threshold into a brightly lit office whose usual personnel had obviously been recently and hurriedly ousted, "I wish I knew."

The phone they escorted him to was attached to something bulky, a big cube like a safe, which in turn was bolted to the floor—a secure phone of antiquated design. The CIA man, an unremarkable presence with bags under his brown eyes and a receding hairline, sat on the edge of the desk and waved Wolfe to an old leather chair on wheels. "Be our guest, dial your number."

And that was a problem, giving up the number in such company—making such a call from hostile territory.

But Wolfe could see *MEDUSA* in his mind's eye and he could see the Berlin Wall with his heart's eye.

He dialed.

And spoke to operators on both sides of Checkpoint Charlie.

And waited.

And heard a click and a voice answering sleepily, an annoyed voice that said, *"Da,"* instead of *"Ja."*

Then, with a feeling he'd never had before because he'd never given up a single secret in all his life, Wolfe spoke code phrases and began to explain, in Russian, what he had seen and what he wanted his KGB contact to do.

When he'd finished, the man on the other end said, "You must be sick in your mind, Wolfe. They will not—cannot—stop, not now, not for any reason, especially an American threat transmitted by a captured agent. You must realize this."

Wolfe did. He said implacably, "This is not a decision for you to make. Transmit my message to . . ." He gave the code name for the KGB chairman, and followed it with a single word that invoked emergency priority procedures. "And when you have done that, you may say that for all our sakes, it would be best if I am out of American hands by morning."

At this, the CIA man revealed the extent of his Russian by the wince and the sour look on his face, as well as by a hand that reached for the phone and then stopped, halfway to Wolfe.

Wolfe put out his own hand, forestalling: This was not treachery; it was necessary to persuade the toad on the other end of the line to relay his message. No midlevel KGB man could know the mind of his superiors, let alone the determination of PKO; the CIA operative must grasp this fact.

When the call was done and the receiver placed in the glittering palm of the CIA man, who still held out a steady hand toward him, Wolfe shook his head. "I do not know what good we've done here."

And the other answered, "Yes, I gathered that. Let's talk about fallbacks—about the offer we can make you. Defection might be your best hope, especially if your Soviet case officer doesn't relay, or PKO ignores the message."

Wolfe found himself nodding. "It cannot hurt to discuss it," he said glumly, wishing there were a window in this room through which he could see the night sky.

Chapter Twenty-Nine

Robinson was trying to get into the OMV, but there was space fungus all over everything—black spots and red spots the color of blood. The spots were all over his hands and his uniform and they danced in his vision.

He was so glad the OMV was there. It was his escape from this prison of cold and dark, where everything was slimy and contaminated. He couldn't even go into the command module—there was something horrible in there. He'd bolted the door shut and welded it to boot. The space fungus in there couldn't be allowed to spread, that was why he'd done it.

He couldn't seem to make Holly Gold understand that, so he'd had to tie her up. She kept yelling at him, so then he'd gagged her—once he'd gotten Alpert inside and realized that Alpert had been taken over by the space fungus, he'd had to do something with her. Because once a man's mind was eaten up by the space fungus, he wasn't a man anymore, and Alpert kept trying to attack him, so that meant Alpert wasn't in control of his body—that the space fungus had gotten to him, too.

He didn't mind about spacing Alpert—it was easy enough to do, because Robinson was suited up and much bigger and stronger then the crippled, arthritic body that the space fungus was using, the body with Alpert's name on it. . . .

And Holly Gold just kept screaming and yelling at him, so he'd tied her up—hit her first, too.

Then she'd been quiet.

But was that after, or before, he'd been battling the space fungus/Alpert in the cargo bay where the OMV was stowed?

He couldn't remember.

Canfield would take care of Holly Gold, make her say something, make her move, when he came back from . . . where the hell *was* Can, anyway?

He couldn't remember.

But he'd be back, that was sure. And Holly Gold would wake up, and she'd be okay. She wasn't contaminated yet.

He'd written Can a note, telling all about the space fungus and the trouble he'd had with Alpert and why he'd spaced the little guy. He didn't feel bad about it as he got into the OMV and started to punch at the emergency control panel.

He was going home. Somebody had to warn the world, and he was the only man left to do it, because Can was . . . Can had to stay with his ship—with the station. That was it. That was why he had left Can behind.

He wished he had help. He wished Holly Gold would wake up so that he could use the remote-pilotry electronics. It was going to be tough, flying home to Earth in the OMV. He didn't remember if anybody had ever done it, but you must be able to do it. There was no other escape. And the heat of reentry on the unprotected shell of the OMV would sterilize it. There'd be no fungus left on the ship.

And it was a ship, he was sure. They'd just never told the crew that the OMV could be used as a reentry craft, because they didn't want people leaving *Skylab* at random.

He wasn't sure he had enough oxygen, but he'd breathe shallowly . . . he'd make it. He'd be a hero. His wife and kids would be proud of him. Anything was better than staying in that contaminated space station where the fungus was growing and Holly Gold wasn't moving and Can couldn't be found anywhere. . . .

He was crying, but he couldn't wipe the tears away unless he took off his helmet. And he couldn't take off his helmet until he'd piloted the OMV clear of *Skylab*.

In the near distance, he fancied he could see the Russian space station. *Salyut*, they called it. Holly Gold had said something—yelled something—about the Russians and Soviet sabotage.

But the Russians weren't smart enough to have created the space fungus. What Holly Gold didn't know was that the space fungus had probably eaten away the Russians' brains; that they weren't human any longer; that they were the slaves of the space fungus.

For some reason this revelation suddenly became very important: The Russian satellite was inhabited by the same monstrous aliens that had destroyed everything aboard Skylab.

Alpert floated by, in a decaying orbit, stiff and

still, his ruptured suit trailed by ice globules of blood. Alpert was going to burn up in the atmosphere, just like Robinson. . . .

He wiped the faceplate of the suit with his elbow, but it didn't help the fog his tears were making. Maybe he'd go over to the *Salyut* station—maybe it was more important to save the world from the space fungus—even the Soviet world. If their station personnel were contaminated, too, only he was in a position to help the USSR. Its crew would never admit they were possessed by alien beings until it was too late. . . .

There was a way, although the OMV carried no weapons, to make sure that the *Salyut* crew never snuck back to Earth, carrying the space fungus with them. There was a way, but it meant that Robinson would have to sacrifice himself.

He wasn't sure if he was capable of such a heroic act, until he got the OMV clear of *Skylab* and looked at his gauges. It was simple mathematics, really. The amount of air and power available, the distance to Earth and the distance to *Salyut*. . . .

Robinson paused, his hands on the emergency control bank, and said out loud, "What the hell are you doing, fool? You go back to your own module, get a good night's rest, and decide in the morning."

Yeah, that made good sense. If he was going to ram the *Salyut* station, he didn't need to be aboard the OMV to do it. Even if Holly Gold wouldn't wake up, he could remotely pilot the OMV onto a collision course with *Salyut*. And if he decided to break for Earth, he could do that tomorrow.

He was getting too tired, his faceplate was too full of tears, and he didn't think he had enough power to make it to Earth. He would run a projection on one of the big computers, he thought, forgetting he'd welded the command module shut. He'd go back in and ask Alpert what he thought, he decided, forgetting he'd just seen Alpert float by.

He wanted to kiss Holly Gold goodbye properly, anyhow.

He turned the OMV and made for the cargo bay adjacent to the docking area. He couldn't raise Holly on the radio—she was still asleep. Luckily, he could get in without help from anyone aboard. Let 'em sleep. They deserved a rest. And they knew that he was reliable—they all trusted him with their lives.

It was just the space fungus that was the problem. He saw it again, smearing the camera lenses as he judiciously jockeyed his way into the cargo bay, where he could affix the OMV to the inner hull, repressurize the bay, and make his way inside.

Space fungus . . . wouldn't you know it would happen on his watch?

He heard the satisfying *thunk* as the hull of the OMV connected with the docking facility/cargo bay attached to the science module. Then he pushed the buttons that secured the OMV to the inner hull and waited while the cargo-bay doors came down automatically and the locks matched up and repressurization began.

When all that was done and his EXIT light came on, green and comforting, he unclamped the manual seals and stepped into the lock that connected to the science module, where Holly Gold still lay unmoving, her eyes staring above her gag.

He didn't like women who slept with their eyes

open. As soon as he got his suit off, he was going to wake her up and tell her to close her goddamn eyes when she slept.

The Soviet crew of *Salyut* saw the blip come up out of West German airspace at phenomenal speed, on such a vector and displaying such an attitude as no space shuttle or missile could. The blip was on course for the American *Skylab*, still jammed and very quiet, except for two sorties of its OMV.

The Soviet mission commander called the data in, and received only an acknowledgment—no request for supplementary tracking data. This was odd, the commander thought, but not too odd under the circumstances: They would track the blip and keep Ground Control informed of its progress without being asked—communications could always be monitored.

Secrecy was of the utmost importance, especially now, because of the jamming, the aggression he'd undertaken in his country's behalf. He was expecting an order to cease jamming; he'd expected the order by now. Didn't they understand down there that some Western craft was coming up to take a look?

Or didn't they care?

His crew was nervous—there were whispered comments and mumbled fears. This was as close to war as any of them could remember having come. Ever. They didn't want to be up here, if worse came to worst and everything erupted into chaos. It was a bird's-eye view no man wanted to have.

And then his electronics specialist came with a clipboard and a quiet voice, bringing to his attention diffidently—oh, so diffidently—signatures coming up from the Sea of Japan military reservation.

The Soviet commander sat back with chills running over him, looking at the data. He told his subordinate to say nothing. Then he considered ceasing his jamming of Skylab without orders.

But he couldn't do that.

What were they doing down there?

He thought about it, watching the speeding blip that would soon be at *Skylab*, thinking about the OMV that for a few minutes had seemed to be on a collision course with *Salyut*, before it returned to *Skylab*.

One never knew what one did not need to know, but the mission commander had a certain degree of autonomy. And he used it, then, to put in a request: He asked for permission to cease jamming activities, stating baldly that it was in the interest of Soviet security, and citing the approach of an unidentified Western space vehicle with previously undreamed-of capabilities to prove his point.

As the unidentified space vehicle arced up out of atmosphere, he received permission to cease "electronic experimental activities."

Nothing more.

Thinking of the opaque material spattered over *Skylab*, and what its presence there might mean to the beautiful blue world below, the Soviet mission commander did exactly what he was bid. There was nothing more he could do. He couldn't demand to know what was going on down there, or on *Skylab*, or even in the minds of the PKO generals who ultimately controlled *Salyut*'s destiny.

He was a soldier. Until further orders came, there was nothing he could do but wait.

And watch.

Chapter Thirty

Munro Hayes was watching the gauges glowing on his heads-up display and, beyond them, through the windshield, the distant stars burning above the last wisps of Earth's atmosphere.

He was talking to his AI computer almost exclusively now; it was the AI, the "tie breaker," that spoke in quick, digital pulses to Vandenberg and Houston. He'd spoken directly to Houston during takeoff and intermittently thereafter, when the vibration was worse than it ought to have been. *MEDUSA* wasn't quite perfect—at escape velocity, she shivered like a frightened horse.

He'd thought of Amy, again wondering if he'd had any right to bring her along. But he'd been too busy overriding the autopilot function to talk to her then, and now the TAV was behaving normally.

For the first time in minutes, he spoke to the woman in the copilot's seat: "Hey, Amy, ain't it pretty down there?"

And Amy, whose gilded faceplate reflected the LASER/ARMED light, replied, "It's the most beautiful thing I've ever seen, Ro. How're we doing?" in a clipped voice distorted by the com system.

"Okay, not bad." When he talked to her, he held the AUDIO OVERRIDE button down, as he'd done when he was on a direct link to Ground Control: the autopilot otherwise was continually engaged during this part of the mission, its voice-recognition system on line, waiting for commands.

There were lots of eleven-inch-plus nanoseconds between *MEDUSA* and Ground Control now as they approached Low Earth Orbit; so many that the transmission delay became noticeable. Ground Control might be able to fly *MEDUSA* by wire, but the onboard pilot and his computerized copilot were palpably faster.

"Good," Amy sighed, and Ro sensed that she'd realized something was wrong—perhaps from the conversation he'd had with Houston, perhaps from the vibration itself.

He said, "I want to explain to you about the AI and the fly-by-wire," and started to do that so she'd understand what she was hearing, and realize that he wasn't talking to himself when he used the voice-actuation systems, and because she was a part of this mission, not a useless passenger, and he wanted her to understand.

He was about finished explaining how, if for some reason he was incapacitated, *MEDUSA* could be remotely piloted from Ground Control, when one of his electronic sweeps of *Skylab* produced an unexpected result:

Skylab answered.

At the same time that Ro received this verbal response, his ECM monitors told him there was no electromagnetic interference—no jamming—and

Ground Control crackled into his circuit, wanting to know if he got the same readings they did. He verified and told the AI to vector him in and "ready docking procedures."

Seconds later, *Skylab* separated from more-distant stars and began taking on the characteristic erector-set shape of manned stations in space.

"Good God," Amy whispered, and he glanced at her out of the corner of his eye, a slight figure in her pressure suit, her hands carefully folded in her lap to avoid touching anything she shouldn't.

He said, "All right, Amy, time to earn your ride. Talk to *Skylab* for me—get a situation report and let them know we're coming after them. We want them suited up and ready to evacuate." He told her what to do to activate a com channel to *Skylab* while he was on another to Ground Control, and watched her for a moment to make sure she hit the proper buttons.

The AI did the rest: *Skylab* was entered in her automated system; all frequency designation, modulation, scrambling, and locking was done by *MEDUSA*.

He listened briefly as Amy began to speak to *Skylab* and someone named Robinson responded. Then, satisfied, he went back to his ground link; he couldn't break off ground contact even for a moment, and he wanted Amy on a different bandwidth.

What he was hearing from down there sounded very much like the scramble he'd been waiting for: He was beginning to get status reports on the bogey everybody had been predicting.

The DefCon status bumped, as he listened, to Defensive Condition Three: The Soviet launch was confirmed. One missile, somewhere down there, was rising in a billow of exhaust.

His stomach wrenched and adrenaline goosed him.

He'd already snapped through the docking procedures and regained manual control of *MEDUSA*, vectoring away from *Skylab* (so close now that he could see the U.S.A. on her Spacehab modules) in a smooth tracking arc, before he thought to warn Amy.

"Amy, tell *Skylab* we're going to burn that bogey and then be back for them—tell them not to sweat it."

"Ro! Ro, God, don't go away yet—I mean, don't get off this channel." Her voice was tense, almost brittle with strain. "Or tell me how to switch back to you."

He had his hands full; he didn't have time to talk to her. He had six onboard computers and the AI to deal with; he had to get into sync with the missile he was just beginning to track, and facilitate his ground-tracking link.

He felt like a one-armed paperhanger, but he said, "No time, just tell me the problem."

His eyes were on his heads-up; he stabbed the AI's autopilot, letting *MEDUSA* choose her vector, and saw the targeting array come up to center, green and red, on his windshield. When *MEDUSA* put a target into those cross hairs and centered it in a circle, Ro Hayes was going to be in the middle of his own private war.

Amy was saying, "Robinson says there's contamination aboard *Skylab*. Look and you can see the black stuff on the outside of—"

"Later," he said. "We'll worry about him later."

He patched her into his channel for the duration, adding only "Don't say anything unless you have to—*MEDUSA* takes verbal orders, remember. And lean your head back, sit still—we're going to find out what that pressure suit's good for."

And they were: The TAV was diving like a hawk after a sparrow, locked on target, down toward the atmosphere-swathed ball that was Earth, looking for her bogey.

Then there was just Ground Control and the AI and that sense of becoming one with his controls, waiting for the right blip in his cross hairs, and that vaguely uncomfortable sensation that came from the strain: Physically and mentally, *MEDUSA* was playing him for all he was worth.

His breathing became labored as the TAV taught him a new respect for physics: His own pressure suit wasn't cutting him much slack; his ribs felt compacted and he couldn't have turned his head if his life depended on it while *MEDUSA* spat fire from her tail and power-dived toward the upper reaches of the atmosphere.

He still couldn't see the target, but he could see the leading edge of his wings, and *MEDUSA*'s nose. He was watching his heat shield glow—a visible reddening as they skipped along Earth's atmosphere like a stone over water.

Damned AI didn't care if it killed him, or disintegrated itself, as long as it made its kill.

He kept up a running banter with Ground Control, telling them what kind of vibration he was getting and what his wing and nose temperatures were, all the while hearing Amy's breathing and his own like some horror-movie soundtrack.

He was about to tell Ground Control that he

was going to override and pull *MEDUSA*'s nose up
before she melted in his hands when the damned
target came blasting into view, closer than any
sane pilot would have chosen, and he said between gritted teeth, "Hold on, sweet thing," to
Amy.

Then everything blacked out for him but the
target; he was in a world defined by his heads-up
displays and in which the only other entity that
mattered was *MEDUSA*'s AI, to whom he talked,
oblivious of who might hear.

The missile came rocketing up out of the ozone,
clear and tiny, and *MEDUSA* reared up on her
tail and shook off the last wisps of atmosphere like
a dog shaking off water. "Fire orders commencing:
Chemical lasers: Fire bursts of three . . . commencing *now!*"

The three-burst firing sequence served a masking purpose, and he had plenty of bursts at his
disposal, enough that he didn't care if the first
couple hit the target: The residues from the firing
of chemical lasers produced a change in the "media"
—the characteristics of the very space in which
both craft traveled.

Sensors—tracking devices—of an entirely different type were needed to "see" through the chafflike
effects of the chemical residue from Ro's three-
shot laser bursts. No one below, now, could track
him until he came out of the trail the first burst
left.

His second "Fire three" order came with his
visual tracking aid depressed: *MEDUSA* was taking her readings off Ro Hayes's eyeballs as they
locked on the missile targeted in his display's cross
hairs.

The first burst caught the tail, he thought, of the Soviet missile, halfway to *Skylab* so that he could have seen its fiery plume if he'd dared take his eyes off his projected heads-up display.

But he didn't. He was staring concertedly at the bogey centered by the circle projected on his windshield, and when the second and third bursts hit that blip, it blew apart in clear and certain computer simulation of a kill.

He must have whooped for joy, because Amy yelled, "What? Did we get it?"

He yelled back, "Hell, yeah, what did you think we came up here for?" as *MEDUSA* veered sharply away from the explosion before her and his stomach lurched because he'd never been in an aircraft that could handle the sort of gyrations that the AI autopilot was demanding of *MEDUSA*. Ro Hayes's twenty years of piloting told him in no uncertain terms that *MEDUSA* couldn't take this sort of punishment, that she was going to shake apart right under him.

He had just enough time to stab and punch and grunt out orders that would return control of the TAV to manual before she dived nose-first back into atmosphere at a speed and vector that no aircraft or spacecraft could possibly survive.

Struggling manually to pull her nose up and punch in *Skylab* as her next port of call, he promised himself that he was going to let Taylor know that *MEDUSA*'s damned AI still had a whole lot of bugs in it, just as soon as he got a chance.

Chapter Thirty-One

Stewart hadn't even finished his after-dinner speech when one of his aides had come in and hustled him down to the Situation Room.

Now he sat, his hands folded so their tremors wouldn't be visible, and listened, and took reports as they came in.

And watched the second hand sweep around his wristwatch. He had fifty seconds left of the seven minutes during which he could alter the destiny of the world.

His Hippo Wallow had gone operational as soon as there was a confirmed launch from the Soviet site. His personal decision, implemented by Hippo 1, was speeding toward Moscow. If he didn't countermand within the next fifty . . . now forty-six seconds, that missile's nuclear warhead would automatically be armed.

He'd chosen Hippo 1 carefully, for exactly this reason: to give him time for second thoughts, time to decide whether he wanted to nuke Moscow. Newer missiles would not have allowed him this time, or this luxurious option.

Perspiration was soaking him as his principles and his pragmatism collided.

He said to his Hippo Herd man (the only other man in the Situation Room to whom the single launch was no mystery), "We're not going to go nuclear. Understand?" They'd worked this part out, Stewart and the single man who knew the truth about Hippo Wallow—they had code words and a game plan. "Abort the arming of the missile," said the president sternly. "You *can* do that, can't you?"

And the man who'd volunteered to take the blame for the "mistake" nodded and reached for the red phone, while all around Stewart at the table, National Security Council honchos tore their hair and sweated bullets.

The real decision made, Stewart sat back, not really listening to his advisers as they all talked at once about how this "terrible error" could be minimized, since a Soviet "error" had triggered it.

Stewart knew all that. Everyone in the room, with the exception of himself and his Hippo Herd specialist, was reacting exactly as Stewart had predicted. There were no surprises here—not among the reactions presented by the Joint Chiefs of Staff or the State Department or the DOD.

No surprises, except within Stewart himself. He hadn't been sure, until forty-one seconds remained of the seven minutes he'd allotted himself for a safety margin, what he'd do about the warhead Hippo 1 carried.

But that would be someone else's problem. He had to deal with his own problems, now, in the real world: He had to talk to the Soviet general secretary on the hot line and pretend that he was sorry, while his opposite in Moscow foisted a parallel ploy on the Western world. He had to do it now, before the Russians could think to deny their own launch, or their attempt to destroy *Skylab*.

While Stewart was sitting there, staring at his white knuckles, an aide came in with a note that said Classic Thunder had succeeded. Stewart sat back, the note in his hand, and found that his throat was aching. Hayes had done it—he'd flown *MEDUSA* to a perfect intercept. He'd destroyed the Soviet missile on the fly.

That changed things. It changed the conversation he was about to have with a man in Moscow, and it changed the world forever.

The U.S. had just demonstrated its ability to destroy a missile aimed at an American target. The Strategic Defense Initiative had just payed off in spades. No matter what it had cost in intelligence to do it—no matter how much the Soviets had learned as America's space tracking and space defenses went on line—it had *worked*.

Stewart said out loud, "Get me Moscow," and found it in his heart to hope that the Russians' point defense around Moscow would work well enough to destroy the one inert incoming missile that he had sent there.

Parity. It was the most important thing in the world, especially because there was no way to know whether the electromagnetic umbrella shielding Washington would really hold.

Wondering if he had any right to feel as good as he did, when civilization was still at risk, Stewart took the phone that was handed him and began to rehearse what he would say when he got his Soviet counterpart on the line.

Chapter Thirty-Two

In *Salyut*, the mission commander watched with astonishment and horror as some superplane destroyed a "runaway" missile and changed course for *Skylab*.

On *Skylab*'s cameras was proof of Soviet foul play.

The mission commander did not know the minds of his superiors, but he knew an advanced weapons platform when he saw one. If an order came from PKO to fire upon the death-dealing spaceplane with kinetic weapons, the fate of *Salyut* and its crew was sealed.

The commander was not a coward, but he knew his weapons' capabilities. There was very little chance that he could destroy the spaceplane.

And then the spaceplane would destroy *Salyut*.

He could hardly track it. It was swathed in some sort of chaff—it had clouds of electronics-resistant material around it. The clouds were opaque to his scanners, so that he saw the plane clearly only when it had exceeded the envelope of the material it seemed to spew out. He could track it by the clouds, of course, but if he was ordered to fire, he would need a better target than a half-mile-wide wake of impenetrable masking material.

So he sat, and sweated, and watched the clouds drift and the spaceplane appear for moments, then disappear again in its foglike shield. He watched and waited, his ears superacute as he anticipated a fire order. And while he tracked it, the spaceplane pulled up beside the *Skylab* station and seemed to drift there, as if it were about to dock. Then, before his eyes, a cloud of this chemical chaff—for that was what analysis told him the material was—surrounded the space station, so that there was nothing at all to see there.

When the inevitable request for data came up and an assessment was demanded, the Soviet commander had to say that he estimated his chances of destroying the spaceplane at no better than fifty-fifty. He could hear the fury in the voice that asked the questions, that voice from so far below. But he was a soldier, trained to evaluate and report. It was not his failure if Soviet equipment was not capable of surpassing American equipment.

He half-expected to be told to fire anyway, to use kinetic weaponry, to jockey an exploding killer satellite into position, using *Skylab*'s coordinates and the half-mile cloud as his target.

A minute passed, and another, and the order to fire did not come. Perhaps, thought the Soviet mission commander, those on the ground were more concerned with the single missile headed toward Moscow that his electronics expert had verified and was tracking.

The Soviet mission commander pushed back from his console and designated another to sit there.

He had saved a ration of vodka for just such a moment, and as ranking officer he could visit the toilet whenever he chose. He chose to visit it now: He and his vodka ration would have a few minutes together, to think about what it was going to mean if the American missile turned Moscow into a mushroom cloud and then more missiles flew, and more. . . .

He could think, too, about what it would mean if World War III were averted, and he was the poor fool who had been in command of *Salyut* when the Americans unveiled their most secret weapon, against which, in his estimation, the USSR had no effective defense.

Because that was what he would say, if anyone asked him, once he had drunk his vodka and was back at his console. Despite the consequences, he would tell the truth. Telling the truth was no way to get ahead in the Russian army; he'd always known that.

Chapter Thirty-Three

Amy was trying to explain the uneasy feeling she had to Ro, and he kept telling her that what she was experiencing was a natural reaction to weightlessness.

"That may be," she said, trying to sound patient when what she wanted was to ring Munro Hayes's neck. "Maybe you're right—maybe it's the docking maneuver, the floating sensation, the fact that you've just cut the engines and we're just fucking hanging here in space. . . ."

"But you don't think so." Hayes was out of his safety harness, floating a few inches above his seat, turned away from her as he got out the "Mini MMUs"—the manned maneuvering units he'd said he didn't think they'd need because the docking tube had connected flawlessly to *MEDUSA*'s belly.

"That's right, I don't," Amy said. "You didn't talk to this Robinson. You didn't listen to him. 'Contamination' . . . something about fungus . . . Soviet sabotage . . . I'm just saying that it doesn't

feel right. I may not know anything about air-
planes—"

"Spaceplanes," Hayes corrected as he pushed
one of the MMUs toward her and started unfold-
ing his own with instructive gestures.

"All right, *space*planes, then. I may not know
much about your damned aircraft, but I know
men. I've been trained to listen, and to know
when somebody's lying or hiding something. And
what I'm telling you is—for God's sake, Ro, listen
to me: There's something wrong in there." She
indicated *Skylab* with an inclination of her helmeted head.

The pilot, looking like some kind of giant insect
with one golden eye, turned toward her slowly.
She had his attention, finally.

"Let's talk to Ground Control," she suggested.
"They'll have heard from this Robinson, too, now
that communications have been reestablished. Let's
check it out."

"I would, sweet thing, except that I know what
they're going to say, especially if they're wondering the way you are. They'll tell us to go take a
look. So let's save one step. Now, about these
MMUs . . . like this, and this . . ."

He was implacable. She slipped into the spidery
little emergency maneuvering unit, which so much
resembled a stiff parachute harness with flexible
armrests, and listened while he explained that she
shouldn't touch the buttons under her fingers unless she wanted to engage the nitrogen thruster
system: The left-hand buttons controlled "transac-
tion"—forward movement; the right-hand buttons
controlled rotation and attitude; and stabilization
was maintained by a minicomputer in the backpack.

"But what do we *need* these for?" she demanded, looking out the window where the docking tube, like some gigantic vacuum-cleaner hose, stretched between the *Skylab* science module and *MEDUSA*.

"You saw that black stuff—the stuff Robinson was talking about, the stuff that's on the cameras. Well, I'm going to take a sample while you take pictures of me taking a sample." From his tone of voice, there was a sardonic grin on his face behind the opaque faceplate of his helmet.

"No," she said with all the finality she could muster. "I forbid it. First of all, they've got samples in there—Robinson told me they did. Second, if anything happens to you, I can't fly this thing. You don't want the Soviets to get a hands-on look at *MEDUSA*, do you? I couldn't stop them, and *Salyut*'s just over there."

She was grasping at straws, looking for valid reasons. Not because she was afraid of floating out there with Munro Hayes taking snapshots for their album—she trusted him implicitly—but because her instinct was telling her that there was something very wrong in *Skylab*. That velvet voice she'd heard had been too rigidly controlled, and too full of suppressed emotion.

She pushed the MMU away and it floated between them, rejected. His helmet inclined toward her, and for a long moment all they could hear was each other's breathing in their phones. Then he said, "Okay, lady. Want me to take my arsenal?"

"Yessir, major. I'm bringing mine." She knew it sounded foolish. She wasn't even sure what would happen if she shot her gun in the space station—something terrible, probably: depressurization, flying sparks and exploding electronics and heaven knew what else.

But Hayes had brought special weapons: special loads for his handgun and a stunner that shot wires along which 40,000 volts of electricity traveled to immobilize an antagonist—she'd seen it in his flight bag.

"Unless I can have that Taser you brought."

"Take it," he said with a quizzical edge to his voice, "but I promise I won't give you any trouble, lady. . . . Look, Amy, if there *is* something wrong in there, we'll handle it, all right? Calling Houston might be just the wrong thing to do. *Skylab* has pretty sophisticated surveillance equipment; I don't know that they couldn't listen to any transmission I sent out. *MEDUSA*'s encoding is good, but it's not meant to get over on our own team. You copy? So let's go see what's what."

"Okay," she agreed, and finally pressed the release button that loosed her safety harness.

And felt her stomach tumble, end over end, as she floated slightly away from her cushioned seat. "The Taser." She held out her gloved hand.

"Right, right. As soon as you put on your MMU."

Bastard. She couldn't imagine a situation in which she'd be evacuating *Skylab* without him, or trying to get to *MEDUSA* if the docking tube wasn't engaged—what would be the point?

But she did what he asked, and he did what she asked, and finally they were ready. He spun locks and released seals and slid back the partition that sealed off *MEDUSA*'s cargo bay, where the evacuees would ride on the trip back to Earth. There wasn't much room in there for people; the chemical laser fuel tanks took up most of the space, but there were web carrier strips attached to the curved walls that would do in an emergency.

As far as Ground Control was concerned, *Skylab* was still an emergency—the second stage of the Classic Thunder mission remained unchanged: Evacuate the *Skylab* personnel. And Ro didn't want to call down for clarification.

Amy wouldn't have wanted to ride back to Earth in that cargo bay, held in straps not meant for humans—it was tough enough sitting in the copilot's seat. But Hayes reminded her that the *Skylab* personnel all had real space suits that were capable of withstanding tougher takeoffs than *MEDUSA*'s had been; these people had all ridden a rocket up here when they'd climbed aboard a space shuttle piggybacked to a booster.

They weren't her problem—yet.

Then it struck her and she reached forward to touch Ro's shoulder before he slid back the cargobay door to which the docking tube had been remotely attached. "Ro, we haven't heard a peep from anybody else on the station—there are four of them, right?"

"Jesus, Amy, stop worrying. You've got your Taser. You're giving me the creeps. Don't talk about it—if there's trouble, we don't have to tell them we're expecting it."

Them. She hoped there was a "them." She'd been worried about the Soviet-sabotage angle, and still was. For all she knew, there were Soviets aboard the station. Robinson had said something about Soviet sabotage, and the jamming of *Skylab*'s electronics had confirmed that.

But the other stuff . . . the black stuff . . . the contamination . . .

She tugged on the straps of her MMU and prayed that Ro was just being his normally over-cautious self—the same guy who'd insisted she pass a punch-out test—and that she was simply back into the paranoid swing of things. There certainly was black goop on the cameras, as well as spattered on the curving hull (was that what you called it?) of the science module.

Please, God, she prayed silently, *let me just get home in one piece.* Home, in this instance, was the entire Earth.

And then Ro had the door open and was preceding her along the tube, pushing occasionally with one gloved hand. She heard him say, "Switching to *Skylab* com frequency," and did likewise, catching the tail end of his greeting, ". . . come to get ya, fellas. Taxi service, door to door, courtesy of the United States Air Force. . . ."

She pushed too hard as she followed him, having nightmares of somehow tearing the tube and plummeting through the stars, and tumbled. An upside-down glance back at *MEDUSA* showed her that the cargo hatch had shut, automatically—Ro had a remote with him.

Once she'd stabilized, Amy saw that Ro had reached a similar hatch on the science module, which had "Spacehab" stenciled on it in NASA-type script.

It opened as he reached for it. There was a big black figure in the hatchway, and she heard "I'm Robinson. You must be the space patrol." As she shoved herself along the tube, she could see Robinson raise his hand, as if in greeting.

Then everything became very vivid: The black man was wearing a helmet and a suit of some kind, but the helmet was transparent—that was why he looked so huge. On the front of his blue suit there were stains, reddish black, getting larger as Amy's momentum propelled her toward the science module. And in Robinson's hand was a long wrench, as if he'd been fixing something.

Amy could hear her pulse hammering in her ears as Hayes reached the threshold and the black man stepped back a pace. Then her own feet hit clumsily on the metal of the threshold and she was blinking in her helmet. Behind them, the hatch closed. A red light came on as regular illumination blacked out; then it turned green for an instant and she heard Ro mutter, "Damn," and grunt as if in surprise.

Her eyes were adjusting. Ro was doubling over as if he'd dropped something, or gotten a stomach cramp. . . . Robinson had the wrench in his hand, and he was raising it high.

Amy didn't even think, she just pointed the Taser and squeezed.

She couldn't see the wires snap out, but she'd felt the trigger pull through and she saw Robinson's face and saw the wrench go spinning as Robinson began to thrash and gyrate.

Too soon, she realized—she'd acted too soon: In the lock, with this man who must be crazy, and who was convulsing wildly, quarters were too close for the Taser. Robinson reached out with clawed hands, seeming to pull himself along the walls toward her. She was afraid that the big black man was going to reach her and squash her.

She had nowhere to run, and no idea whether a second jolt from the Taser would do any good. But she fired anyway.

The big man kept coming, but his eyes were all whites, staring.

Now Ro was straightening up, floating toward her, yelling, "Don't shoot him again—he's out. He's probably dead."

Amy had barely sufficient presence of mind to slide out of Robinson's way as he floated by. He hit the lock and stopped. Then Hayes was beside her, his fingers wrestling the Taser from her grasp.

Robinson's now-limp body, rents showing in the material covering his chest, drifted toward them again. Amy was desperately sure she was going to be sick in her suit. She fought the urge. And won.

By the time she was capable of saying "Ro, are you okay?" the pilot was crouched over Robinson's still-floating form.

"I'm not getting any signs of life—but then, he tried to bash my brains out." Ro's helmeted head turned toward Amy. "You did good. You did great. I'm sorry I didn't trust your instinct. Want to tie this guy up, or what?"

She wished she could see his face, tell if he was making fun of her. She said, "Well, there's air in here now—that's what the green light means, right? Let's see if he's alive. Hell, yes, tie him up if he is." Her voice was trembling.

Ro heard and reached out a gloved hand to touch her, a clumsy movement because of the MMU attached to him like scaffolding. "I said you did great. I'm just worried that the rest of them in there might be waiting to try the same thing on us."

One knee on Robinson, to keep the body from moving, he examined the Taser critically, then handed it back. "You've got a good three-quarters charge left, Dead-eye, if you need it again." He reached into a pocket of his suit leg and pulled out his own handgun, shoved it through his equipment belt. "Now," came his voice in her phones, a self-deprecating chuckle, "I'll be ready for whatever. Thanks to you."

He stripped off Robinson's helmet and fussed over the body, finally using the man's faceplate to check for any misting of breath. "Dead, unless I've forgotten how to tell. Can't check for pulse in these gloves, but he ain't breathing. . . . Bad heart, as likely as anything you and your Taser did."

"Don't sugarcoat it. I can handle killing him. He was going to kill *you*."

"Yeah." Hayes discarded the helmet and it floated by Robinson's head.

"And if you were dead, how would I ever get home?" Her voice was too defensive. She knew it, but the words were already echoing in his helmet's phones.

"Oh, *MEDUSA* likes you. She'd get you home. Just hit the autopilot and talk nice to her," Hayes said. "You don't need me. I wish I could say the same."

"Screw you, major," she murmured.

"You keep promising, but you don't come through."

"We never get the spare time," she shot back, feeling somewhat better. She'd killed a man. She remembered the huge wrench, and Ro doubling over. What else could she have done? Tasers weren't normally lethal, not single jolts, anyway, but . . . Could she have been wrong?

No, there was Ro here to prove it. Ro, who'd been nearly bludgeoned by the wrench. There

was no time to regret it—he was doing his best to
make her realize that. She wanted to thank him.
She didn't have the words. She reached out to
touch him with her own gloved hand, but he was
already slapping a button that opened the hatch to
the interior of the science lab.

"Shit," he said softly.

His form blocked her view. She had to step over
Robinson's still body to get to the hatchway—her
foot slipped, and she stepped on the dead man. A
little squeak of panic came out of her mouth, but
then she was floating toward Ro, her head for an
instant above the line of his shoulder, and she saw
a woman, eyes wide open, gagged and bound and
indubitably dead of the same sort of violence Robinson had attempted to perpetrate on Munro Hayes.

"Shit," said Hayes again, the single word carrying volumes: hardness, disgust, regret, alertness.

His gun was out, its muzzle questing.

They were there a very long time, trying to get
the command module open. Someone had welded
it shut. When they did get it open, Hayes said,
"Amy, you don't want to see this. Keep watch—we
still don't know where this Alpert guy is."

He didn't have to ask her twice. She watched.
And she saw, eventually, while Hayes was in the
command module, exactly where Alpert was: She
saw the body float by, surrounded by ice like
planetary rings of rubies.

She screamed then, and Hayes was there in an
instant. He had his helmet off now; so did she.
She lay her head against his shoulder and blub-
bered like a baby: "There's somebody out there,
covered with frozen blood, all around. . . ."

Ro looked out the porthole, or window, or whatever it was, and squinted, and then said, "Yeah, I'll get a picture when he comes by again—if he does; that's a very elliptical orbit he's on."

Then the pilot's hand was in her hair, and his chin rested on the top of her head for a moment before he said, "Hey, Amy, look at me."

She did, and very slowly and gently Ro Hayes, staring into her eyes, leaned down and began to kiss her on the lips.

Chapter Thirty-Four

Marcus Wolfe was still in the same room at Ramstein, still being subjected to extensive debriefing, when Forrestal came in.

Wolfe paused and looked around at the lesser interrogators. Forrestal blinked once, as if he were about to rub his eyes like some ancient, sleepy child.

The two men had been archrivals for years; they had described the limits of counterintelligence; pushed the envelope of espionage to new frontiers.

The others in the room sensed something of what the two men must be feeling—their rivalry had been legend. Slowly, the air force and CIA and State Department intelligence officers drifted toward the door.

Neither Forrestal nor Wolfe said anything whatsoever until the door had closed on the last of those men, who whispered as if in a church, "Here's everything we have so far, director," and put a manila envelope in Forrestal's hands.

"*Guten abend*," said Forrestal to Wolfe. "It's gratifying to meet you at last."

"A quick trip, and I assume a pleasant one," Wolfe replied.

"We've got a mutual problem, Herr Wolfe; I haven't time to mince words. We've got to get you in touch with the KGB chairman directly, or you and I won't have time to strike the deal of the century." Forrestal moved now, taking a seat behind the desk that Wolfe sat before.

Wolfe nodded. "Concise and to the point. You will have to explain to me more exactly—your underlings have been less than forthcoming about what subsequent troubles have developed since *MEDUSA* took off."

Forrestal began to explain about Stewart's "knee-jerk" reaction and the single, unarmed missile called Hippo 1 launched on Moscow.

Wolfe nodded complacently and waited until Forrestal had finished. Then he said, "My friend—I have always thought of you as a friend. A man like myself has so few peers that, in my mind, we two have been long engaged in this very special game of chess. . . ."

In the pause, Forrestal only watched Wolfe steadily, offering neither affirmation nor denial.

So the East German continued. "There is no way to determine—or condition—a Soviet reaction, you know that. Have they shot down the missile, or did it strike the city?"

"We think they got it, about seventy miles above the city."

"Good. Good. Then shall we suggest that we—that *you*"—a flicker of a death's-head smile came and went as Wolfe corrected his own grammar—"that you and they concoct a joint explanation—they will take longer to release any news than your people—one with which both nations can concur, in which neither side seems foolish or profligate with its population's safety?"

"Something like that," Forrestal said slowly, "might do the trick. We have evidence of Soviet sabotage of our *Skylab*, which we'll willingly suppress for the right incentive."

"Such as?"

"Such as, we've got a crippled space installation up there, casualties on board for which the Soviets aren't directly responsible, but *MEDUSA*'s there, too. We don't want *Salyut* shooting at our plane. We don't want to have to shoot back. And we definitely don't want any more missiles launched from either side."

"This last, I am sure, they don't want either. No one wants a war between the superpowers, Director Forrestal."

"I'm hoping like hell that's the case, Herr Wolfe. Will you help us? We're willing to admit we have an electromagnetic shield up over certain of our major cities and strategic installations—there's a good chance it's working. Both nations are reaping an intelligence bonanza. It ought to be enough."

"And you want only a cessation of hostilities? A return to the *status quo ante*?"

"I want my plane to come home without its having to blow *Salyut* to bits." Forrestal sat back in the chair, his eyes slitted, his cards on the table.

"Well said, but we shall not say that to the chairman of KGB, you understand. And I? What do I receive if I do this ultimate favor for your nation, if I negotiate a suitable solution for both sides, in which each can claim a victorious 'test' of its own equipment and neither must admit that the world has nearly slid into the war from which our poor planet would never recover?"

"Wolfe," Forrestal sighed, "you old shark, you know you'll be able to write your own contract—if you stay. You can probably get out of here by sunup, if you want that, though why you would is beyond me. They'll never trust you again, and we can offer you the moon."

Wolfe frowned. "The moon?"

"A figure of speech, Herr Wolfe. A figure of speech. Anything you want—a fine home, money, security, a new identity if you want that, a consulting position to our government if you wish prestigious employment."

"Ah, like Gehlen, you will embrace me?"

"Not exactly—we don't think we can go quite that far. And we think you'd be safer in the continental U.S. But," and Forrestal's pale, thin face grew dark, "we're not having much luck assuring anything like a peaceful resolution to this, with Stewart and the Soviet premier yelling at each other on the hot line. So you're in the rather enviable position of being able to pretty much call your own shots."

"Yes, I thought it might end this way."

"You're ready to make that call?"

"My friend, I have been ready for at least half an hour. I thought you would never get here."

And with a short, barking laugh that had very little humor in it, Forrestal handed Marcus Wolfe the receiver of Ramstein's antiquated secure phone.

Chapter Thirty-Five

Ro Hayes found himself thinking about his ex-wife and kids, in the hills above Santa Barbara, and about his cabin near Vandenberg, and about Amy Brecker as he sat in the science station wrestling with the remote-pilotry function of the OMV.

He'd cannibalized some circuit boards from the command module and patched together, under the guidance of Ground Control, a working power unit for the science module so that he didn't have to rely on the depleted batteries. The unused boards hadn't been pulsed, and the system was drawing power from the solar panels.

The jury-rig had seemed like the hardest part of the job, until he sat down at the console and began trying to remotely fly the damned OMV so that he could snag Alpert, the orbital corpse. Then things really got tough. The OMV was far from easy to pilot, and his nerves were frayed—he didn't like taking rote instructions from console jockeys down at Houston. He'd probably never hear the end of it.

But eventually he got the remote arm to grab

Alpert, and the rest wasn't too bad—or wouldn't have been, if he weren't acutely conscious that everybody down there was still worrying that the Soviets in *Salyut* were going to open fire on the station any minute, or maneuver a killer sat into *whammo* range, or use this opportunity to see if any of their other antisatellite kinetic kill devices—their rail guns and such—could take out *MEDUSA* and *Skylab* in one fell swoop.

He didn't like playing high-tech undertaker. He'd said so, but nobody down there seemed willing to let these bodies sit until a shuttle could come up to get them. The brass wanted "the evidence."

Hayes didn't like the sound of that at all.

Intermittently, Amy would float over, unaware that he'd saved her worse trouble: If not for the ground link and his on-the-job training in OMV pilotry, one or both of them would have been out there in the MMUs on tethers, trying to snare Alpert's mobile corpse.

Whenever she appeared, his mind would wander back to the mess he always liked to leave on the ground, far behind him: his personal life.

She brought him a squeeze container of coffee once, and he touched her hand, then they both backed off. It really didn't seem like the time or the place for the sort of conversation he thought he wanted to have with her. She'd given him no indication that it was necessary, either. There was no reason to assume that they had anything to talk about; people on these sorts of missions developed instant bonding; afterward, you never saw the guy again.

Guy. That was part of the problem: Amy Brecker

wasn't one. She was female, indubitably. He told himself he'd get out of this without making a fool of himself or embarrassing her, and never take a mission like this again, where he was working this closely with some lady spook.

It bothered the hell out of him that she'd shot Robinson, once everything calmed down and he had time to think about it. She could have held her fire; maybe he could have subdued the other man. But she'd blasted away like some cowboy, and it scared him. Worse, it reminded him that he didn't know a damned thing about her, and probably never would. You couldn't get all protective about somebody like Brecker. For all he knew, she blew away guys like Robinson routinely, before breakfast, to keep in practice.

Anyway, he'd had one wife; he had a terrible track record with women in general; and what he'd told her at the beginning of this mission (so long ago, it seemed like years) had really been the truth: Spooks scared him to death.

But he couldn't stop thinking about it, and that scared him worse than anything else.

She was a potent distraction, and he still had to fly his headstrong, air-breathing *MEDUSA* home— nasty vibration, suicidal AI, and all. If he didn't make it, he wouldn't have to worry about what, if anything, he was going to do about Brecker in the future. They wouldn't have one.

So he bitched about having to play garbage man, and argued about the various touchdown windows open to him. As a matter of fact, he was bitching about everything those desk jockeys added to his work load, so that finally they rounded up Taylor and he got an earful from Terrible about being "flexible."

He wanted to put down at Vandenberg, fade into the woods, and finish reassembling the Blazer's carburetor. It wasn't a whole hell of a lot to ask, considering. But Taylor was saying, "Look, Ro, we want those bodies, and we want the samples and the pictures you've got—the real film, not just what you've sent, because computer take can be argued, faked, what have you. So that's Langley, and I don't want to hear another word about it. And it's ASAP as well, for obvious reasons."

The "obvious reasons" were all too obvious: There was still a chance that things weren't going to stop at one missile lobbed per side.

He couldn't monitor commercial or military channels; he was too busy with the OMV, bringing it into the cargo bay with Alpert pincered by the manipulator arm like some damned specimen. But Amy wasn't too busy to keep abreast of current events. She'd come in once or twice in the last few minutes, silent now except to ask how he was doing, lots of urgency in what she wasn't saying. He kept wanting to hug her and tell her it would be okay. Which was bullshit. He didn't know it would. He didn't know anything of the kind.

Finally, he had Alpert inside and the cargo-bay doors closed and the OMV secured, so he called her on the intercom and said, "Okay, sweet thing. Ten minutes to go if we're in the window Houston wants. Suit up, get everything you're bringing, and meet me back here when you're ready. And bring Canfield with you."

He wished they'd had proper body bags. He'd stifled the impulse to spare her the ghoulish stuff.

She'd been talking to her people while he'd been talking to his. Doing whatever spooks in space did, up there in the command module where the surveillance gear was still on emergency power but capable of spitting out all sorts of spy goodies if you knew what to do. And her people knew exactly what to tell her to do.

He'd wrapped Canfield, Robinson, and the dead woman, Holly Gold, in silver space blankets. There was no reason to shield Amy from any of this; she had her own job to do, and retrieving the corpses was as much her business as his.

He signed off with Ground Control, telling them that the next time they heard from him, he'd be in *MEDUSA* headed home, and went to help her, fitting his helmet and repressurizing his suit as he did so.

He met her in the hatchway. She had her helmet on and was pushing one of the silver corpses before her with no more apparent concern than she'd have shown for a supermarket cart.

He kept underestimating her; or overestimating the humanity in there, somewhere, behind the years of government service.

He said into her phones, staring at her gilded faceplate as if by trying hard enough he could see through it, "Okay? Ready? We'll tie all three together, go back through the science module into *MEDUSA*'s cargo bay. You'll secure these while I get Alpert. Questions?"

"Nope." She had a thick case in one hand, the sort pilots carried for their air sectionals. He ignored it; whatever was in there wasn't any of his business.

He pushed back and bumped the wall, making

room for her to precede him with her wrapped corpse, then followed.

She still had the Taser.

He wished he could forget about the incident in the airlock. He knew he'd say just what she'd want him to, even if they had to debrief under polygraphs. No matter how he felt about it, there was no way you could determine that she'd been wrong to kill Robinson. Like she said, it would have been real tough for her to fly *MEDUSA* home alone.

He wasn't overly confident about the TAV's reentry himself; he wished the spaceplane didn't shiver like that. If her engines "unstarted"—if she swallowed too much grit coming back into atmosphere, or if she stalled too badly and he had to argue with those onboard computers—no fly-bywire desk jockey down there was going to have fast enough reflexes to be of any help to him.

In the years he'd been flying, Ro Hayes had encountered nothing so demanding of speedy response time. And he didn't trust the computer quorum's judgment worth a damn.

But he'd make it, he always did.

It was bound to be easier than acting like a waldo while Ground Control flew the OMV through him. Anything would be.

He followed Amy down the corridor, a slight figure in a pressure suit that couldn't disguise her female attributes enough for him, right then; telling himself that it shouldn't matter who or what she was—his own ass ought to be his first priority, not hers.

Damned confusing mission. If they grounded him after this one, because of the Lutz fiasco or anything else, he wasn't going to argue. Not this

time. He was going to sit under his trees and
screw around with the Pig until he got her running right. Then he was going to drive up the
coast, maybe as far as Alaska when the weather
broke, rent some pack horses and get away from
anything that so much as lit up when you turned it
on.

By himself.

That was what he needed—some time alone to
shake things out.

But first he had to tie those three corpses together like so much inert baggage, and he'd been
in too many shooting wars down below not to get
the shakes when he hooked that bunch together.

Then off went Nurse Amy with her macabre
bundle, toward the hatch, and he saw her through
the lock and waited until he knew she was safe in
MEDUSA before he went to get Alpert, space
blanket in his belt. Alone with that particular corpse,
all smashed up and eloquent in its rigor mortis, he
had the worst moments of the entire mission. First
he couldn't get the manipulator arm to let Alpert
go; then he couldn't get the man's limbs to bend
into anything like a compact package.

He was perspiring in his suit by the time he'd
gotten Alpert's corpse wrapped up. It wasn't a
pretty sight—this one looked very much like a
dead person and not nearly enough like a generic
piece of dross wrapped in silver. But Amy would
be up front in *MEDUSA* by now. He checked with
her verbally to make sure, and heard her relieved
voice in his ear: She wanted him to come aboard.

"On my way, sweet thing," he said, and heard
his own act wearing thin.

Oh, well, you did the best you could.

This station ought to be sealed up and left as a memorial to something or other—man's inability to do anything right, maybe. Or as a sacrifice to the gods of space. Or to Murphy. Or because it all might just work: Kill a few guys and scare the piss out of the bureaucrats because what you had to do was remind them that things tended to get real, outside of Washington and Moscow, where nothing ever got real at all, and maybe they'd remember.

For a while.

For long enough to get SDI finished, anyhow.

Both nations were in up to their necks, now. The Russians knew what the U.S. had; the U.S. knew what the Russians had. It was a kind of intelligence detente that resulted from putting all that equipment on line. Both governments had enough to chew on that they could give their spooks a couple years off with pay while the analysts analyzed and the politicians tried to read the reports shot their way.

Maybe this time they'd understand.

Ro didn't mind the concept of war in space—it sure beat war on Earth. But he much preferred machine wars to human wars. He didn't like casualties—he'd accounted for too many of them. He'd been hoping—he still hoped—that SDI would eventually not involve men on site.

But, as *MEDUSA* proved, computers couldn't be trusted, not wholly, and not to make superfast decisions when the results of those decisions cost lives if they were wrong. So the human component would always be necessary.

Pushing Alpert, looking as much like a crippled arthritic in death as he must have in life, along the docking tube toward *MEDUSA*'s hold, he was acutely aware that Alpert and Gold and Robinson and Canfield all had families who probably hadn't expected to have their loved ones come home in makeshift body bags. Damned space station wasn't supposed to be a goddamned war zone.

But it was human nature that did that, not any computer or any glitch in the math.

It always was, really. Otherwise, there would be no need for men like Munro Hayes, who never went operational until a number of bad decisions had been made and things were in their "consequential" stages.

He understood why the brass—why the president himself, if Terrible was telling the truth, which Terrible usually did—wanted the physical remains. Remains meant a lot to families. And to the press, if there was going to be any press. But remains didn't mean squat to the poor sucker who'd been killed.

Amy had blown Robinson away without even a second thought. And she hadn't come apart afterward, not for a long time.

He wished he knew how he felt about that.

He knew how he felt when he pushed Alpert the rest of the way into *MEDUSA*'s hold and cut loose the docking tube after he'd shut his own cargo-bay doors. The damned place looked like some high-tech mausoleum. Amy had stowed each corpse in webbing. It was so creepy that his breathing must have escalated, for her voice broke into his reverie: "Ro? Ro, is everything all right back there?"

"You bet. I'm on my way up now. Strap in; we're going to make it out of here just under the wire."

And that was true: The earth's rotation was no inconsiderable factor when deciding where to land. Getting the corpses to Langley on the East Coast was what he'd promised, though, and he was going to do it with . . . He checked his wrist chronometer as he pulled himself into *MEDUSA*'s cockpit. He was going to make it with one minute, thirty-five seconds to spare.

If *MEDUSA* fired up okay.

With the panel bolted behind him, he slid into his seat and began his preflight checks.

He noticed the case Amy had brought with her, snuggled between her knees. "Under the seat with that. Put your feet on it. Things get rough and it flies around, it could be worse than a bird coming through the windshield at Mach four."

She didn't answer. He could tell she was tense.

But then he'd finished his preflight and *MEDUSA* came to life under his hands and he could hear Amy's whispered "Thank God" as the TAV surged under them, on her way home, all her countermeasures up and running, alert to any possible foul play from *Salyut* or from the beautiful blue planet below.

Minutes later, as the atmosphere came up to greet him and he started to feel the vibration he'd kept hoping wouldn't be there, he called in to Langley, saying, "Classic Thunder to Lightning Rod. Get that shield down, folks, or I'm going to splatter this billion-dollar piece of junk all over the neighborhood."

You could never be too careful with little details like the electromagnetic shield the SDI boys had thrown up over Washington and everything from Pax River to Langley.

                    *   *   *

The *Salyut* mission commander watched the
American weapons platform disappear into the atmosphere with his every hackle raised.

Salyut was still tracking it, of course, waiting for
a destruct order.

But the order never came.

Chapter Thirty-Six

President Stewart got the calls he'd been waiting for in the situation room.

It was the middle of the night—the longest night of his life.

The first call was from Forrestal, confirming Wolfe's cooperation and reporting a successful interchange with KGB.

It burned Stewart's butt to have KGB to thank for something, and he had them to thank for everything. Impeachment would have been easier to take.

The second was from Langley, where Terrible Taylor was encamped, demanding that the electromagnetic shield around Washington come down.

The third was from his national security advisers' representative at Cheyenne Mountain, confirming that the shield was down.

The fourth was from Langley Control, giving an approximate time for *MEDUSA's* touchdown.

When the fifth call came, Stewart already was reaching for his coat, and the heads of his national security advisers were already together, concocting damage-limitation scenarios to prevent their commander in chief's impeachment.

"Damn it," said Stewart to no one in particular, "I'm going to Langley. I want to be there when that plane touches down."

On his way out, Stewart diverted only long enough to tiptoe into Lincoln's bedroom, where he placed a tender kiss on Susan's sleeping lips.

And then, suddenly weak in the knees, he sat down on the edge of the bed.

His wife awoke, rolled over, and said sleepily, "See, dear? Everything's fine, isn't it? I told you, it was just another crisis."

"Yes, dear, everything's fine. You were right," Stewart said, although things still might be far from right for him personally.

But he had a staff to deal with that. And he had a pilot to greet who was still under the shadow of a murder he didn't commit (according to Marcus Wolfe), and a few spooks to talk to, and a press conference to arrange, and a vice president who was at this moment cutting a deal with Moscow to determine exactly what would, and would not, be said in that press release.

And then he'd have the grieving relatives to console.

Sometimes, life just didn't seem fair.

But Stewart had won the big one—the price for that win was expensive only in retrospect, now that he was reasonably sure he hadn't started World War III.

He patted his wife on the knee and got up, leaving her snoring prettily in FDR's bed.

Chapter Thirty-Seven

Amy Brecker hadn't let out the breath she'd been holding throughout Ro's final approach until *MEDUSA*'s nosewheel hit the runway with a satisfying jolt.

Then she realized how much she needed to find a bathroom, how much she wanted a cigarette, and how terrified she'd been that the vibration Ro kept talking about to Langley Control (with his test pilot's analytic insouciance that made her want to scream) would cause *MEDUSA* to disintegrate under them and spread her and her case full of intelligence all over the West Virginia landscape.

In the case were not only the samples *Skylab*'s crew had taken of the black material the Russians had sprayed on the station's cameras, but all the data Canfield had collected, which were too secret to risk burst-transmitting. It might be enough, she told herself, to get her off the hook for Lutz, and for the hijacking of Dietrich's plane. They'd brought in Marcus Wolfe, after all.

But how much and what kind of blame Amy

Brecker took was going to depend on what kind of deal had been struck between the superpowers.

That some kind of deal *was* being struck, she was sure from what she'd heard, and not heard, from her controller on the ground while she'd been cleaning out the classified data in the command module.

When your earthly CIA station was overrun by a hostile horde, you needed only a quick and efficient document shredder. When your orbital intelligence-gathering station was integral to the command module of a putatively NASA enterprise, you needed somebody like Amy Brecker: a cleaning woman among the stars.

Wouldn't you know that was what she'd end up doing—domestic work in outer space?

Still, she had the goodies. And she was determined to make the best of things. Ro would back her claim that Robinson's death had been necessary and appropriate. He'd said so.

As the TAV taxied along the black runway in the blacker night toward a hangar crowded with black cars and lit with floodlights, her stomach began to doubt her intellect. She remembered Hayes telling her that if they won big enough, they'd be okay. She cast a surreptitious glance at the pilot, busy shutting down the TAV and bantering with Langley Control. They were walking into an extensive debriefing, she knew. Probably separately. And after that, they would in all likelihood never see one another again.

With trembling hands, as Hayes touched a final bank of toggles and *MEDUSA*'s engines died, Amy fumbled with her helmet, then eased it up and off

her head. After shaking out her hair, she got a
grip on one glove's finger and began pulling it
off.

When she'd done that, she saw Ro's helmeted
head turned her way. He held up a hand: wait.
And took off his own helmet so that she could hear
whatever he was going to say, while outside Amy
glimpsed a presidential limo pull up and Secret
Service types swarm the tarmac around it.

She saw something in Ro's stubbled jaw that she
didn't understand—a tightness, as if he were fighting to get words to form. Then he said, "Got your
case? It'll be fine. We did good. We did great."

"I know," she said, feeling her own throat close
up. He wouldn't say anything in here, not if it was
personal or important, especially not if it was private and the cockpit recorder was still running.

He squeezed her arm with a quick move and
then went back to his controls. MEDUSA's ladder
whirred down and they uncoupled their safety
harnesses, and the cold night air rushed into the
cockpit, and suddenly all she could think about
was what lay in MEDUSA's hold: four corpses
wrapped in silver blankets.

The first thing she did when her feet touched
the runway and men with CIA credentials hanging
around their necks on silver chains surrounded
her was to ask, "Anybody got a cigarette?"

And when she looked up, exhaling smoke, Hayes
was shaking General Taylor's hand and there were
too many strangers between them for her to protest as the air force general hustled his pilot off
toward the presidential limo and her own people
urged her discreetly toward a nondescript car wait-

ing, its motor idling, on a shadowed part of the runway.

In it, to her surprise, Jeremy Pratt was sitting with a concerned and proprietary smile on his diplomat's face.

Epilogue

Hayes was out in the California sun, packing up the Blazer. It had taken a week to get it running right, but now the Pig was ready to go.

And so was he.

He'd followed the news—or lack of news—for a few days after the extended debriefing that had lasted until sunup. It wasn't much different from what he'd expected: The Soviets and the Americans had both announced successful tests of classified SDI components; NASA had reported four casualties sustained during a routine but also classified mission; Stewart had gone on TV and presented the astronauts' families with neatly folded flags and posthumous medals.

Ro had gotten a medal, too, unexpected and unappreciated, from President Stewart himself. He couldn't very well refuse it, under the circumstances, there on the tarmac, but it had been a CIA medal. Just because Taylor and Forrestal had made some sort of deal, that didn't mean CIA had any right to commend an air force pilot, any more than they'd have had a right to discipline him. But you didn't turn down a decoration from your president, even though you were sure that all medals were bad luck.

So he had this thing, something called a Distinguished Intelligence Cross, for "exceptional heroism involving acceptance of existing dangers with conspicuous fortitude and exemplary courage."

Bullshit.

He'd thought about sending it to Amy Brecker, who probably deserved one and just as probably hadn't gotten one. It had the eagle/shield medallion and it said "For Valor" in raised letters; the ribbon was blue with a thin red/white/black strip in the middle. She really would have liked something like that.

But he hadn't seen her since they deplaned and he didn't know where to send the damned thing. Except to Langley, c/o the Agency. And he wasn't about to do that.

He'd put it in his safe-deposit box, where he kept stuff his kids might want someday. It would bitch his ex-wife something fierce the day she found it; Jenny would automatically assume that it represented one more part of his life that he hadn't "leveled" with her about.

He'd seen Reinhardt Dietrich on the six o'clock news, bold as brass, castigating the U.S. for putting more troops into Nicaragua—up to his old tricks. It seemed that in the interest of international relations, Dietrich and Hoffman had been treated as hijacking victims and returned with "apologies" to Germany the same night Ro had brought them in.

You couldn't figure these political types: Crimes

weren't defined by actions as much as by convenience.

It had made him so angry, he'd pushed up his departure date. He knew what he was feeling was more than his typical between-mission sulk—it had begun too early and it was lasting too long. He'd even been snippy to Taylor, who'd offered him six weeks in Bahrain that he'd normally have jumped at: He liked the venue, he liked the weather, and he liked casinos.

But nobody would tell him anything about how Brecker was doing or where she was or whether she'd come through her part of the debrief all right. He really didn't like the people she worked for; he didn't trust them worth a damn. He especially didn't like it when they told him his inquiries were inappropriate—that he was to forget all about her; that he could impair her ability to do her job otherwise.

He knew that was a pile of crap. He didn't believe for a second that Brecker was off on some other assignment, not with the mess the two of them had made.

They should have treated her better. She should have been standing there with him when Stewart got all friendly. If Stewart could come through this smelling like a rose partly because of Amy's sweat, he could at least have had the courtesy to thank her. Bringing in Wolfe should have been enough to make up for whatever rules she'd broken. She'd have played it by her rule book except for him.

He'd said that to anyone who'd listen, until Taylor personally told him to stop. If she wanted to get in touch with him, Terrible had said with that gentleness that always surprised Hayes when it surfaced, Taylor would see to it that she could. Otherwise, it wasn't any of Ro's business.

So he was doing what he'd decided to do when he was packing up the dead guys littering *Skylab:* getting the hell away for a while. He was going to get as far away as he could from a world in which Reinhardt Dietrich could play both sides of the fence, and Marcus Wolfe could end up with a Miami mansion, and gunslingers like Stewart could manhandle reality to save face, but people like Amy Brecker got hustled off in gray midsize sedans because they'd committed errors in procedure.

He just hoped that she wasn't having trouble, or at least that if she was, it wasn't because of him. He simply couldn't play by her rules. He'd never promised he would.

He started tossing things into the Blazer through its open tailgate.

A friend of his in Anchorage had said he could bush-pilot up there for as long as he pleased if he decided to stay on. He doubted that Taylor wouldn't have something to say about that, but he was content to pretend it might work. Decompression was what he needed, and he was expert at taking care of Ro Hayes's needs.

He'd told Jenny he didn't know how long he'd be gone, set up lines of communication through Taylor's office for her, said goodbye to the kids. There wasn't anything to keep him here, unless it was so cold up north that Bahrain started sounding a lot better than it did now.

He was chucking the last duffel bag into the Blazer when his remote phone bleeped.

He let it ring. He didn't want to talk to anybody right now. That was the damned point. And he wanted to get on the road before dark.

He went inside, taking a final inventory, making sure he'd closed all the windows and left the bathroom faucet running so his pipes wouldn't freeze in case there was a cold snap. He tromped through the three-room cabin, sparsely furnished, nothing special or personal except for a few PR photos of aircraft he'd flown before they'd reached the PR-photo stage, and it wasn't any emptier in there than he felt.

He ought to stop doing this sort of work if it kept bothering him like this. When he came back, he'd tell Taylor he wanted straight testing work.

Sure he would.

He paused before the door, setting the motion detector twice before he got it armed. Then he had thirty seconds to pick up the handgun on the lamp table, get outside, and lock up.

The gun was the custom piece he'd taken on Classic Thunder. Still had the nonstandard loads. He didn't think he'd need it, but he wasn't about to leave it in the cabin and he was licensed to take it wherever he damn well pleased—one of the perks that came with his job. He sauntered over to the Blazer and slipped the handgun into the glove compartment, and just sat there in the passenger seat awhile, looking at the trees.

And then he heard the car laboring up the dirt road that went nowhere but here.

"Shit," he told the Pig. Taylor wasn't going to let him get out clean after all.

He walked down to the bend that shielded the

cabin from the road, and waited. This wasn't any time for Terrible to have a great idea about what Ro ought to do with his downtime. But Jenny wouldn't be coming up here, and Ro had a good ear for engines; it wasn't any car he could recognize.

And that was true: What came nosing up the drive was a gray Plymouth with rental plates.

Some things never changed.

He hunkered down where he was, breaking off a piece of tall brown grass as the car with its woman driver slowed, and stopped, and its door opened.

"Hey," said Amy Brecker as she got out, dressed in jeans and an Irish sweater.

"Hey yourself," he said, straightening up. "You okay?"

She hesitated then. The smile on her face was strained and she seemed uncertain about coming any closer. "Sure. I heard you were asking, so I thought I'd come tell you myself. . . ."

"Come here," he suggested.

But she was looking at the Pig. "Taylor said you were leaving, going on some kind of vacation. I've got some time off, too."

Very tense. Her shoulders were hunched and she jammed her hands in her pockets as she took two steps toward him.

"That's right," he said, deciding to meet her halfway. Otherwise, he'd be kicking himself for the rest of his life. "Alaska. The slow way. Want to come?"

She grinned at him mischievously and cocked one hip, looking at the ground, where one booted foot dug in the dirt. "I'm all packed," she admitted.

He laughed, reaching out to grab for her. "Pretty sure of yourself, 'sweet thing.'"

She didn't dodge, and his arms went around her. "Screw you, Major Hayes," she retorted.

"We'll see what we can do about that, too," he promised, thinking that Taylor probably never had been serious about Bahrain.

For
Fiction with Real Science In It, and Fantasy That Touches The Heart of The Human Soul . . .

Baen Books bring you Poul Anderson, Marion Zimmer Bradley, C.J. Cherryh, Gordon R. Dickson, David Drake, Robert L. Forward, Janet Morris, Jerry Pournelle, Fred Saberhagen, Michael Reaves, Jack Vance . . . all top names in science fiction and fantasy, plus new writers destined to reach the top of their fields. For a free catalog of all Baen Books, send three 22-cent stamps, plus your name and address, to

Baen Books
260 Fifth Avenue, Suite 3S
New York, N.Y. 10001

Announcing one hell of a shared universe!

OF COURSE IT'S A FANTASY . . . ISN'T IT?

Alexander the Great teams up with Julius Caesar and Achilles to refight the Trojan War—with Machiavelli as their intelligence officer and Cleopatra in charge of R&R . . . Yuri Andropov learns to Love the Bomb with the aid of The Blond Bombshell (she is the Devil's *very* private secretary) . . . Che Guevara Ups the Revolution with the help of Isaac Newton, Hemingway, and Confucius . . . And no less a bard than Homer records their adventures for posterity: of *course* it's a fantasy. It has to be, if you don't believe in Hell.

ALL YOU REALLY NEED IS FAITH . . .

But award-winning authors Gregory Benford, C. J. Cherryh, Janet Morris, and David Drake, co-creators of this multi-volume epic, insist that *Heroes in Hell* ® is something more. They say that all you really need is Faith, that if you accept the single postulate that Hell exists, your imagination will soar, taking you to a realm more magical and strangely satisfying than you would have believed possible.

COME TO HELL . . .

. . . where the battle of Good and Evil goes on apace in the most biased possible venue. There's no rougher, tougher place in the Known Universe of Discourse, and you *wouldn't* want to live there, but . . .

IT'S BRIGHT . . . FRESH . . . LIBERATING . . . AS HELL!

Co-created by some of the finest, most imaginative

talents writing today, *Heroes in Hell* ® offers a milieu more exciting than anything in American fiction since *A Connecticut Yankee in King Arthur's Court*. As bright and fresh a vision as any conceived by Borges, it's as accessible—and American—as apple pie.

EVERYONE WHO WAS ANYONE DOES IT

In fact, Janet Morris's Hell is so liberating to the imaginations of the authors involved that nearly a dozen major talents have vowed to join her for at least eight subsequent excursions to the Underworld, where—even as you read this—everyone who was anyone is meeting to hatch new plots, conquer new empires, and test the very limits of creation.

YOU'VE HEARD ABOUT IT—NOW GO THERE!

Join the finest writers, scientists, statesmen, strategists, and villains of history in Morris's Hell. The first volume, co-created by Janet Morris with C. J. Cherryh, Gregory Benford, and David Drake, will be on sale in March as the mass-market lead from Baen Books, and in April Baen will publish in hardcover the first *Heroes in Hell* spin-off novel, *The Gates of Hell*, by C. J. Cherryh and Janet Morris. We can promise you one Hell of a good time.

FOR A DOSE OF THAT OLD-TIME RELIGION (TO A MODERN BEAT), READ—

HEROES IN HELL®	THE GATES OF HELL
March 1986	April 1986 Hardcover
65555-8 • 288 pp. • $3.50	65561-2 • 256 pp. • $14.95